MURDER ON THE MIDWAY

The Complete

Cases of the Human Encyclopedia

1936–38

FRANK GRUBER

introduction by Keith Alan Deutsch

illustrations by Wynne W. Davies,
Harold Heffernan & Arthur Rodman Bowker

cover by J. George Janes

BLACK MASK
2022

Table of Contents

Introduction

FRANK GRUBER (1902–1969) was one of the most successful and prolific writers of the pulp era. At his peak he produced three or four full-length novels a year, many about series characters Johnny Fletcher and his sidekick Sam Cragg. Each year Gruber also wrote numerous short stories, many featuring Oliver Quade, "The Human Encyclopedia," that is arguably his most warmly remembered series character.

By the late 1930s Gruber had visited Hollywood, and sold the screen rights to Oliver Quade with hopes that a regular series of films would be made. Unfortunately only one lackluster Quade film was made. However, within a few years, Gruber was writing successful screenplays almost every year, including such major features as *The Mask of Dimitrios, Terror by Night* (one of two superior Sherlock Holmes scripts for Basil Rathbone), and with his companion and fellow *Black Mask* contributor, Steve Fisher, the classic noir thriller *Johnny Angel.* This last film was based on the novel *Mr. Angel Comes Aboard* by fellow *Black Mask* writer Charles G. Booth.

Although Gruber had a light touch, and successfully combined humorous characters with authentic hard-boiled milieus, a technique that was a major influence on later mystery writers like Craig Rice, Gruber claimed that he, Steve Fisher, and Cornell Woolrich became great friends at *Black Mask* and together developed the noir thriller under the brilliant hand of editor Fanny Ellsworth. Ellsworth was the great woman editor of the pulps who took over *Black Mask* from Captain Joseph

Shaw in 1936 and promoted a kind of dark, psychologically centered emotional tale in *Black Mask,* often of innocent men trapped by fate. Gruber describes his writing friendships in his colorful autobiography, *The Pulp Jungle,* which is also an informal history of pulp magazines, and the era in which they flourished.

Gruber wrote more than three hundred stories, sixty novels, and more than two hundred television and film scripts, mostly mystery and western tales. Perhaps his most beloved character is Oliver Quade, the Human Encyclopedia, whose seemingly infinite knowledge of even the most arcane subjects helps him solve crimes in a long series of pulp stories.

According to an early reminiscence called *The Starving Writer,* published in *The Writer* (July 1948), Gruber arrived in New York in 1934 one month after Steve Fisher. They had been corresponding and met up in Ed Bodin's office; Bodin was literary agent for both friends at the time. Gruber, like Fisher, arrived alone with a typewriter, a suitcase, and a few dollars. As Gruber noted in many reminiscences, "I had one thing else… the will to succeed." Both Gruber and Fisher shared this powerful desire.

After a few dry months, Fisher and Gruber began to sell the occasional story. In 1936, Fisher married Edythe (Edie) Syme, an editor at Popular Publications, Inc. Gruber and his wife often went to dinner with Fisher and Edie.

By then, Fisher and Gruber had become close friends with Cornell Woolrich with whom they occasionally had dinner on those rare occasions when they were able to sidestep Woolrich's restrictive, overbearing mother.

Fisher, Gruber, and Woolrich all started to sell to *Black Mask* after Fanny Ellsworth took over editorial reign. In *The Life and Times of the Pulp Story* in *Brass Knuckles* (1966) Gruber claims that he and Fisher managed to take the reclusive Woolrich to a party where they all got drunk. The next day Fanny Ellsworth called Gruber and reported that Woolrich had come tearing into the *Black Mask* offices threatening never to write for the magazine again because Fisher and Gruber had told him that they were getting three times the word rate for their stories than Fanny was giving Woolrich. Fisher and Gruber had been too drunk to remember the hoax!

Gruber knew Ellsworth well from selling lead rangeland novels to her during the years she ran the very successful, *Ranch Romances*. Gruber thought Ellsworth an extremely erudite and perceptive editor who could have run *The Atlantic Monthly* or *Harpers*. In *The Life and Times of the Pulp Story* Gruber claims that he introduced Fisher to Ellsworth and helped him break into *Black Mask*. Both Gruber and Fisher credit Ellsworth with deliberately and perceptively changing the course of the magazine.

It is difficult to remember seventy-five years after the revolution, but Steve Fisher, Cornell Woolrich, and Frank Gruber lead the second wave of *Black Mask* boys in the late 1930s and ushered in a sea change in crime fiction narration. Fanny Ellsworth, who became editor at *Black Mask* with a new strategy, favored a change from the objective, hard-boiled writing promoted by Joseph Shaw and the earlier editors of *Black Mask* to the subjective, psychologically and emotionally heightened writing that came in vogue under her guidance.

This little-noticed shift in style in *Black Mask* fiction, "The Ellsworth Shift," led to the creation of the film genre we now know as noir through the writings of Steve Fisher, particularly in his film scripts, and through the novels and short fiction of Cornell Woolrich, whose writings we now also call noir, although the term was originally applied only to film.

This dark new style and psychology in crime fiction narration jumped from magazine and book publications into screenplays, and led in the 1940s to the emergence in Hollywood of the classic age of the noir film thriller.

The obsessive, dreamlike narration favored by Fisher and Woolrich in their tense crime tales was a perfect match for the dark shadows, and frightening, expressive camera angles developed in German and Hollywood horror cinema. Narrative fiction style, and camera photography styles, played against and enriched each other in the development of this new film genre.

In his seminal essay, "Pulp Literature: Subculture Revolution in the Late 1930s," from *The Armchair Detective* published in the 1970s, Fisher was the first to note this paradigm shift in *Black Mask* fiction. The gifted new woman editor, Fanny Ellsworth, used Fisher, Woolrich, and occasionally Gruber, who also supplied humor to the emotional new mix.

Humor was another taboo under the old Shaw regime. Most effectively through the art of Woolrich and Fisher, Fanny Ellsworth turned the emphasis in *Black Mask* fiction away from the objective, unemotional, hard-boiled writing style Hammett and the first wave of *Black Mask* writers introduced to the magazine, and for which *Black Mask* is celebrated.

Black Mask author William Brandon provides us with the most revealing portrait I know of Joseph Shaw discussing the art of objective writing in the early 1930s when he was at the height of his influence. Brandon recounts many conversations he had with Shaw in his little-known memoir, "Back in the Old Black Mask" *(The Massachusetts Review,* Winter 1987):

> Shaw wanted action, naturally, as did any right-thinking pulp, but what Shaw wanted most of all was style.
>
> Objectivity was part of what Shaw meant by style—a clean page, a clean line, an uncluttered phrase.
>
> Even the illustrations—Shaw called them 'end pieces'—that Shaw liked were of a certain elegance and were meant to excite the imagination rather than a surface emotion. But traditionally the pulps left nothing to the imagination and the cruder the emotion the better. I think Shaw would have argued for hard and cruel emotion too but I think he felt it was better effected by clean and plausible and objective subtlety.

Brandon makes it very clear that Shaw was not interested in character expressed through psychology, but only as it was expressed through external action.

Shaw didn't buy any of Brandon's detective stories, but he introduced him to "Fanny Ellsworth across the hall, a pretty and witty and red-haired young woman who edited *Ranch Romances* ("Love Stories of the Real West"), and Fanny started buying—at rare intervals—western stories I wrote in what I thought was a humorous vein."

Fanny was comfortable with complexity in the stories she edited. She liked strong emotion and humor in a story, regardless of its genre.

Shaw was uncomfortable with humor and he mistrusted complexity in his narratives, whether in plot or in psychological states.

By all contemporary accounts, Fanny Ellsworth was one of the great fiction editors of all time. Frank Gruber describes her as one of the brightest, most urbane people he met in New York. Gruber and Steve Fisher both assert that when Fanny Ellsworth took over control of *Black Mask* she came with a well-mapped vision for a change in the kind of crime fiction the famous magazine would feature.

Ellsworth immediately started to buy stories from Frank Gruber, who wrote lead stories for her *Ranch Romances* pulp, and also Steve Fisher, who she recognized had a natural talent for expressing strong and complex emotions. She also increased the number of stories she purchased from Cornell Woolrich, who also had a natural way with twisted, pathological emotional states presented in strange, dark, haunted plots.

Ellsworth quickly established a much more subjective, emotionally driven style of crime writing than Shaw. Commentators on *Black Mask's* influence on film and popular culture have not often noticed these changes in style and direction.

Certainly, Curt Siodmak's science fiction noir masterpiece, *Donovan's Brain,* the darkest of obsessive, subjective, first person narratives, serialized in *Black Mask* in 1942, years after Fanny Ellsworth had left, would not have made it into *Black Mask* if the talents of Fisher (nine stories from August 1937 to April 1939) and of Woolrich (twenty-two original stories from January of 1937 to June of 1944) had not first been let loose on its pages.

Black Mask writers and genres influenced Hollywood in more ways than hard-boiled dialogue and tough-guy detection of films based on Hammett, Chandler, and similar writers.

The late Curt Siodmak's work on horror films, especially at

Universal scripting and creating *The Wolf Man* (1941), and with Val Lewton at RKO scripting *I Walked with a Zombie* (1943), is of interest, particularly with regard to the emergence of a noir film aesthetic from out of the shadows of the "horror" films of the 1930s and 1940s Hollywood.

Once the noir film emerged at the beginning of the 1940s with the production of Steve Fisher's novel, *I Wake Up Screaming* (1941), Fisher's and Woolrich's noir work flooded Hollywood.

In 1943 the great run of more than two-dozen noir films based on works by Cornell Woolrich, the genius of the dark thriller, began when Val Lewton produced *The Leopard Man* (1943); Robert Siodmak (Curt's brother) directed *Phantom Lady* (1944); *The Mark of the Whistler* (1944) followed; Clifford Odets scripted *Deadline at Dawn* (1946); then came *Black Angel* (1946); and *The Chase* (1946); followed by *The Guilty* (1947); and *Fear in the Night* (1947).

Steve Fisher scripted Cornell Woolrich's *I Wouldn't Be in Your Shoes* (1948) with a telephone call assist from his pal Woolrich. When Fisher couldn't come up with an appropriate ending for *I Wouldn't Be in Your Shoes*, Woolrich suggested that Fisher resurrect the sexually obsessive, psychotic cop from *I Wake Up Screaming* and turn him into the culprit, motivated by his lust for the framed man's wife. Ironically, Fisher originally had based that haunting and haunted police detective, Ed Cornell, on his friend Cornell Woolrich.

The most famous Woolrich inspired film, of course, is Alfred Hitchcock's 1954 classic, *Rear Window*.

Frank Gruber and Steve Fisher always remarked on this change in the aesthetic of the crime thriller that started to take place in pulp fiction (and some would argue in American cinema) in the late 1930s, and which came of age in Hollywood films in the 1940s; and to note *Black Mask's* and Fanny Ellsworth's role in that change.

In *Black Mask*, Fisher and Woolrich shared a talent for presenting aberrant mental states, and for casting suspenseful plots with inventive, obsessive incidents.

Frank Gruber, who more than any other *Black Mask* writer encouraged Fanny Ellsworth's influence among his writing peers, had a flair for introducing humor into classic hardboiled and noir thriller situations. And so even though he did not have the dark, obsessive, natural noir talents his best friends Fisher and Woolrich possessed, Gruber was still able to make significant and influential contributions during Ellsworth's heightened emotional reign over *Black Mask's* narratives.

Gruber's natural sense of humor heightened and relieved the tension in hardboiled and noir thrillers and influenced many writers to follow him. Craig Rice even adopted character duos of a sharp, super smart and fast-talking detective partnered with a slow-witted, always hungry, funny foil of a sidekick. One of Rice's characters even had a photographic memory.

More modern stylists who owe much to Gruber's sense of comic complications, and humorous dialogue are Donald E. Westlake, and the much more sinister Elmore Leonard. Gruber credits Fanny Ellsworth with allowing *Black Mask* authors to relax and explore their sense of narrative humor.

Under Captain Shaw, brilliantly funny narrators like Norbert Davis had to sneak their more zany sides into more traditional tough guy stories. We can see the long distance result of Gruber's influence in the movement toward screwball mysteries in the films of the late 1930s and the 1940s, especially in the better film work of Bob Hope and Red Skeleton.

Even the great Dashiell Hammett in his late career brought the genre its greatest recipe for mixing humor with mystery in the Thin Man films. Nick and Nora Charles were presented on screen as a classic screwball loving couple as they romped through an iconic tough guy crime universe of cops, criminals, and corpses with a charming élan that became Hammett's most enduring commercial creation.

Even more important than Ellsworth's encouragement of humorous turns in classic *Black Mask* mysteries, Fanny Ellsworth was the inspiration for the full emergence of the psychologically heightened noir genre that has had an enduring and thrilling impact on film and fiction in popular American and world-wide entertainment.

Brass Knuckles

Oliver Quade, the Human Encyclopedia, Steers a
Mob of Criminal Parasites into a Bloody Waterloo!

QUADE WAS IN his element. Standing on an overturned soap box he was talking to an audience as only Quade, himself, could talk. Oliver Quade, the greatest book salesman of the day. A lean, hungry looking man, standing about five feet ten and weighing less than a hundred and forty, dressed in the black and white checked suit that was a badge of his vocation. Against his soft white shirt a red tie flamed and in the tie a big diamond horseshoe stickpin caught the sun. That was Oliver Quade, exhorting in a voice that was famous throughout the country.

"Ask me any question, friends, any question at all—history, economics, science or general interest—and I'll answer it. They call me the Human Encyclopedia and I want to prove that I really am— Yes, what was the question?"

"How fast does light travel?" asked a nondescript man in the crowd.

"How fast does light travel?" Quade repeated, a wide grin spreading across his face. "One hundred and eighty-six thousand miles per second. Am I right?"

No one disputed the answer, but a woman in the audience spoke up. "What are the chances of my getting thirteen spades in a bridge game?"

"What are your chances of getting thirteen spades in a bridge game? One chance in sixty-two billion. Don't take my word for it, either. It's here in this book!" Quade smacked his right palm on a thick volume he was holding in his right hand. "Shepard, the great bridge expert and mathematician, has figured it out for you. Next question."

"When was the Battle of Hastings?"

"In the year 1066; it decided the supremacy of the Normans in England. Next."

THE QUESTIONS BEGAN to come faster.

"How can I remove ink spots from a white dress?"

"Who was vice-president during Wilson's first administration?"

Quade shot back the answers as fast as the questions were hurled at him. Correctly, too, for he knew them all. He had read the *Encyclopedia Americana,* from cover to cover four times; had read every book he had ever sold in fifteen years. The nickname, the Human Encyclopedia, was his deservedly. History, science, craftsmanship, economics, Quade had a smattering of them all.

He entertained the crowd, too. *"The Compendium of Human Knowledge,* friends, the knowledge of the ages, condensed, all in this one volume. Twelve hundred pages, a complete high school education in one volume—for the amazing, stupendously low sum of one dollar and ninety-five cents."

"I want a college education," piped up a wag in the crowd. "Haven't you a book for that?"

"Four years for high school, four for college," Quade shot back at him. "Buy two of these books and you'll have both."

A roar of laughter greeted this retort and the heckler retired in confusion.

Quade launched into his sales talk; three minutes of it and he'd pass out the books; forty or fifty persons listening—unless he'd lost his marvelous gift of talk and he knew he hadn't—at

least ten of these would shell out one dollar and ninety-five cents.

Alas, however, this was one of the few occasions that Quade, having built up his audience to the buying pitch, could not cash in. Looking out beyond the crowd he saw the familiar figure of Joe Simmons coming toward him. Simmons was about fifty feet away and as Quade looked, he stopped in his stride.

A battered taxicab had pulled up to the curb. Two men climbed out and accosted Simmons. With *The Compendium of Human Knowledge* open in his left hand, Quade suddenly paused in his harangue. The two men were quarreling with his friend. Simmons was talking defensively and backing away, the men crowding him closely. Then suddenly one of them, a short chunky fellow, lashed out with his right fist and struck Simmons right in the face.

Quade let out a yell of protest. He leaped straight from his soap box perch into the crowd surrounding him.

"Let me through!" he cried. "Let me through. They're beating up a pal of mine!"

The crowd jostled and milled. Quade got through at the expense of a couple of buttons from his dark coat. Simmons was down on the sidewalk vainly trying to protect his head with his arms. Quade's thin figure fairly skimmed the sidewalk toward the brawl. He caught the gleam of brass knuckles and groaned.

"Hey, you guys!" he yelled.

The man with the brass knuckles jerked sidewards, shot, a look at Quade, then turned and smashed the brass-knuckled fist down on the top of Joe Simmons' head. At a distance of a dozen feet Quade heard the crunch of bone. He dove into a flying tackle.

HIS HEAD AND shoulders hit the man with the knuckles in the small of the back. The man let out a *"whoof"* and flew forward on his face.

Quade sprawled on the sidewalk after him. He scrambled up quickly however and turned to meet a fist smashed into his face. Off balance, he fell. By that time the other pug was back in the fight. Quade saw the brass knuckles and winced. A crowd was collecting, he saw in a flashing look, but he knew, too, that he could expect no assistance. City crowds were that way.

Well—

Quade eluded a kick from the chunky man and got to his feet. He charged the other fellow, a big bruiser, but his fists were unclenched. Instead his fingers were spread out. He dodged under the swinging fist of the big fellow, poked savagely with his outspread fingers at the man's throat. His fingers made stiff contact and the big man fell back, a scream of anguish forced from his throat.

But the move cost Quade plenty. Brass knuckles in the rear charged! Quade ducked, but the knuckles connected with the side of his jaw, a tearing, vicious blow. Quade staggered; flashing pain through his head blinding him for an instant. He covered up instinctively, but a terrific blow on his chest smashed him to the sidewalk.

Dimly he heard a police whistle. He struggled to his feet and covered up, expecting another brutal attack. But there was none. He forced his eyes wide open and saw the chunky bruiser just piling into the open door of the cab. The big man was already inside.

In a second the cab was whirling away.

Quade jerked a white silk handkerchief from his breast pocket and wiped blood from his chin. A burly cop forced his way through the crowd.

"What's goin' on here?" he demanded.

Quade said, "Hello, Murphy. You came a couple minutes too late."

The cop peered at him. "Ah, 'tis the Human Encyclypedy. Begorra, an' it looks like matter has done triumphed over mind! An' what kind of trouble have you been in now?"

"The trouble wasn't mine, Murphy," said Quade very grimly. He dropped to his knees beside the huddled figure of Joe Simmons. "Those thugs—God!" He broke off, for his questing hand had touched Simmons' heart. There was no beat! Simmons was dead.

"He's—dead!" he cried, passionately. "Those bruisers killed him!"

The cop dropped down beside Quade. "Dead is right," he snarled. "His head's smashed. What did it?"

"Brass knuckles!" Oliver Quade rose to his feet, his eyes bleak. Joe Simmons dead! Killed by a set of brass knuckles on the fist of a dirty thug. Joe Simmons, Quade's friend. Well—they'd pay for it, the chunky thug and his big partner.

No man had ever yet committed a crime against Quade or one of his friends and got away with it. Everyone who knew Oliver Quade knew that. Quade wasn't a big man physically. But he was an enemy to be feared. Stored up in that fine brain of his was loyalty to his friends, a passionate devotion to law and order and an amazing knowledge.

The men who had killed Joe Simmons, beat up Oliver Quade himself, would suffer, if it were humanly possible for Quade to bring them to grief.

"All right, Murphy," he said quietly. "I'll appear at the inquest. I've got to be going now—patch myself up. You know where to find me."

"Sure, Mr. Quade," replied Murphy. "And I'm sorry. I knew Joe Simmons. A good lad, even if the breaks was against him."

Dabbing at his bloody face Quade pushed through the crowd. Fifty feet away, he had left a huge grip full of books, copies of *The Compendium of Human Knowledge*. The sample volume Quade had dropped when he'd charged at the thugs was gone, the grip was broken open; a few books were scattered on the sidewalk. More than twenty had been stolen by persons in the crowd when Quade had deserted his stand.

Quade shook his head wryly. "At any rate, I made a good spiel. Sold them on the book."

He gathered up the few remaining volumes, put them in the grip. It was still heavy, but Quade hefted it as if it were empty. Lean and consumptive looking he was, when dressed in his street clothing, but the body underneath was a mass of sinew and iron muscles.

QUADE WAS IN the pink of condition. Years ago he'd started a set of exercises—gleaned from a physique building book he'd sold at the time—and he still kept up the exercises. He disdained to use fists in a street brawl—no point to injuring, perhaps breaking knuckles. He always avoided fist fights. When it was absolutely necessary to defend himself he used jiu-jitsu and only Japanese exponents of the art were his equal.

Two blocks away in a shabby boarding house, Quade was making his temporary headquarters. There was a sizable sum of money in a trust fund uptown and the bank account in Quade's name was a respectable one, but he lived in cheap places, where he could meet prospective customers of his knowledge books and who in moments of recreation could tilt verbally with Quade. He had once lived uptown but had found little worthy competition for his mental powers. Down on Twelfth Street, he enjoyed himself.

Quade lugged the grip of books up to his room on the second floor front and deposited the bag on the floor. Then, going into the bathroom, he examined in the mirror the ugly cut on his face. He washed the blood away, daubed iodine on the cut, then covered it with adhesive tape.

There was blood on his shirt; he'd have to remove it. He took off his coat, stopped. On his white shirt, a half inch or so to the right of his vivid red tie was a peculiar red mark. A thin red circle with two initials inside of it—*N.B.*

Quade looked at the mark for a moment, while his keen brain raced. Of course, that last smashing blow on the chest; a fist. There had been a ring on the fist, the flesh underneath the shirt and undershirt was bruised. It had been a ring all right, a ring with a circle and the initials. And either blood or ink on the ring had stamped the initials on the shirt.

"Very well, *N.B.*, you're in for it," Quade told himself grimly. "I'll get you—and I'll get your murderous pal."

A half hour later, Quade rang the bell of a brownstone house near Sixth Avenue. A tear-stained lad of about twelve opened the door.

"Your mother, is she home?" Quade asked gently.

"Y-yes," blubbered the boy. "But she's crying. Dad was killed."

"I know, son, and I'm terribly sorry. You're the man of the family now—and you've got to buck up. Let your mother see that you're going to face the world like a man. Like your father."

The lad stopped blubbering. The tone of Quade's voice had gripped him. "Yes, sir, I'll be brave."

"That's the stuff. Now go in and tell your mother that Oliver Quade is here and would like to ask her one or two questions. And son—wait until I leave. I'll have something for you."

A MOMENT LATER he went into the shabby living room to face the faded woman who was trying to dry her tears.

"Mrs. Simmons, I'm terribly sorry," he began. "I was there when it happened, tried to prevent it. Got this cut on my face from the same skunks. There's just one thing I want to know.

Did Joe have an enemy?"

Mrs. Simmons shook her head. "No, he hadn't an enemy in the world that I know of. I don't know who could have done this terrible thing."

"I don't either, but I'm going to find out. Tell me—was Joe in any trouble?"

Mrs. Simmons bit her lip. Finally she volunteered. "He seemed a lot worried about something lately—a bill we owed. But of course that couldn't have anything to do with this."

"Forgive me if I am meddling in personal things. But Joe was a friend of mine. I can't overlook any chances. To whom did he owe this bill?"

"Why—why he borrowed some money from one of those loan men who walk the streets."

A warning bell rang in the back of Quade's head. He knew of the loan usurers, human sharks who carried their offices under their hats, sought out prospective victims, loaned them money at exorbitant rates, then heckled their victims ever after. Was Joe Simmons a victim of one of these sharks?

"How much did he borrow and how much had he repaid?"

Mrs. Simmons' lips trembled. "Joe borrowed fifty dollars almost a year ago when young Jimmy was hurt in the auto accident. He was to pay five dollars interest a week. I—Joe paid back almost two hundred dollars in interest, but still owes the fifty dollars. You see, Joe earned only a small salary and even paying five dollars a week was a hardship. The man has been pressing him lately."

Two hundred dollars interest in a year on a fifty dollar loan! Oliver Quade's blood ran cold as he thought of it. He knew about this extortion racket from newspapers, magazines and talk with many men who were hard up. Cold, merciless leeches sucking the blood of their victims. It was estimated that they took ten million a year from the poor in New York City alone.

"The man's name, Mrs. Simmons?" he asked softly, but there was metal in the tone.

"Well, Joe used to talk about a Nate Burger. Whenever he paid off some money he got a little receipt which had just the man's initials—N.B."

N.B.—the initials in the little red circle on Quade's soiled white shirt—from the signet ring of one of the two men who had killed Joe Simmons!

"You have some of those receipts here?"

Mrs. Simmons rose. From a cheap bureau she pulled out a handful of small square pieces of paper, torn from a tiny pad. Each sheet was about an inch and a half in diameter.

Quade took them from the woman's hand. He looked at one. All that was on it was the amount, "$5," written in pencil, and a red circle with the initials N.B. inside.

"Can I have one of these, Mrs. Simmons?" he asked.

She nodded. "They're no good to me now. I couldn't possibly repay the loan and I don't believe I would if I could. You think this might have something to do with Joe's—"

Quade pocketed the little square of paper. "I believe it has. Thank you, Mrs. Simmons. I'll get in touch with you later. Good-by."

Out in the hallway Quade ran into young Jimmy Simmons. Quade drew a thick roll of bills from his pocket. He peeled off a half dozen twenties. "Here, son, give this to your mother."

The boy's eyes bulged. It was more money than he'd ever seen. He hesitated for a moment, then suddenly seized the bills and ran into the next room, crying out excitedly. Quade slipped outside.

A BLOCK AWAY he entered a corner saloon. He had a glass of beer and sipped it slowly. It was the slack time of day and the bartender lingered for a bit of conversation.

"Haven't seen you for some time, Mr. Quade. Could you be telling me now what's the biggest breed of chickens? There was an argyment here last night."

"The Jersey Giant is the largest standard-bred fowl, according to the American Standard of Perfection," Quade replied automatically. "Standard weight for cocks is fourteen pounds. Next in size comes the Orpington—but hell, what am I starting?"

He looked up into the delighted face of the bartender. "And sure, Mr. Quade is there anything in this world you don't know about?"

"Yes," said Quade, "I don't know much about these usurers—the loan sharks who walk the streets."

"Ah g'wan," said the bartender. "Everybody knows about them. There must be a hundred of them on the East Side alone. They hang around the places where they's a lot of low-paid men working. Lend 'em money; five dollars, and the poor fish pays back six dollars for a week's loan of the five."

"I know about that," said Quade. "But surely there must be some system to that racket. Why it's a gold mine; the racketeers wouldn't let a bunch of small time crooks get away with such a business very long."

"They haven't," said the man behind the bar. "Sure and almost everyone knows that these loan sharks all work for the same mob."

"Is that so? I hadn't known. What mob is it?"

The barkeeper shrugged. "Who would it be but the Austrian's mob?"

"Max Wagendorf?"

"Of course."

That was something else. Wagendorf, the biggest racketeer in the city; the man who controlled the gigantic numbers and lottery rackets, who owned night clubs and breweries. Max, the Austrian. So he'd muscled into the usury racket.

Quade sipped a second glass of beer slowly. Then he left the saloon. In a little stationery store a few blocks away he produced the square little piece of paper. "How much would it cost me for a rubber stamp like this?"

The proprietor looked at the red-inked design. "Seventy cents."

"When can I get it?"

"Tomorrow: We don't make them here, you know. The rubber stamp company calls for the orders."

Quade looked at the clock. Two-thirty.

"Have one of these rubber stamps here for me in one hour and I'll pay ten dollars for it. Can do?"

The proprietor looked startled, but nodded quickly.

"I'll close up the store and take it over to the factory myself. At three-thirty."

At three-thirty-two Quade walked again into the stationery store. The proprietor had a small newly-made rubber stamp ready for him.

"Now let's see a stamp pad, one with the same color ink as on that sample."

The man produced an ink pad from a showcase. Quade

pressed the rubber stamp on the pad, then transferred it to a sheet of paper on the counter. He looked at the result and nodded with satisfaction.

"Now some paper," he said.

A half hour later Quade sat at a desk in his room. Before him lay more than fifty square pieces of paper. Each had "$5" written on it in a coarse pencil and the mark of the rubber stamp, a circle with the initials N.B. inside. Quade's eyes were slitted as he stuffed the sheaf of slips into a manila envelope. He picked up a large sheet of paper then, wrote a brief note with his fountain pen and folded it into the envelope. He sealed it and wrote on the front, "Number 1."

With the letter in his coat pocket he left the room. Outside he walked slowly along Third Avenue until he came to the block in which Joe Simmons had been killed that morning. It was a block of big loft buildings where thousands of low wage men and women worked. Good hunting grounds for loan sharks.

Quade stopped in the middle of the sidewalk. The short hair on the back of his neck rose slowly. For there, walking casually in company with another man was N.B., the man who had slugged Quade that morning—the man who had killed Quade's friend, Joe Simmons.

Unperturbed, the wolf was back on his beat, looking for new victims, new men to rob, beat up and kill. The big fellow who had wielded the brass knuckles wasn't with him this time, but the skinny, dark man walking with his hands in his pockets beside N.B. was more deadly. Quade recognized the man's vocation immediately. He knew that the man had more than his hands in his pockets.

SO QUADE WALKED up the street to meet the two men.

N.B. didn't recognize Quade until the latter planted himself in his path. Then he stopped and sneered. "The buttinsky!"

"You know, of course, that the man you beat up this morning died?" Quade asked calmly. Men who had had dealings before with Quade would have recognized the ominous calmness of his tone and would have become wary. But N.B. didn't know Quade.

"You want to make something of it?" he demanded, truculently.

"I suppose you have six men all ready to swear that you were up in the Bronx all morning?"

The usurer looked coolly at Quade. "I have—and what's more I got friends in the right places. So what?"

The dark man nudged N.B. with his right elbow, keeping his hand in his coat pocket.

"Don't you like this fellow, Nate?" he asked.

Nate laughed shortly. "I don't like his manners. It ain't polite to butt into other people's business. Get the idea, fella?"

"I get it," said Quade. He brushed past N.B. He did not look back, but he knew he was being watched out of sight. And he knew, too, that from that moment on his life was in danger. N.B.'s kind didn't like healthy witnesses to their killings.

He turned the corner, crossed the street and walked rapidly up the block. At the next corner he entered a saloon and slipped out of the side entrance immediately. Five minutes later he entered the office of a young attorney several blocks away. The office was on the second floor of a shabby building. Morris Moskowitz was a shabbily dressed young man, but his eyes behind a pair of thick-lens glasses were intelligent.

"Hello, Quade, aren't you in the wrong place?"

"No, Morris, I came to get some information from you."

"You're kidding. You know more about law than I do."

"I didn't come to ask about law. I came to ask how a man can find someone in this city who doesn't have a regular address. Someone who doesn't like people to know where he lives."

Moskowitz' smile became a bit frozen. "Who do you mean?"

"Max Wagendorf."

Moskowitz sat down in his swivel chair and looked up at Quade very shrewdly. "Why would you be wanting to see Max Wagendorf?"

Quade pulled the manila envelope from his pocket. "I have a letter for him—a personal letter."

Moskowitz took the envelope, creased it between his fingers then turned it over and stared at it. "Important?"

"Yes, but I'd rather Max didn't know who it came from. If you know what I mean."

The lawyer rubbed a bristly chin and looked out of the window. "All right," he said, "I'll see that he gets the letter. I owe you a favor or two."

"Thanks, Morris," Quade said warmly. "I'd appreciate if it was delivered soon."

Moskowitz nodded. "Okay. And come around some time, Ollie. I've been reading up on Epictetus. I'll give you an argument."

Quade grinned. "You haven't got a chance. Epictetus was a student of Epicurus, who founded the Epicurean school of philosophy in the first century B.C. The modern version of the Epicurean philosophy is, 'Eat, drink, and be merry for tomorrow ye die'—which reminds me I forgot my lunch. See you later, Morris."

He walked home so wrapped in thought that he was almost struck by a truck while crossing the street The moment he entered his room he went to his bookcase which contained a complete set of the *Encyclopedia Americana*. He took out two volumes, read in each for five minutes, making notes as he read. Then he returned the volumes to the case and left the room.

At the corner drugstore he made purchases amounting to almost ten dollars. In his room again, he took off his coat and rolled up his shirt sleeves. Then he unwrapped the parcels, revealing four or five bottles of liquids and a couple of small cartons containing powders. He worked over the sink, mixing liquids of three of the bottles. The result was a cupful of a very black liquid. He drained his fountain pen, washed it and filled it with the liquid he had just concocted.

Then he got out a large tin basin and began a really serious job of mixing liquids and powders. The task absorbed him for more than an hour. The finished job was a thick pasty substance reeking of sulphur. Gingerly he patted the paste into the bottom of an empty cigar box to a depth of a half inch. He spent another fifteen minutes fitting a dummy bottom into the box, over the layer of paste. He nodded with satisfaction when he was through. Into the box he put the rubber stamp, stamp pad and the remaining little square slips of paper. He closed the box, then, sat down at his desk and wrote a letter—in pencil. A phone call brought a Western Union messenger. Quade gave the boy five dollars and explicit directions as to where to find the addressee of the letter.

An hour later there was a knock on the door of Quade's room. Quade called, "Come in."

The door opened and Brass Knuckles entered. Behind him

was N.B. Brass Knuckles looked in the bathroom and in the closet, then shook his head at N.B. The latter kicked the door shut and nodded toward Quade.

"Frisk him."

Quade rose to his feet and permitted himself to be patted for weapons.

"I've never carried a gun," he said.

"You depend on your brains?" sneered N.B. "Yah, I been checking up on you. You're supposed to be a smart guy. Well, the dumbest thing you ever done in your life was getting mixed up with me. Come on now, come clean."

"Did you bring the money?" Quade asked. "In my letter I said it would cost you five thousand dollars to square yourself for killing Joe Simmons."

N.B. cursed luridly. "You numbskull, did you think I came here to *give you money?*"

"Why of course. Joe Simmons' widow is destitute. You and this gorilla killed Joe—"

"T'hell with that," snarled N.B. "I'm not interested in any widows. I'm interested in knowing what you blabbed to the boss."

"Why I just sent him a bunch of receipts and said that I'd paid you about three hundred smackers, but you were holding out; wouldn't give me back my I.O.U. Anything wrong?"

N.B.'s face turned a sickly green. "*Wrong?* Why you—" A foul string of oaths turned the air of the room blue for a moment Then the loan shark recovered himself. "You know damn well you never borrowed any money from me."

"I know, but does Max know that? He figures you've been making loans on your own hook and holding out on him." Quade smiled.

"That's a lie!" cried N.B. "I never held out a dollar on the chief. I know better than to try it."

"But Max is sure now that you *did* hold out on him. So what?"

N.B.'s face worked spasmodically. "He's—he's threatened to knock me off."

"That wouldn't be nice," Quade chuckled.

THE BIG THUG reached a meaty hand into his pocket and produced a handful of gleaming brass. Quade looked at it, interested. "Brass knuckles. What you figure on doing with them?"

"I'm going to give you a good working over," Brass Knuckles said, pleasure in his voice.

"Like you gave Joe Simmons?"

"Yeah, but I'm going to hit you easier. It hurts more that way. No fun in knocking you out right away."

Quade looked at his wrist-watch. "It's seven forty-two."

"What the devil do I care what time it is?" snarled N.B. "Now sit down at that desk and write a letter to the chief, saying what you wrote about me was a damn lie. On the same kind of paper and with the same kind of ink you wrote the other letter."

Quade looked at his writing desk and pursed his lips. Then he looked again at his wrist-watch. "It's seven forty-three."

"You told me the time a minute ago!" yelped N.B. "Sit down and write."

"Somehow I don't feel like writing this evening," replied Quade. "And you *should* be interested in the time. I would be if I were in your shoes."

A startled look shot into N.B.'s eyes. "Why?"

"Because at exactly eight o'clock Max Wagendorf is coming to see me. Won't he be surprised meeting you here?"

"*What?*" The word wailed through N.B.'s throat. "He's coming *here?*"

"Yes, I asked him to. Told him I was having a bit of a party. Just you and maybe another friend."

"You damned—" yelped Brass "Knuckles. "This is your finish."

Oliver Quade shook his head. He watched Knuckles out of the corner of his eye. The bruiser had slipped the brass on his fist and was crouched, prepared to leap on Quade.

"Take it easy!" Quade snapped, his voice rising for the first time since he'd entered the room. "You touch me and you'll never be able to square yourself with Austrian Max. You know that. No matter where you go, he'll find you sooner or later. It's seven forty-five. Only ten minutes."

N.B. waved Brass Knuckles back. Quade knew then that he had won. N.B. knew his boss.

"You'll square me with him?" N.B. begged hoarsely. "I won't touch you if you will."

"You won't anyway," snapped Quade. "How much money have you got on you?"

The usurer's eyes lit up. "A couple of grand. And listen, it's all yours if you'll only write that letter. Here!"

N.B. jerked out a thick wad of bills. He held them out to Quade. "Take it, only hurry up. Write that letter."

Quade took the money from the loan shark's shaking hands. "It's not enough, but I'll let it ride. This money is going to Joe Simmons' widow."

"Sure, sure, anything you say!" babbled N.B. "Hurry up."

Quade sat down at his writing desk, unscrewed his fountain pen and wrote:

Max Wagendorff:

I'm sorry I wrote that letter about Nate Burger holding out on you. I was mad at him about something. Him and me have made up so now I want to square him. I'm sending the proof along by him with this letter. Quade.

N.B. was reading over Quade's shoulder. "What proof?" he chirped eagerly. Quade reached into a drawer of the desk and pulled out the cigar box containing the slips, rubber stamps— and something else.

"This'll square you with the Austrian."

N.B. let out a tremendous sigh. "Will it!" he exulted. An unholy light came into his eyes. "Gimme back my dough."

Quade got up from his chair and faced the two hoodlums. "So you're going to welsh, are you!"

Brass Knuckles went into a crouch. His lips bared and he growled ominously. Quade reached out his left hand, picked up a heavy cane that was leaning against the wall. He twisted the grip and an eighteen inch steel blade was bared. "Okay, Brass Knuckles!" he invited. "Come on, you with the knucks and me with the steel."

Brass Knuckles cursed. "You should have brung a gat, boss," he whined. "Then we could have fixed him for good."

N.B. looked at the steel and backed to the door. "The devil with him, Knucks. He ain't as smart as he thinks he is. Wait'll Max sees this stuff. The chump! He don't know that Max don't like jokes like this. He'll be getting measured for a wooden kimono tomorrow."

Brass Knuckles' face lightened. "Say—I never thought of that," he chortled. "Let's beat it."

"Don't hang around waiting for Max," Quade said after them. "He's not coming here. That was a stall to get some action out of you."

"You'll get the action," Brass Knuckles promised. "Mebbe not now, but later. You can't hide from Max."

THEY WERE GONE then. Quade looked at the door and shook his head.

Quade spent the evening reading the *Encyclopedia Americana*. At eleven-thirty he heard a boy calling outside "Extra." He opened the window and yelled to the boy. A minute later he closed the window and sat down in his big Morris chair. A headline screamed at him:

Austrian Max Killed

Two Aides Also Die as Bomb Shatters Headquarters of Mob

Max Wagendorff, Czar of the numbers, lotteries and small usury rackets, and two of his aides, Nate Burger and Abe Jones, were literally blown to bits about nine o'clock this evening when a bomb exploded in Austrian Max's apartment in the Bronx. Police were unable to determine—

Quade put down the newspaper. The police didn't know how Austrian Max and his aides had come to their deaths. They would probably never know. But Oliver Quade, the Human Encyclopedia, knew. The books in his bookcase knew too, for from them Quade had got the formulas—the one for making black ink which faded and became invisible as soon as it had dried.

Quade visualized the scene in Austrian Max's apartment. N.B. and Brass Knuckles bursting in with the cigar box containing the "proof" and the letter of confession. He could almost see Austrian Max's face as he opened the letter and found a blank sheet of paper. Well—if Austrian Max hadn't been a killer nothing else would have happened.

But he'd pulled a gun and shot N.B. And the sharp vibration blast of the pistol had exploded the bomb Quade had cunningly concealed in a false bottom of the cigar box.

Quade smiled complacently as he thought of how his passion for encyclopedia reading had helped him. Not one person in a thousand knew that if you added a bit of iodine solution to ammonia, the resulting damp brown paste, when dried, in powder form, was a highly sensitive and lethal explosive. Concocted in the proper dilutions, this seemingly harmless powder had the potentialities of TNT. Only the whiplike, cracking report of a gun-blast would cause sufficient vibrations to bring about the needed concussion and explode the powder.

By firing a gun Austrian Max had irrevocably signed his death warrant—something the law and courts had been unable to do in years, although his life had been forfeit a dozen times over.

Quade went to the bookcase and got out one of the volumes. He sank himself into his easy chair and thumbed pages until he came to *Proboscidea, Elephants.*

He sighed contentedly and began reading.

Death at the Main

OLIVER QUADE HAD perused both the *Social Register* and *Bradstreet's Journal* on a number of occasions and he calculated mentally that there was easily a billion dollars worth of blue blood here tonight in this big renovated barn. Reggie Ragsdale, the host, was worth a hundred million if he was worth a cent; the average fortune of the two hundred-odd other men could be estimated conservatively at five million.

Long Island didn't see many cocking mains. Cocking wasn't a gentleman's sport like horse racing and fox hunting. In fact, many of Long Island's blue-bloods had shaken their heads when Young Ragsdale took up cock fighting. But they had eagerly accepted invitations to the Ragsdale estate to witness the great cocking main between Ragsdale's birds and the best of the Old South, the feathered warriors of George Treadwell.

Ragsdale had cleared out this large barn, had built tiers of seats in the form of a big bowl surrounding the cockpit. The place was ablaze with lights, and servants in uniforms scampered about with liquid refreshments for the guests.

Oliver Quade had crashed the gate and was enjoying himself immensely. He'd heard of the cocking main quite by accident; and being a Southerner by birth and a cocking enthusiast, he'd "crashed." He'd brought along a bagful of books, too. After a long and varied career he never knew when the opportunity might present itself to dispose of a few volumes and he wanted to be prepared for any contingency.

He chuckled at the thought of it. Two hundred millionaires

protected daily by business managers, secretaries and servants; few of them had ever been compelled—or privileged, depending upon your viewpoint—to listen to a really good book salesman. And Quade *was* a good book salesman, the best in the country. Oliver Quade, the Human Encyclopedia, who traveled the country from coast to coast, selling books and salting away twenty thousand dollars every year.

The fights had already been started when Quade bluffed the doorkeeper into letting him into the Ragsdale barn. For an hour he rubbed elbows with the Long Island aristocrats, talked with them and cheered with them while the feathered warriors in the pit fought and bled and died.

The score stood at eight-all now, with the seventeenth and last bout of the evening to come up, which would decide the superiority of Ragsdale's Jungle Shawls and the Whitehackles of George Treadwell. Ragsdale rose to make an announcement as the handlers carried out the birds after the sixteenth fight.

"There'll be a short intermission of ten minutes before the final bout, gentlemen."

Quade's eyes sparkled. This was his golden chance, the one he'd waited for all evening. Perhaps they'd throw him out, but Quade had been thrown out of places before. Chuckling, he climbed upon a bench. He held out his hands in a supplicating gesture.

"Gentlemen," he cried out suddenly in a booming voice that surprised people who heard it issue from such a lean body, "give me your attention for a minute. I'm going to entertain you— something entirely new and different."

A couple of attendants looked with surprised eyes at Quade. Reggie Ragsdale, on the other side of the pit, frowned. Quade knew that he'd have to talk fast—catch the interest of the audience before Ragsdale tried to stop him. He had confidence in his oratorical powers.

"Gentlemen," he continued in his rich, penetrating voice. "I'm Oliver Quade, the Human Encyclopedia. I have the greatest brain in the United States, probably the greatest in the world. I know the answers to all questions; what came first, the chicken or the egg; the population of Sydney, Australia; the dates of every battle from the beginning of history; the founders of your family fortunes. Try me out, gentlemen. Any question at all—any! History, science, mathematics, general interest. You, sir, ask me a question!"

Quade, knowing the hesitation of any audience to get started, pointed to a man close to him, whose mouth was agape.

The man flushed, stammered. "Why, uh—I don't know anything I want to ask—Yes, I do! At what price did N.T.&T. close today?"

"Easy!" cried Quade. "You could read that in today's newspaper. National Telephone and Telegraph closed today at 187 ½. A year ago today it was 153. Ask me something harder. You, sir," he pointed. "A question; history, science, mathematics—"

"What is the distance to the moon?"

"From the center of the earth to the center of the moon the distance is approximately 238,857 miles. Next question!"

The game was catching on. Quade didn't have to point at anyone now. The audience had gathered its wits and the next question came promptly.

"What is ambergris?"

"Ambergris is a greasy substance spewed up by sick whales and is used in the manufacture of perfumes. It comes in lumps and is extremely valuable, a chunk of approximately thirty pounds recently found in the North Atlantic bringing $5,200. Next!"

"How do you measure the thickness of leather?" That was evidently a wealthy shoe manufacturer, but his question didn't phase Quade in the least.

"By irons," he shot back. "An iron is one seventy-second of an inch. The ordinary shoe sole is eight irons thick, although some run as thick as twelve irons and those on dancing pumps as thin as four irons—And now—"

Quade stooped, snapped open his suitcase and extracted a thick volume from it. He held it aloft. "And now I'm going to give each and every gentleman here tonight an opportunity to learn the answers *themselves* to any question that may arise, today, tomorrow or any time during the year. This book has the answers to ALL questions. *The Compendium of Human Knowledge,* the knowledge of the ages crammed into one volume, two thousand pages. Classified, condensed and abbreviated."

Quade paused for a brief breath and shot a glance at Reggie Ragsdale. The young millionaire, who had assumed a tolerant, amused expression a few moments ago when he saw that Quade's game was catching with the guests was frowning again. Entertaining the guests was all right, but selling something to them, that was different! Quade knew that he'd have to work even faster.

He launched again into his sales talk, exhorting in a vibrant, penetrating voice that was famous throughout the country. "The price of this magnificent volume is not twenty-five dollars as you might expect, not even fifteen or ten dollars, but a paltry two ninety-five. It sounds preposterous, I know, but it's really true. The knowledge of the ages for only two ninety-five! Yes, Mr. Ragsdale, you want to ask a question before you purchase one of these marvelous books?"

"I don't want to buy your confounded book!" cried Ragsdale. "I want to know how you got in here?"

Quade chuckled. "Why, your doorkeeper let me in. I told him I was a book salesman and thought this gathering would be ideal for selling books. Really, Mr. Ragsdale, that's exactly what I told him and he let me in. Of course, if he didn't believe me, that's not my fault."

A roar of laughter swept the audience. None doubted that Quade had actually made his entrance in that manner. His audacity appealed to the thrill-jaded aristocrats. Even Ragsdale grinned.

"All right, you can stay. But put up your books now; they're coming in with the birds for the last fight. After it, you can sell your books. I'll even buy one myself."

Quade was disappointed. He'd made his pitch, built up his audience to the selling point and he didn't like to quit before collecting. But he couldn't very well cross Ragsdale—and sight of the handlers coming in with the birds was making the sportsmen turn to the pit. The best book in the world couldn't compete against a couple of fighting roosters.

Quade closed his sample case, walked down to Reggie Ragsdale's ringside seat and prepared to watch the last fight of the evening. Ragsdale grinned at him.

The handlers were down in the pit now. Ragsdale's handler, Tom Dodd, carried a huge, red Jungle Shawl and Treadwell's handler, Cleve Storm, a fierce-looking Whitehackle.

"Treadwell must have a lot of confidence in that Whitehackle," Quade remarked. "He's battle-scarred. Been in at least four professional fights."

Ragsdale looked at Quade in surprise. "Ah, you know that cocks are at their best in their first fight?"

"Of course," said Quade. "I was raised down in Alabama and fought a few cocks of my own. That Whitehackle must be one of those rare ones that's improved with every fight instead of deteriorated. Ah!"

The referee had finished giving the handlers their instructions and Storm and Dodd retired to opposite sides of the sand-covered pit.

The referee looked at first one handler, then another. He hesitated a moment, then cried, "Time!"

Both handlers released their birds. There was a fluttering of wings, a rushing of air from both directions—and a sudden rumbling of voices from the audience. For the Jungle Shawl faltered in his charge—turned yellow. An unforgivable weakness in a fighting bird.

It cost the Shawl his life, for with a squawk and flutter of wings the Whitehackle hurtled through the air and pounced on his opponent. His vicious beak hooked into the hackle of the Shawl and for a second he straddled the bird, then the two-inch steel gaffe slashed down—and the Jungle Shawl was dead!

"Hung!" cried Tom Dodd.

Both handlers rushed forward. Quade looked at Reggie Ragsdale. The young millionaire was rising to his feet, his lips twisted into a wry grin. Quade looked across the cockpit at George Treadwell—and gasped.

Treadwell was still seated, but his arms and head hung over

the top of the pit and even as Quade looked, his hat fell from his head and dropped to the sandy floor. At the distance Quade could see that Treadwell's eyes were glassy.

"Treadwell!" Reggie Ragsdale exclaimed. He, too, had glanced across the pit.

Ragsdale brushed past Quade and hurried around the pit to Treadwell's side, Quade following. Other spectators saw Treadwell then and a bedlam of noise went up.

"Don't anyone leave!" thundered Ragsdale, his bored manner gone. "Treadwell is dead!"

"He's been murdered!"

The three words rang out above the rumble of noise. Quade looked down into the pit at the awe-stricken face of Cleve Storm, Treadwell's handler.

"Don't be a fool, man!" he cautioned. "You can't make an accusation like that! Mr. Treadwell probably died of heart failure."

"He's been murdered, I tell you!" cried Storm. "There wasn't nothin' the matter with his heart."

Ragsdale straightened beside Quade. "Doctor Pardley!" he called.

A middle-aged man with a grey-flecked Vandyke came up. He made a quick examination of George Treadwell, without touching the body. Then he frowned at Ragsdale. "Hard to say, Reggie. Might have been apoplexy—except that he's not the type."

Ragsdale blinked. "He was a dead-game sportsman—I'll see that his widow receives my check at once."

"That ain't gonna bring him back to life!" cried Cleve Storm. "I—I warned him not to come up here."

"Why?" snapped Ragsdale testily.

Cleve Storm looked around the circle of hostile faces, for most of the men here were personal friends of Ragsdale. He gulped. "Because he didn't have a chance—not against your money. You—you always win."

Ragsdale winced. It was the deadliest insult any man could have hurled at him: to accuse him of not being a real sportsman. His lips tightened.

Quade came to Ragsdale's assistance. "I'd advise you to keep your opinions—for the cops."

Ragsdale flashed him a wan smile of thanks. "That's right, we've got to call the police. And when the newspapers hear of this!"

Quade knew what he meant. Cock fighting was an undercover sport. A murder on the Ragsdale estate—cock fighting. The tabloids would have a scoop.

Ragsdale signaled to a steward. "Telephone for the Charlton police, Louis," he ordered. "Tell them someone died here—might possibly be a murder." He did not spare himself.

Quade looked at his leather case full of books and shook his head. Well, this shattered his hopes of making sales. The prospective customers wouldn't be in the mood now for buying books, even if Quade had the bad taste to try selling them with a corpse just a few feet away.

Wait—a thought struck Quade. The police! They'd be here in a few minutes. This might be a murder after all and everyone here knew everyone else—except Quade. He was a gatecrasher—and he was *not* a millionaire. Why—why, he might even have some very bad moments trying to explain his presence here.

The police came, four of them, led by Chief Kells. With them came the county medical examiner. There was deference in the chief's manner as he approached Ragsdale.

"Cock fighting, sir? It's going to make quite a stir in town. It's—it's against the law!"

"I know," replied Ragsdale wearily. "Go ahead, do your duty."

The chief looked importantly at the medical examiner who was already going over the body of George Treadwell. "Very well, sir, you might begin by telling me just what happened."

Ragsdale sighed. "Our birds were fighting in the pit—the last bout. My bird lost. When I looked across the pit, there was Treadwell, head hanging over the railing, dead."

"Who was beside him?" asked the chief.

Ragsdale shook his head. "I don't know, several of my guests, I suppose. I know only that I was directly opposite him across the width of the pit. But no one—excepting myself—had any motive for wishing his death."

"And why yourself?" The chief pounced on Ragsdale's self-accusal.

"Because I had a bet with Treadwell and lost."

The chief looked worried, but just then the medical examiner came up. He, too, was frowning. "Not a mark on him," he said. "Yet I'd swear that it wasn't apoplexy or heart failure. Symptoms indicate he's been poisoned, but I can't find anything on him. I'll have to do a post-mortem."

Cleve Storm, who had released his Whitehackle in the pit and come up, sprang forward. "I knew he was poisoned. I knew it."

"How did you know it?" asked Chief Kells sharply. "And who are you anyway?"

"He was Treadwell's trainer," explained Ragsdale. "A loyal employee."

Kells shrugged his shoulders hopelessly. "It would have to be murder. All right, Mr. Ragsdale. I've got to do some questioning. How much money did you have bet on the final outcome of these cock fights?"

"Ten thousand—no, wait. Thirty-five thousand altogether. Ten thousand with Treadwell and twenty-five thousand with a man down in the South."

"Who? Is he here?"

"No, and I really don't know the man except by reputation. The bet was made through correspondence. A cocking enthusiast who lives in Nashville; C. Pitts is the name."

The chief's eyes narrowed. "That sounds screwy. You mean this Pitts guy just up and sent you twenty-five thousand as a bet?"

"Not exactly. Pitts sent the money to the editor of the *Feathered Fighter*," explained Ragsdale. "I gave my own check to Mr. Morgan when he arrived here."

"That's true," said a heavy-set man, stepping forward. "I have both checks in my pocket right now."

Kells bit his lip. "You know this Pitts fellow?"

"Not personally," said the magazine man, "but by reputation. He bets on many of the cocking mains and I've held stakes for him before. The arrangements have always been made by mail."

Kells grunted. "How long you been raising roosters, Mr. Ragsdale? I thought horses was your game."

"They are, but a few months ago Treadwell got me interested in game cocks. To tell you the truth, I've only raised a few birds and they're still too young to fight. All the cocks I fought here tonight were purchased specially for the occasion. It's quite ethical, I assure you."

Quade perked up his ears. This was ironical indeed. Ragsdale with millions at his command and intensely interested in winning in everything he did, had probably spent an enormous sum for his fighting birds—and yet they'd lost, against ordinary fighting birds raised by Treadwell himself. Quade began to take a more serious interest in the situation. There might be something here yet that would prove interesting, perhaps afford Quade an opportunity to use that marvelous brain of his.

"From whom did you buy your roosters?" Kells again.

"Terence Walcott, who lives in the state of Oregon. Tom Dodd brought the birds east and handled them for me, during the fights. Dodd!"

Tom Dodd came forward. He was a little bandy-legged man of about forty.

"You the chap who raises these roosters?" questioned the chief.

"Yes, I work for Mr. Terence Walcott of Corvallis, Oregon. I been working around game cocks all my life."

"Where were you when Treadwell was kil—died?"

"In the pit, of course."

Kells looked at Ragsdale for confirmation. The latter nodded. "That's right. He was down in the pit. In the opposite corner from Treadwell. Treadwell's handler, Cleve Storm, was in the other corner, just under Treadwell's seat. Federle, the referee, was all around the pit."

"And everybody was watching them? That sorta lets those three out. Well, who was close by Treadwell at the moment?"

"I was," a lean, middle-aged man spoke up. "I was right beside him on his left. I was so excited over the fights down in the pit, however, that I didn't even know anything had happened to poor George Treadwell until Ragsdale came dashing around."

The chief looked at the man with suspicion-laden eyes. "What's your name?"

"Ralph Wilcoxson. Treadwell was my business partner. Treadwell & Wilcoxson, Lumber."

The chief looked even more hostile than before. "And who was on the other side of him?"

"I was," said Morgan, the editor of the *Feathered Fighter*.

The chief snorted in disgust. "Hell, everyone here is a friend of someone and respectable as a deacon. What chance have I got?"

Louis, the steward, who was standing behind his master, coughed. "Pardon, sir, everyone here isn't a friend. I—I let the gentlemen in at the door—and one of them didn't have a card."

Quade swore softly. Ragsdale, the sportsman, hadn't seen fit to betray him, but the servant who'd been the butt of Quade's harmless joke awhile ago, couldn't take it. This was his revenge.

"He means me, Chief," he said, beating the traitorous steward to the punch.

The chief's shoulders hunched, and his teeth bared. Here was someone who didn't belong. "Who are you?" he asked, in a voice that almost shook the rafters.

Quade grinned impudently. "Oliver Quade, the Human Encyclopedia, the man who knows the answers to all questions." The introduction rolled glibly off Quade's tongue. It was part of his showmanship.

The chief's mouth dropped open. "Human Encyclopedia! What the hell you talkin' about?"

"Just what I said. I'm the Human Encyclopedia who knows everything."

"Ask him who killed Treadwell," called out a wag in the crowd.

Quade winced. His wits had been wool-gathering, otherwise he'd never have left himself open for that. The chief pounced on it, too. "All right, Mr. Encyclopedia—who and what killed Treadwell?"

Quade gulped. "Ah, now, Chief, you're not playing fair! Even Human Encyclopedias have a code of professional ethics. We don't go into competition with other professions. You wouldn't think it fair for cops to take in laundry on the side or sell moth tabs from door to door?"

Chief Kells tried to look stern but made a failure of it. "So you're not so smart after all."

"Well," said Quade, "it's against union rules, but I'll help out a bit." He pointed at the body of Treadwell. "Notice how the arms are hanging over the pit. I suggest you look at the hands!"

The medical examiner sprang forward, reached down and picked up Treadwell's limp arms. He exclaimed almost immediately. "He's right. There's a tiny spot of blood right in the palm of his right hand. And it's inflamed. Looks like he's been struck with a hypodermic!"

The chief whirled and leveled a finger at Cleve Storm. "You—you're the man!"

The cock handler's jaw dropped and his eyes threatened to pop from his head. "Me?" he cried.

"Yes, you! You been doing all the hollering about murder around here and you're the only one *could* have done it!"

"I could not!" screamed Storm, suddenly panic-stricken that

the tables had been turned on him. "I was down in the pit when he was killed."

The chief nodded grimly. "That's why I'm accusing you. Look," he pointed at the body of Treadwell. "He's hanging over the pit right over the side where you was waiting while the roosters were fighting. Dodd was over on Ragsdale's side, so it couldn't have been him. And the referee was moving all around, which lets him out."

The chief's reasoning was sound, but the expression on Cleve Storm's face caused Quade to pucker up his brow. Storm didn't act like a murderer—and if he really was, he'd been damned dumb awhile ago to insist on murder when everyone else was willing to let it go as heart failure.

He looked down into the cockpit. The Whitehackle was still down there and was now quietly scratching away in the sand, hopefully trying to find a worm or bug. But where was the Jungle Shawl's carcass?

Chief Kells spat out a stream of tobacco juice. "I'm arresting you, Storm. If I find a hypodermic anywhere around here you're as good as burned right now. Oscar!" He signaled to one of his policemen. "Go over that pit down there, inch by inch. Look for a needle or hypodermic. You, Myers and Coons, you go over this place with a fine-tooth comb!"

Kells turned to Reggie Ragsdale. "I don't believe there'll be any more now, Mr. Ragsdale. Of course you know I got to bring charges about the cock fighting. That'll mean maybe a small fine or suspended sentence. You'll be notified when to appear in court."

Ragsdale nodded. "Of course, Chief, and thanks for the way you've handled things here. I'll speak to the board of council-men about you."

The chief's eyes glowed. He rubbed his hands together and began shouting orders. Men bustled around. The body of Treadwell was carried out on a stretcher. Cleve Storm, still protesting his innocence, was led out. Guests began to leave.

Quade gathered up his bagful of books and topcoat. He walked over to Ragsdale. "Sorry about the trouble. Hope everything will work out all right."

"Thanks." The young sportsman smiled wanly.

Quade nodded and swung around. His topcoat caught on the top of the railing. He gave it a jerk and it came away with a slight ripping sound. Quade swore softly. The coat was only about a year old. He reached out to touch a nail on which the coat had caught.

He stopped his fingers an inch from the point and his eyes narrowed suddenly. It wasn't a nail on which the coat had caught, but a needle. It stuck up about a sixteenth of an inch from the top of the flat railing. This was the exact spot behind which Treadwell had sat.

At that moment one of the policemen down in the pit yelled. "I've found it!" He held aloft a shiny hypodermic needle. The medical examiner hurried down into the pit and took the needle from the policeman's hand. He sniffed at it. "Not sure," he said, "but it smells like *curare,* that stuff the South American Indians put on their blow-gun arrows. Kills instantly. Figured it was something like this that killed Treadwell," he said triumphantly.

Quade shook his head. *Curare* at a cock fight! Things were getting complicated. A scrap of information in the back of Quade's head bothered him. He had a habit of filing away odd bits of information in his encyclopedic brain, and when he had time, marshaling them together like the pieces of a crossword puzzle. A marvelous memory and this faculty of fitting together apparently irrelevant bits of information was largely responsible for his nickname—the Human Encyclopedia.

Quade deserved that name. Fifteen years ago he'd come into possession of a set of the *Encyclopedia Americana,* twenty-five large volumes. Quade read all the volumes from *A* to *Z* and then when he had finished, began at *A* again. He was now at *PU* on the fifth trip through the volumes. Fifteen years of reading the encyclopedias, plus extensive reading of other books had given him a truly encyclopedic brain.

What was this odd bit of information that puzzled him? It had something to do with the mix-up here tonight—something he'd observed or heard. Storm? No, because Quade was quite sure Storm was innocent. Something about the birds?

He hesitated for a moment, then sauntered over to the rear door of the barn. He slipped out quietly.

The yard was pitch dark. In the front of the building he could hear voices and automobiles, but back here it was as still and dark as the inside of a pocket. There was no moon or stars. A long black shadow loomed up ahead. Quade made his way toward it.

As he approached the building he recognized it for a Cornell type laying house. There was a door at one end of the building. Quade set down his bag and tried it. It was unlocked. He pushed it open. He stepped inside and struck a match. By the light of it he saw a light switch beside the door. He turned it and electric lights sprang on.

Quade saw that the building was evidently used as a conditioning room for poultry. Wire coops, sacks of feed, a bench on which stood cans of oil, remedies, tonics and other para-phernalia. Quade examined the objects and grinned. There was even a box of face rouge. Having raised birds himself he knew that breeders often used rouge to touch up the ear lobes of the birds. Baking soda was used to bring out the color of the red Jungle Shawl birds. The oil was for slicking up the feathers.

A large gunny sack on the floor caught his eye. There was a small pool of dark liquid beside the sack. Quade stooped and picked up the shawl. He dumped out the contents—four Jungle Shawl cocks—dead.

Four? Nine of Ragsdale's birds had met defeat. Quade hadn't seen all the bouts, but he'd been informed by other spectators that six of the losing Shawls had been killed, three merely wounded. Well, where were the other two carcasses? The bag was large enough to have held all of them. That didn't make sense. If Tom Dodd had brought the carcasses here why hadn't he brought them all? Or hadn't Dodd brought them here?

A sound behind him caused Quade to whirl. He was just in time to see the door push open and a couple of hairy arms reach in. The hands held a huge, red fighting cock. Even as Quade looked, the cock was dropped to the floor and the door slammed shut. Quade heard the hasp rattle outside and knew that the person who had thrown in the Jungle Shawl had locked the door on the outside.

Quade's eyes were focused on the fighting cock. The bird was ruffling up his hackles and uttering warning squawks. Quade gasped. He'd known game cocks down in the South to kill full-grown sheep with their naked spurs—and those were ordinary games. These Jungle Shawls were only one generation removed from the wild ancestors of the Malay jungles.

This particular cock was well equipped for fighting. It had needle pointed steel gaffs on his spurs which seemed to Quade longer than those the birds in the pits had used. They were at least three inches long.

One slash of those powerful legs and the needles would rip through clothing, skin and flesh. They would lay open a thigh to the bone.

Quade was given no time for thought. With a sudden vicious squawk the Jungle Shawl hurled himself at Quade, half running, half flying. Quade sprang backward and collided with a sack of egg-mash. He stumbled on it and tripped to the floor. He rolled over on his side as quickly as he could and just missed the attack of the angry rooster. One wing brushed his face. He sprang to his feet and put a safe distance between himself and the bird.

The cock whirled and uttered a defiant screech. Then it charged again. Quade sidestepped and began stripping off his topcoat which he'd donned before leaving the big barn. He held the coat a foot or so before him and waited.

The bird charged. Quade flicked out the coat like a bull fighter teasing a bull and lashed out with his foot at the same time. The bird hit the coat and there was the ripping sound of cloth. At the same moment Quade's foot caught something solid and a sharp streak of pain shot through his leg.

The kick hurled the bird several feet backward and Quade looked down. The steel gaffs had slashed the topcoat clean through, pierced Quade's trouser leg and the skin underneath. Quade felt the warm blood course down his shin and cursed aloud.

He was fighting a losing fight, he knew. The bird seemed

hurt by the kick but was preparing for another charge. Quade tossed his coat aside and sprang across the room for a heavy broom that stood against the wall.

Glass tinkled as Quade hefted the broom. His eyes shot to the little window beside the door. A red galvanized pail appeared in the opening and its liquid contents poured in to the floor with a tremendous splash. The fumes of gasoline hit Quade's nostrils and he gasped. The distraction fortunately had also attracted the attention of the fighting cock, for if it had charged just then it would have been too bad for Quade.

The hair on Quade's neck bristled. He had a feeling that he was in the most dangerous spot of his entire life. In front of him a fighting cock—and on the side—?

The rooster was cackling again. Quade took the fight to the bird now. He rushed across the room and met him in full charge. The smack of the broom as it hit the rooster could have been heard a hundred yards away. The cock screeched as it was lifted off its feet and hurled against the wall. Quade followed up his attack, smashed the bird again as it hit the floor.

Then—then the entire room shot up in one terrific blaze of fire. The attacker outside the shed had tossed a blazing piece of newspaper into the gasoline. One entire side of the room was a sheet of flame, from floor to ceiling. Quade rushed back from the crippled bird and stared, panic-stricken, at the fire.

The door was locked on the outside. The windows were small and had wire mesh nailed outside of the glass. He could never get through one of them—not in time at least. This building was made of dry spruce boards. It would be in ashes inside of ten minutes.

Quade was trapped.

Heat from the huge flames scorched Quade's face. Fire! Of what use now was his encyclopedia knowledge when he was trapped in a burning building? Was there anything in the *Encyclopedia Americana* that would tell him how to get out of such a predicament?

Fire—what would extinguish a fire? Water. There was none in here. Chemicals. There were none—Wait!

Chemicals—no—but baking soda! Why, there were three large cartons of it right here behind him on the bench. Baking soda, one of the finest dry fire extinguishers in the world. Quade had read about it in his encyclopedias and had tried it out—as he had many other things that particularly interested him. He'd built a fire of charcoal wood and paper, had let it blaze fiercely. Then with an ordinary carton of baking soda he'd put out the fire in an instant. That had been an experiment on a small scale, however; would it work on a large scale—when it was an absolute necessity?

Quade reached behind him and snatched up a five-pound carton of baking soda. He reached in, drew out a handful and hurled it into the midst of the big blaze. A flash of white leaped high and was followed by greyish smoke. Quade's eyes, looking sharply at the floor where the soda fell, saw that the fire burned less fiercely there.

He advanced on the fire then. It seared his face and hands, but he threw the baking soda full into the flames, handful after handful. Then, finally, with a desperate gesture, he emptied the box. He whirled his back on the fire and started back for the second box. He caught it up, ripped open the cover and turned it on the fire.

A wild surge of joy rose in him. Why, there was a wide swath of blackened flooring now leading to the door. The fire still blazed around the edges but the heart was cut out of it. Quade attacked the fire with renewed effort. He hurled soda right and left. His eyes smarted, his lungs choked and his skin was scorched, but he persisted. The second box of soda went and now the fire was but a few flickering flames around the edges. It required only a few handfuls from the third box to put out the last little flame.

Quade surveyed the fire-blackened wreckage and let out a tremendous sigh of relief. A stench of burnt flesh penetrated his nostrils. A mass of smoking flesh and feathers told of the fate of the fighting cock that had attacked him.

Five minutes later Quade leaned against the doorbell of the big Ragsdale residence. A butler opened the door, gasped and tried to close the door again, but Quade shoved it open smartly and stepped into the hallway.

"Mr. Ragsdale in?"

The butler rolled his eyes wildly. "Why—uh—I don't think so."

Quade heard voices and the tinkling of glasses ahead. He brushed past the butler. A wide door opened off the hallway into a luxuriously furnished room, containing about twenty men. Ragsdale, standing just inside the door, caught sight of Quade and cried out in astonishment. "Why—it's Oliver Quade. Good Lord, man, what happened to you?"

Quade walked into the room. His eyes searched the crowd, picking out familiar faces—Morgan, Wilcoxson, the medical examiner, even Tom Dodd. Then his eyes came back to Ragsdale. "One of your hen houses caught on fire and I put it out," he explained.

"Good for you!" exclaimed Ragsdale. "We all left the barn right after the police found the hypodermic which pinned Treadwell's murder on Cleve Storm."

"Storm didn't kill Treadwell," Quade said bluntly. "The murderer is right here in this room. He's the same man who poisoned your Jungle Shawls and made you lose the cocking main."

"He's a liar!" Tom Dodd, face black as a thundercloud, came forward. "Your birds weren't poisoned, Mr. Ragsdale. I handled them myself and examined each one before I pitted them."

Quade looked insolently at the furious handler. "I didn't see all the bouts, but I did see four Shawls in a row get killed—and each one of them was killed because he apparently turned yellow—and faltered. But they didn't really falter. They were poisoned—"

"That's a lie!" screamed Tom Dodd. "The Shawls lost because they were up against better birds."

Quade grinned wolfishly. "Say—whose side are *you* on?" he asked. "You brought those Shawls here and claimed they were the best in the world."

"That's right!" snapped Ragsdale. "I paid Walcott a fancy price for those birds and he guaranteed them to beat the best in the country."

"I think they would have," Quade assured him. "They were real fighters. One of them almost killed me—but let that pass for the moment. Mr. Ragsdale, just to prove my point, pick up that phone there and call Mr. Terence Walcott, of Corvallis, Oregon."

"Why should he call up the boss?" cried Dodd. "I'm the handler. I've raised fighting cocks all my life!"

"Have you?" Quade didn't seem impressed. "I've raised a few birds myself. By the way, have you gentlemen noticed that we Southerners use different cocking terms than Northerners? For example, up here you say, 'stuck' when a bird is wounded. Down South we say 'hung.' Am I right, Mr. Morgan?"

"That's right, Mr. Quade," the editor replied. "There's quite a difference in the terminology of the South and North. I've published articles on the subject in my magazines."

"Well, did any of you notice that every time a Jungle Shawl was hung, Tom Dodd cried out, 'Hung'? Yet Mr. Dodd says he comes from the *North!*"

The silence in the room was suddenly so profound that Tom Dodd's hoarse breathing sounded like a rasping cough. Quade broke the silence. "By the way, Dodd, that's a peculiar ring you're wearing. Mind letting me take a look at it?"

Tom Dodd looked down at the ring on his left hand. His lips moved silently for a moment, then he looked at Quade. "No—I don't mind. Here—"

He started toward Quade who, to the surprise of everyone in the room, suddenly lashed out with his right fist. He put everything into the blow, the pent-up emotion and anger he'd accumulated in the burning poultry house. The fist caught Dodd on the point of the jaw, smashed him back into a couple of the guests. They made no move to catch him and Dodd slid off them to the floor. He lay in a huddle, quiet.

"There's your murderer!" cried Quade, blowing on his fist.

That broke the spell. Men began shouting questions. Quade stooped down, slipped the ornate ring from Dodd's finger. He held it up for all to see. "See this little needle that shoots out on the inside of the ring?" Heads craned forward.

"That's why those birds of yours died without fighting, Mr. Ragsdale," Quade explained. "Just as Dodd would let them go, he'd prick them with this needle. There's poison on it, which took effect almost instantly."

Ragsdale shook his head in bewilderment. "But Treadwell—"

"Was killed in a similar fashion, but not with the ring. Remember there was an intermission before the last fight—during which I tried to sell you men a few books," Quade grinned. "That's when Dodd stuck a little poisoned needle into the flat top of the railing where Treadwell sat. Perhaps he'd noticed Treadwell eyeing him with suspicion. Suspecting that he was poisoning the cocks. Dodd worked out the whole thing pretty cleverly. Took no chances. Witness the hypodermic which he tossed into the sand. That was for a blind.

"He'd figured out that when Treadwell's bird won the last and deciding bout that Treadwell would probably smack the railing in his excitement—maybe he'd watched him doing it after other bouts. Well, that's exactly what Treadwell did. The needle's still in the railing. I ripped my coat on it when I started to leave."

"But what made you suspect Dodd?" asked Ragsdale.

Quade grinned. "My encyclopedic brain, I guess. In the excitement of learning that Treadwell was murdered, Dodd was still cool enough to remove the carcass of the Shawl. That was the first thing that got me to thinking. Then the matter of terminology stuck in my mind. I didn't catch it at first. Dodd cried out 'hung' every time. Well, that's a Southern term and Dodd was supposed to have come from Oregon: claimed he'd lived there all his life."

"You mean to say that Dodd does not actually come from

Oregon?" exclaimed Ragsdale. "Why—that would mean that he isn't really Dodd at all?"

"Right," said Quade. "And Treadwell must have known that. He'd probably met the right Dodd at some time or other. I suspect you'll learn after talking to Walcott on the phone that the real Dodd doesn't look like this one at all. Where he is, I don't know. This chap may have bought him off, murdered him perhaps. That isn't so important because he'll burn for the murder of Treadwell anyway. It's enough that we know this chap took the real Dodd's place somewhere between Oregon and here."

"Yes—but who is he?" asked Ragsdale.

Quade screwed up his lips. "I think you'll find that he sometimes uses the name of C. Pitts. In fact, I'm willing to lay odds that a hand writing expert will declare the signature on that check Morgan has, was made by this chap. Twenty-five thousand is a lot of money and Mr. Pitts wanted to make sure he won."

"I'll be damned!" said Ragsdale. "You've certainly figured everything out. And—I believe you. I can understand now why they call you the Human Encyclopedia."

Quade's eyes lit up. "That reminds me—I didn't get finished out there in the barn. So if you have no objections, I'll continue with my little talk about *The Compendium of Human Knowledge*. 'All the knowledge of the ages condensed into one volume.'"

Murder on the Midway

The Human Encyclopedia Spins a Whirlwind Roundup and Dazzles a Killer!

THE RUMBLING OF machinery, the roaring of the "Crack-the-Whip" cars, the squealing of many thrill seekers failed to drown out Oliver Quade's stentorian voice. Quade, tall and lean and wearing a loud checked suit, was on a three-foot platform making a high pitch. His booming voice, famous from coast to coast, had attracted an audience of more than a hundred.

Quade strutted, waved his arms and stamped about the platform.

"I'm Oliver Quade, the Human Encyclopedia," he boomed. "I know the answer to all questions—history, science, mathematics, general knowledge. Anything at all. Ask me a question, someone!"

A pause, during which the clamor from the tent just behind caused Quade's audience to move uneasily. Then Quade pointed at a man in the front of the crowd.

"You, sir," he roared. "Ask me a question. On any subject under the sun. I'll answer—and correctly. History, science, mathematics, general— Ah!"

The man said something in a tone too low for the crowd to hear, but Quade's sharp ears picked it up.

"Who was the nineteen-twenty Olympic four-hundred-meter hurdles champion?" he repeated it aloud. He paused dramatically, his face breaking into a huge smile. "The nineteen-twenty Olympic four-hundred-meter hurdles champion was Frank Loomis of Chicago, a member of the Chicago

Athletic Association. His time—fifty-four seconds, not a world's record, shaving been surpassed several times before and since— Look it up in the sporting records, or your encyclopedia if you have one— All right, ask me another question, friends; sports, science, economics—"

"Who invented the periscope?" someone in the middle of the crowd asked.

QUADE'S EYES FLASHED. "That's a bad one to answer, friend," he shot back. "Because no patent for the periscope was ever issued. But— Morgan Robertson, who posthumously received fame as an author of sea stories, is generally considered to be the inventor of the periscope. He worked twenty years perfecting it and all modern periscopes are built on his basic principles. Robertson was refused a patent because another storyteller, Jules Verne of France, in his book, *Twenty Thousand Leagues Under the Sea*, described a fictitious periscope— Next question."

The audience was catching on now. "What's the hardest metal?" someone yelled.

"Tungsten," Quade shot back promptly. "Melts at thirty-three hundred and seventy degrees Centigrade. Next!"

"Who were the first civilized people?"

"How far is Chicago from St. Louis?"

"How do you make angel food cake?"

"What's the best way to catch mice?"

The questions came fast and furious. Quade, master showman, orator supreme, answered them all, hopping about on his platform, gesticulating. For five minutes the questions and answered were hurled back and forth, then Quade called a sudden, dramatic halt.

"No more questions for the moment. I have proved to everyone here that I am what I say I am—the Human Encyclopedia. I know the answers to all questions. But listen—" He paused for effect, then he shot out thundering, rapid-fire words. "You—and you—and you—" pointing—"can learn the answers to all these questions yourselves. You can astound your friends by your knowledge of every subject under the sun. You can be the life of the party, the envy of your rivals and the satisfaction of yourselves. Know the answers to everything. Here's how!"

Quade reached into a black bag that was standing open beside him and brought out a thick book.

"By this—the greatest book ever published. *The Compendium of Human Knowledge.* The knowl-

edge of the ages, classified, condensed, abbreviated, all this in one volume. A complete high school education."

Quade's voice dropped but still carried to the farthest away of his audience.

"How much is a high school education worth to you? Five thousand dollars? How much would it cost you to get? One thousand? Two?—No, you don't have to pay that much. Because you can get one by reading that book, the greatest of its kind. And you won't have to pay anywhere near what that high school education would cost. Friends, when I tell you what I'm asking for this book you won't believe me. You'll think it absurd—so much for so little. Twenty-five dollars? Ten? Five? No—no! Only the insignificant, paltry sum of two dollars and ninety-five cents. That's every cent this book will cost. But please—please don't crowd!"

No one crowded. Quade hadn't expected them to. They never did. Master psychologist, keenly aware of his own spell-binding powers, he knew his audience were like sheep, waiting for the bell-wether. And Quade didn't work with a "shill." He didn't need one. He pointed merely at the first person below his stand.

"You! You want this book, of course?"

And the man nodded. Quade dropped from his platform, handed the man a book, accepted a bill and made change. The man next to the first looked timid. Quade forced a book into his hands. After that it was a stampede. Quade sold every volume in the bag, went to the big box under his stand for re-fills and emptied the bag again.

Twenty-eight volumes out of an audience of about a hundred. Not so good; not so bad. The ordinary book pitchman would have sold less than ten. Quade wasn't an ordinary salesman however; he was the greatest book salesman in the country, netting twenty thousand a year.

The crowd was milling about, leaving, new persons were gathering. Confusion. Quade retired to his stand, held out his hand for silence and prepared to launch into another pitch. He never started on it, however.

As Quade mounted his platform a hoodlum at the rear of the crowd cut loose at him with a chunk of stone. It missed Quade by six inches. The hoodlum let fly again. Quade saw it coming and ducked, otherwise it would have struck his head.

"Hey—you damn roughneck!" he thundered. "Cut it out or I'll come out there and tan your hide."

A raucous north-of-Harlem and south-of-White Plains cheer was the answer. The hoodlum, a rat-faced punk who wore a red and yellow turtle-neck sweater, let fly with a stone almost as large as his fist. Quade ducked, whirled and caught the brickbat as it bounced from the tent behind him. Like lightning he fired the stone back at the hoodlum.

"Oh!"

It was a woman who screamed. Quade gasped. For there, a few feet to one side of the hoodlum a man with face suddenly bloody, staggered and pitched to the ground. Quade was dumbfounded. Why—why he had seen *his* stone strike the ground beside the ratty hoodlum. Yet this man had been hit by something thrown.

"He's killed!" somebody cried hysterically.

Quade leaped from the platform, straight into the crowd. It melted before him. In fifteen seconds he reached the fallen man. He looked behind him, saw the hoodlum just disappearing around the African Dodger concession. Quade cursed under his breath and dropped to one knee.

The stricken man was done for, Quade could see that at once. Something had struck him squarely in the forehead, smashed the bone and smeared both eyes. He was a ghastly sight. But disregarding the gore, Quade slipped his hand under the man's head.

"Sorry, old-timer," he said, huskily. "Sorry as hell!"

THE WOUNDED MAN twitched. His bloody jaws worked.

"Aureus—Henry—Clay!" he gurgled, then the mouth dropped wide open. A rattle in the throat forced out confined air and the body went limp.

Quade put the head back on the ground and rose to his feet. Absent-mindedly, he whisked out a handkerchief and wiped his hands. His brain worked like lightning. He knew his stone had not struck this man; someone else therefore had thrown something. But who—and for what reason?

For that matter, why had the hoodlum thrown the stones at Quade? He wasn't just a mischievous boy. Quade had seen him clearly and the man had been over thirty years of age. Why should he single out Quade for a vicious attack? An enemy?

Quade shook his head. He'd traveled the country for fifteen years selling his books in all sections. He'd made enemies, but not more than did the average person. He usually minded his own business, seldom went out of his way for trouble, although he did not avoid it when it came looking for him.

"Who done this?"

The ungrammatical question was barked into Quade's ear.

He turned and looked into the scowling face above a blue uniform. He shrugged.

"A bum threw stones at me," he implied. "I threw one back—and this bum fell over dead."

"So yuh killed him, eh?" The cop's face became grim and he reached for his handcuffs.

"No," Quade replied firmly. "I didn't hit him with my stone. It hit the ground ten feet from this man. Someone else threw something— which hit him."

"Yah," jeered the cop. "You threw a stone and this bloke's head is smashed open. Come on, hold out your dukes."

"What's the trouble here?" snapped a voice of authority.

The newcomer was Gus Conrad, owner of the circus. Quade sighed in relief.

"Hello, Mr. Conrad. I'm glad you're here. Looks like I'm in a jam. This man was killed and I threw a stone at someone." Rapidly he explained what had happened.

When he finished the circus owner shook his head. "Damn! Why do such things always happen to my circus?"

A MAN DRESSED in an ill-fitting suit came up. "I think he's telling the truth. Look at this!"

Quade looked at the object in the man's hand, then stared. The man was holding a stone-composition billiard ball. A black one with a couple of white circles in which were the numeral "8." The eight ball. One of the white spots blurred with a red smear. Blood.

"Where'd you get this?" Quade snapped.

The man jerked his hand to the right. "Over there. It bounced from his head. I picked it up."

"That makes things look different," said Gus Conrad. "If you can prove now that you threw a stone and not a pool ball—"

"I can vouch for that," spoke up another bystander. Quade, who had a camera memory, recognized him at once. This was the man who had been in the front during Quade's pitch, the one who had asked the question about the hurdles champion.

"I was right up in front of him," offered the man. "I saw the stone that guy threw. It was a rough, flat stone. It bounced from the tent wall and Mr. Quade here, caught it and threw it back."

The cop swore. "Damn it, why the hell you want to make it tougher?" he complained to the innocent bystander. "I had it all worked out and—"

"—And you'd just as soon throw an innocent man into the hoosegow as a guilty one," Conrad finished. "Well, you can't do it. I look out for my friends."

Quade thought of the hundred dollar "nut" he had paid for the privilege of working on the grounds of the circus during its four-day stand in this town, he grinned. Well, if it cost a hundred dollars to be a friend of Conrad, all right.

"I'd better call the chief and the Black Maria," said the cop. "The chief will thrash it out with you guys."

Conrad, the policeman, Quade and the material witness adjourned to the front of the circus grounds. There, on a siding, stood a train of special railroad coaches, owned by the circus. Conrad used one of the cars for a combination office and living quarters.

The chief and a couple of detectives tore up in a car just as the little group reached the special car.

"Murder!" the chief greeted the group, belligerently. "I knew it'd happen just as soon as we let the circus into this town."

Conrad's eyes glinted dangerously. "Come on inside the car," he snapped. "We'll thrash this out."

The entire group crowded into the car. Quade noted with surprise that it was quite roomy inside. Conrad dropped into a swivel chair behind a desk at one end of the room. He motioned Quade to a chair beside his desk. The policeman and witnesses gathered on the other side of the desk. The arrangement was obvious. The two circus men opposed against the rest of the assemblage.

They fought it out in that fashion, an hour of bickering, snapping and accusing. The chief threatened two or three times to close down the circus. At one stage of the argument he had Quade already at the door, preparatory to taking him into town.

But in the end, Quade and Conrad prevailed. It was fairly obvious that Quade had not killed the man and the chief knew it. His argument was mainly directed toward the circus as a breeder of viciousness. Conrad chewed up two pencils during his heated defense.

The chief finally drew off his forces with a final warning that if just one more act of violence occurred on the grounds the circus would be closed down.

When they had left Quade picked up a copy of *Billboard* from Conrad's desk and fanned himself with it.

"Phew! What a stubborn crowd! I was afraid any minute they would get onto the identity of the dead man. If the chief had known he was with the show, we'd probably been battling for another couple of hours."

"He wasn't with the show," said Conrad.

"No? I thought I'd seen him around?"

"Yah, sure. It was Charlie Miller, but he wasn't really with the show. He hung around, but that's all. Just one of the riff-raff that always hangs around any show. Sometimes he worked as a shill for a concessionaire, but mostly he did nothing but lift a leather or two. Miller was just no-account."

Quade put the copy of *Billboard* back on the desk and picked up a copy of the *American Numismatist* from the desk.

"Why do you let guys like that hang around your circus?"

"How the hell can I get rid of them?" snorted Conrad. "There's fifty or more of them follow every circus. They're what give a show a bad name. I throw them out whenever I got a legitimate excuse, but I got plenty of other things to look after besides worry about grifters."

Quade could understand that. It had been a tough year for all shows and circuses. Owners were frantic because of poor business.

"Just one thing more," he said to Conrad. "Where would someone pick up a pool ball around here? It isn't the sort of luck-piece a man usually carries around in his pockets."

CONRAD SPREAD OUT his hands. "Anywhere else it might be a strange thing. But not here. There's a half dozen concessionaires use pool balls. Roll-down layouts and such. For that matter, there's a pool table in the employees' recreation car. Anyone in the circus could pick up a ball."

Which made every member of the circus a suspect. Not so good. Quade shook his head and left Conrad in his private car. He returned to the "Crack-the-Whip" tent. His stand was still there, but alas, the books he'd left under it had all disappeared. Proof that his pitch had been a good one. The crowd had just helped themselves.

He had another stock of books at the express office, but it was too late to get them today. It would be dark in a little while. The mishap would cost Quade a hundred dollars or more.

He was annoyed. His encyclopedic brain puzzled over the problem of the killing. It didn't make sense and things that didn't worried him. A student all his life, he always sought the logical explanation for everything.

Fifteen years ago he'd purchased a set of the *Encyclopedia Americana,* a monumental work in twenty-five large volumes. Quade read every volume from cover to cover, then when he had finished "Z" he started all over again with "A." In fifteen years he'd gone through the books four times and was now on "N" on the fifth trip.

That was the secret of his amazing knowledge of almost every subject under the sun. Voracious reading of the *Encyclopedia Americana,* supplemented by other reading.

Why would anyone want deliberately to kill Charles Miller, a circus roustabout? Revenge? The only type of person who'd want to kill Miller for revenge would be in his own social strata—another roustabout. Men like that did not work out such careful plans.

For profit, then? What could a roustabout have that anyone would commit murder to possess?

Those were questions that Quade wanted to answer in his own mind. He drifted about the midway. He stopped at a concession or two. The circus people had heard of the tragedy. Most of the concessionaires sympathized with him. Others were noncommittal. Many of them knew Miller by sight or reputation.

"He wasn't doing anything, just now," one man told Quade.

Another spat in disgust at mention of Miller's name.

"Lousy crook, he had it coming to him. Him and his pals have made it tough for all of us the last four-five towns."

QUADE PRICKED UP his ears. "Pals? Who are they?"

"Some more no-accounts like himself. They got a tent over on the edge of the grounds. Al Dingo, Izzy Klein and a couple more like them."

Quade's eyes became pensive. He nodded to the concessionaire and moved on. He inquired the way to the tent of the roustabouts and found it to be one of several pitched at the far side of the fair grounds on which the circus was located. He found an oddly assorted trio of men loafing in the tent. They had heard about Miller's death and they knew about Oliver Quade. Izzy Klein was brutally frank in speaking their thoughts.

"I think Charlie was conked by your brick."

"I don't care what *you* think," Quade snapped. "I know I didn't hit him and I want to find out who did. It wasn't an accident, of that I'm sure. I'd like to see Charlie's effects."

"There they are," jeered Al Dingo, a sour-faced beanpole of a man. "That's all he owned, except for the clothes he was wearing."

Quade looked at the bunk to which Dingo had pointed. All he saw on the canvas cot was a moth-eaten old army blanket—and a beautiful red Persian cat.

"You mean the cat?"

"Yeah," snorted Izzy. "That's all. A damn cat. He lugged it with him everywhere."

Quade shook his head, puzzled. A roustabout, making a

pet of an aristocratic cat. The animal purred, stretched itself and walked daintily along the bunk to Quade. Quade patted its head and the cat arched its back. Yes, it was a pet all right, for it wore a collar studded with flat, round metal ornaments.

"Any of you fellows know a bird by name of Clay—Henry Clay?" Quade asked the question casually, but he was watching the trio sharply.

Dingo guffawed. "So yuh think Henry Clay killed Miller?"

"I didn't say that," Quade replied. "But—Miller whispered that name to me just before he cashed in his chips."

Dingo looked at Izzy Klein and nodded.

"Well, mebbe you're right," Klein said. "I guess you oughta pinch this Henry Clay."

Quade looked at them suspiciously. "I'm not a cop," he said, steadily. "But I'd like to ask this Henry Clay a couple of questions."

"Go right ahead," snickered Dingo. "You got hold of him."

Quade didn't need a diagram. Henry Clay was the name of Miller's pet, the Persian cat. His only possession, he naturally thought of its welfare with his dying breath. Quade rose to his feet.

"All right, the laugh's on me. Well, I'll be seeing you boys— in jail, I hope."

Jeers followed him outside. Quade walked huffily away from the tent. Henry Clay, a cat. Well, that angle was washed up. Now for that "Aureus." It was getting dark and lights were going on along the midway. Quade made his way to the main gate, found a public telephone booth there. He looked into a directory for a number, then called it.

"Hello, *Chronicle?*" he said a moment later. "Gimme the city desk."

A bored voice said, "Yeah."

"This is the *Buzz-buzzville Daily,*" Quade said, purposely slurring his words. "I want you to tell me if anyone lost an aureus. Sure, I know what an aureus is. You don't? Well, I'll tell—"

The conversation lasted just two minutes, then Quade hung up. When he came out of the booth his face was thoughtful.

Quade walked back along the midway. Lights were blazing brilliantly and the evening crowds were gathering. He stopped at the African Dodger concession, beside the lot where he'd had his own pitch. He surveyed it thoughtfully.

Someone standing at the edge, presumably throwing soft baseballs at the Dodger in the rear of the tent, could by mere side twist heave a ball to the left into the open space where Quade had made his pitch. And suppose the man had a pool ball with him? It wouldn't be hard to mix it with the baseballs without being detected.

A big, hard-faced man was standing inside the counter, ballyhooing for customers.

"Try your skill, folks. Make him dodge. Hit him and you win a cigar. Try your skill—lots of fun!"

The spieler scowled when Quade stopped before him. "Whata you want?"

Quade looked bitterly at him. "Who was standing here heaving balls when Charlie Miller was killed next door?"

"How would I know?" retorted the concessionaire. "There's been a hundred customers here today."

"What's your name?" Quade shot at him suddenly.

"Bauer," said the big man. "Not that it's any of your busi—"

"Bauer," Quade repeated softly. "Dutch Bauer. You pitched for the Three Eye League back in Twenty-four."

Bauer's eyes widened. "How did you know?" he demanded.

"I know everything," said Quade firmly. "I'm the Human Encyclopedia."

"Yeah?" sneered Bauer. "Then you ought to know that I ain't the only former ball player on this lot. Al Dingo caught for a good team, in a bush league four years and even Gus Conrad, the owner, was a high class player before he bought this circus."

Quade nodded. "I know their pedigrees. I even know that you got kicked out of baseball for boozing."

Bauer wet his lips. "But I can still heave a ball," he said boastfully. "Look!" He picked up a baseball from the counter, whirled and threw it suddenly at the African Dodger whose head was stuck through a hole in the canvas rear wall, some forty feet away. The colored man let out a yelp as he saw Bauer throwing at him and tried to jerk his head back through the hole. He didn't make it however. The soft ball hit his skull and bounced back twenty feet.

Then the Dodger jerked his head back through the opening. As he did Quade gave a start. The colored man had revealed the top part of his clothing—a red and white striped turtle-neck sweater!

QUADE NODDED TO Bauer. "Okay, Dutch, I'll be seeing you again."

He started off, then swung around the side of the tent. He hurried to the rear, jerked open a canvas door and stepped into a narrow section behind the canvas backdrop of the concession.

The African Dodger had his head through the hole again, but Quade had been right. The man *was* wearing a red and white turtle-neck sweater, and he was a small man.

Eyes grim, Quade strode up to him. The Dodger heard him and pulled his head back. He choked when he saw Quade.

"Hello, pal," Quade greeted him. "I almost didn't recognize you with that black grease paint on your face."

The Dodger looked suddenly sick. "G'wan, cheese it," he said, half heartedly. "You don't know me—and they ain't no one allowed back here."

"Fine," said Quade. "Then come outside with me. I'd like to have you tell the cops why you threw stones at me."

"You're nuts!" cried the fake Negro. "I never threw no stones at you."

"There were only about one hundred witnesses," said Quade grimly.

"After we wash your face they'll be able to identify you easily. Come along."

"No—no! I didn't do nothing," whined the Dodger. "Honest. A guy gimme ten bucks to break up your pitch. That's all—Honest, I didn't know Charlie Miller was going to get bumped."

"No? Well I'll believe you," said Quade, "if you'll tell me who hired you to throw the stones at me."

"I—I can't tell you!" cried the Dodger, desperately.

"You'll tell," said Quade grimly, "or come along to jail."

Quade reached out for the little man, saw his eyes go wide in fear—and then something swished past Quade's face. There was a loud smack and the features of the Dodger's face suddenly changed. Quade whirled, saw the flap of the door fall into place. He half turned, saw the Dodger crumpling to the ground, then tore out of the tent into the lot where he had that afternoon had his pitch.

Too late! The lot was vacant. The killer might have run any

one of four directions. Quade hesitated uncertainly for a moment, then rushed back into the tent. The Dodger might be able to talk.

But he wasn't—he was dead. Quade knew what had killed him even before he found the weapon. He had seen Charlie Miller's smashed face. He found the pool ball, a red one this time, with the number "3" on it. Quade looked bleakly at it, then dropped the ball into his side coat pocket.

"Hey, Nick!" yelled a voice out front. "Get on the job!"

That was Dutch Bauer, calling for the Dodger to dodge some balls. But the Dodger hadn't been able to dodge a ball, and he would attempt it no more.

Lips thin, Quade ducked out of the tent. Outside, in the darkness he made his way cautiously back to the section where were located the tents of the roustabouts. The tent occupied by Dingo, Klein and the others was dark. The men were no doubt out trying to pick up some leathers from the evening crowds.

Quade opened the door flap and stepped into the darkness. There was a rush of wind and Quade, tensed for something like that, threw himself forward. Something smashed on his right shoulder, numbing it. Quade's face collided with a pair of legs and he wrapped his good arm around them viciously. He tugged and pushed forward at the same time.

A BIG BODY collapsed on top of him. Quade squirmed from under, lashed out in the darkness. His fist met muscle and flesh, but at the same instant something swished out of the darkness again and exploded on Quade's jaw. Lightning shot through his brain from a hundred different directions. He didn't go out, but he lay half-stunned for a minute or two.

Then he groaned and shook his head to clear out the cobwebs. On his knees he reached into his vest pocket and drew out his cigarette lighter. He flicked it into light.

His assailant had fled, but the result of his work here in the tent lay before Quade's hands—a ball of yellow fur. Henry Clay, the Persian cat. It was dead.

Quade reached out and touched the cat. The collar that had been around its neck that afternoon was gone.

"Too late," Quade said under his breath. He started to get up, then saw something on the dirt floor at his feet. He picked it up. It was half of a wooden hexagonal pencil, broken, no doubt in the fight with Quade's assailant. Quade looked at the pencil, then put it into his pocket.

There was a light in Gus Conrad's private car. Gus Conrad looked up from his desk when Quade pushed open the door of the car and entered without knocking.

"What's the idea bustin' in?" he began in his customary blustering tone.

Quade pushed the door shut. "Some things I wanted to tell you, Conrad."

"I was just going to get supper," said the stocky circus owner. "Hurry up and spill what's on your mind."

"Ever see an aureus?" Quade asked deliberately.

For just a second Conrad sat stiff, but then he leaned back in his swivel chair.

"An aureus?" he repeated. "What's that—an animal?"

"No, it's a coin," said Quade. "A gold coin of ancient Rome. It has a value of twenty silver denari—about three dollars and forty cents in modern money."

Conrad screwed up his face. "Come to think of it, I have

heard of an aureus."

Quade pointed at Conrad's desk. "I'm glad you admit it. You see, I happen to know that you subscribe to the *American Numismatist*. A copy is right there on your desk. I saw it there when I was in here before."

Gus Conrad hitched up his chair. "Enough of this cat-and-mouse stuff. Out with what's on your mind!"

"All right!" snapped Quade. "Here it is. Charlie Miller cracked a safe back in Delport a week or two ago. He got only a few dollars in real money—but he also got an aureus, for the man whose safe he happened to crack was Milson, who owned the only Justinian aureus in existence."

"Go on," said Conrad, icily. "You interest me. What did Miller do with this aureus?"

"He put it on his Persian cat's collar. I'm guessing he didn't know the value of the coin, until maybe he got hold of one of your magazines, or maybe he came to you and asked about it. I don't know about that, but I do know that you learned about it in some way and knowing that this particular coin is worth sixty thousand dollars you killed Charlie Miller!"

For just a moment Gus Conrad sat rigidly. Then he laughed. "All right, Quade," he said, shortly. "You win. Here's the damn coin." He pulled open the drawer of the desk.

THE MOVEMENT CAUGHT Quade by surprise. He threw himself forward, saw that he couldn't reach Conrad across the desk in time, then swerved, and hurled himself sideward to the floor.

Conrad's hand streaked from the desk drawer, an automatic clenched in it. Thunder rocked the room. Red hot fire seared

Quade's left ribs. He hit the floor, turned a half somersault and felt a sudden pain in his hip.

He'd been hit there, too. No, he had heard only one shot so far. Ah—the pool ball in his pocket, the ball with which Conrad had killed Nick, the African Dodger. Quade had fallen on it.

He came up on his knees, saw Conrad's gun bearing down on him. Frantically, he threw himself backwards, jerking at his coat pocket at the same time. His hand closed around the hard pool ball, came out with it. The room rocked again to an explosion and Quade winced as a bullet ploughed through his left thigh.

Then his hand was clear of his pocket. Conrad saw the object in Quade's hand and cried aloud. The cry forced back into his throat, for the pool ball, thrown with all of Quade's strength, hit Conrad squarely, on the nose and left cheek bone.

Conrad went back into his chair, teetered with it a moment, then he and the chair both crashed backwards to the floor. Quade limped around the desk.

He looked down at the floor and let out air in a rush of breath. Conrad wasn't a pretty sight. But Miller and the African Dodger hadn't been either. Conrad, at least, was alive, would live to walk up thirteen steps.

Quade dropped to his knees beside the circus owner. He ran his fingers through Conrad's pockets. In the watch pocket he found what he sought—a small, blackened coin; worth by weight, three dollars and forty cents, but as a curio, sixty thousand dollars.

Conrad moaned and his eyes fluttered open. His mouth worked horribly.

"How—did—you—know?" he gasped.

Quade looked bleakly at the wounded man.

"Because I'm the Human Encyclopedia. I knew right from the start what an aureus was; then when I saw that numismatist magazine in here I was pretty sure *you* had killed Miller. But I didn't have the proof, and didn't know where the aureus was."

"What—proof did you have when—you came—in here?" Conrad brought out painfully.

Quade brought from his pocket the broken half of the pencil which he had picked up beside the dead cat. "This. It dropped from your pocket when you fought with me in the dark. Look—it's all marked up with teeth marks. Every pencil on your desk is marked up that way. I noticed you chewing pencils all during the time the chief of police and his cops were here."

Pictures of Death

*The Human Encyclopedia Stumbles on a
"Candid Camera" Blackmail Set-Up!*

QUADE FROWNED AND looked up from the bulky tome on his lap as the door of his room resounded to the staccato rapping of knuckles. He sighed.

"Come in!" he called out.

A wild-eyed young man of about twenty-five stepped nimbly into the room and closed the door carefully behind him.

"Mr. Quade," he cried, "I'm in dutch! You gotta help me."

"What's up, Herman?" Quade asked.

"I want you to keep this for me." Herman Spiess held out a black, box-shaped camera.

Quade looked quizzically at the camera. He knew it was the outfit with which Herman Spiess made his living, for the youth was one of the army of "roving" photographers who infested the streets of New York. They snapped pedestrians and handed out numbered cards, which the subject of the photograph was supposed to send to the firm's main office, along with a quarter. In exchange the person would be rewarded with a "candid" action photograph.

"Sure, just set it down on the table," Quade nodded.

"If anyone asks you for it, don't let 'em have it. No matter who it is. Okay?" said Spiess as he deposited the camera.

"Right," Quade replied. "I'll guard it like the family jewels."

"Thanks, Mr. Quade." Herman Spiess let out a great sigh of relief. "I'll be seein' you." He popped out of the room as abruptly as he had entered.

Quade shook his head and resumed his reading. In every

corner of the United States, Oliver Quade was known as the Human Encyclopedia, extraordinary book salesman. He possessed an encyclopedic brain.

Fifteen years ago he'd purchased a twenty-five volume set of the *Encyclopedia Americana*. He began with Volume One, Page One, and read straight through the entire twenty-five volumes. Then he began again with Volume One. His spare time was devoted to reading every type of book and periodical, from *History of Needlecraft* to *Holstein-Friesian Cattle Breeder*. But always in between he read systematically the *Encyclopedia Americana*.

Thus, he was now reading for the fifth time the biographical sketch of Claudius Ptolemy, the ancient astronomer and geographer. But something annoyed him. He couldn't concentrate on the mathematical equations by which Ptolemy had evolved his star tables.

A vagrant bit of information refused to fall into a groove in his regimented brain. He looked up from his book and his eyes came to rest on Herman Spiess' black camera. Yes, that was it. The camera didn't really belong to Spiess but to the company for which he worked.

Why hadn't he turned it in this afternoon as customary when he quit work?

And why had Spiess acted as if the safety of the thing were a matter of life and death?

The window at Quade's elbow vibrated suddenly to the thundering report of a gun fired on the street. Quade gasped and leaped to his feet, the encyclopedia falling to the floor. He tore at the window shade to let it up—the gun outside thundered again. This time the report was punctuated by a scream of mortal anguish.

The shade wouldn't work—most things didn't in Mrs. Peebles' boarding house—and Quade, cursing softly, tore it down. It fell on his head and shoulders and it took him a moment to fight free of it. But then he was able to jerk up the window and poke out his head.

The first thing he saw was a figure lying on the sidewalk just at the foot of Mrs. Peebles' steps. His eyes lifted to the figure of a man fifty yards away, running swiftly. It didn't require an encyclopedic brain to figure out what had happened. The fleeing man had shot the prone one and was making his getaway.

A whistle blasted down the street and was followed instantly by the roar of a police positive. Quade jerked his head in the other direction and saw a uniformed cop dashing up.

By that time the assassin was out of sight around the corner. The cop came to a halt by the limp body on the sidewalk. He dropped to his knees and turned the body over gingerly.

Light from a street lamp cast its rays upon the face. Quade, craning his neck, gasped. Why—it was Herman Spiess, the young photographer who less than three minutes ago had been in Quade's room!

QUADE SHOVED DOWN the window, sprang for the door. He tore it open and ran out into the hallway. Other roomers, having heard the shots, were dashing outside. Quade joined them.

When they reached the sidewalk, a crowd of more than twenty persons was surrounding the cop and the gruesome object on the sidewalk. Quade had to peer over shoulders. One look was sufficient for him.

Young Herman Spiess was dead.

Well, there was nothing here that he could do. Police reinforcements would come in a little while and there would be questions. Quade had no mind for them. He turned his back on the throng and started back into Mrs. Peebles' boarding house. The hallway was empty.

Quade started for his room, stopped suddenly. He had left his door open when he'd charged out. It was closed now.

Someone had closed the door, was probably inside. With tight lips, Quade tiptoed to the door, twisted the knob and shoved it open.

A hulking stranger, with battered nose and cauliflower ears stood in the middle of the room, holding Herman Spiess' black camera. He let out a startled oath and whisked a blackjack out of his hip pocket.

"Put down that camera!" Quade said.

"Make me," sneered the thug.

Quade weighed 160, stood five feet ten in his shoes, and his body was steel and whipcord—the result of rigid exercises contained in a physical culture book he had once sold. The pug weighed over 200 pounds and was armed.

Quade leaped forward suddenly, ducked his head and swayed sidewards. The blackjack swished over his head, fanning a light breeze on the back of his neck. Then Quade lashed out with his fist, the blow took the bruiser high on the side of his face, rocked him to his heels.

Quade stepped in, to press his advantage. Then the pug brought the blackjack up from underneath. It smashed under Quade's chin while a streak of fire shot to his brain. He gasped and dropped to his knees. It was only by a superhuman effort that he retained consciousness.

He shook his head and fought to get to his feet. The big man let out a grunt and stepped forward. Throwing himself to one side, Quade caught hold of a chair. His attacker let out a yelp and retreated. Quade followed, but the man reached the door, tore it open and leaped out. Quade was too dizzy to follow. He slammed the door shut after the man.

His chin felt as if it had been broken, but careful examination showed that it was merely bruised. His eyes caught sight of the camera on the floor. The pug had dropped it. Well, *that* at least was safe.

He picked it up and looked at it. Then he bit his lower lip. Herman Spiess had been in abject fear when he'd brought in this camera. He'd cautioned Quade to guard it closely. Inside of three minutes Spiess had met his death and a man who had been lurking near had tried to steal the camera.

Quade's forehead washboarded. Shaking his head in perplexity he stripped off his lounging jacket, donned street coat and hat. Then, with the camera under his arm, he left the room. This time he locked the door behind him.

The hallway was still deserted, but Quade heard a police siren out in front and realized that the crowd would be dispersing in a moment or two. He slipped quietly to the rear of the building, down to the basement and let himself out into the tiny back yard. He scaled a fence into the yard of the building next door and in a couple of minutes came out on the street.

TEN MINUTES LATER he stopped in a drug store in the Grand Central district. There he bought pyrogallic acid, sodium thiosulphate, two shallows, enameled pans and a small, but complete photograph printing outfit. Arms loaded with packages, he checked in at a nearby hotel, signing a fictitious name on the register.

The moment he was alone in his room, Quade locked the door and headed for the bathroom. He unscrewed the bulb over the washbowl, put in a red one, a special lamp for a photographic developing room. Then he mixed his chemicals in the enameled pans.

In was the first time in his life that Oliver Quade had ever developed films, but he went at the task like an expert. The *Encyclopedia Americana* contained four pages of fine print on the subject. Quade had read them five times—the last time, within the month, for PHO was within a hundred pages of Ptolemy.

He'd bought the developing chemicals and the other materials from memory. In his brain, the use of pyrogallic acid was registered just as clearly as was the recipe for making Mississippi hoecake, and the names of all the vice-presidents of the United States.

In a half hour Quade had a half dozen strips of wet paper on which were printed dozens of photographs of people walking, some singly, others in pairs. He adjourned to the bedroom, spread the strips of pictures on the bed and began examining them. He ran over them once, sighed, and with a pair of shears snipped them into individual pictures.

Examining the pictures, he sorted out the "types," girls, youths, young men and girls together. He discarded all these as well as snaps of persons who were evidently out-of-town visitors. That left him with less than twenty pictures. He looked at these more carefully.

Suddenly he drew in a sharp gasp of breath. A picture in his hand showed two men seated in chairs, facing each other. It was an interior picture, for a corner of a desk showed at the elbow of one of them. The man seated in this chair was a middle-aged man.

His face wore a pleasant smile and he seemed to be listening to the other man who was talking eagerly. It was the other man's face that had caught Quade's attention. He had seen it before. He stared at it intently—then it clicked in his brain.

This was Frenchy Renard, the city's leading racketeer, the man who controlled the huge "numbers" and "loan shark" rackets. His name and picture had been much in the papers recently for he was on trial for negligence regarding his income tax. He was out on bail now while his attorneys were girding for their struggle.

The other man Quade could not identify, but it was obvious that he was not the same type as Renard. That meant little, however, for Renard had "connections" everywhere.

Quade started to push the other photographs aside, but thought better of it. He couldn't afford to overlook a bet. It was well, for in studying the remaining pictures he noted the familiar gilt-lettered window of the American Central Bank, which he knew was located on the corner of Madison and 43rd.

Quickly he ran through a few more pictures. Partial views showed the same lettered window. Quade's eyes gleamed. It was evident that Spiess had worked in front of the American Central Bank the day before.

Shuffling the smaller pile of snaps together, he scrutinized them again. He picked out one, merely because it was also an interior picture. It was of a lean, hungry looking man seated, facing the camera, accepting or giving a white envelope to an attractively dressed woman whose back was turned to the camera. Quade bit his lips. There was something peculiar about this picture. He studied it a moment then picked up the picture of Renard. His eyes widened.

THIS PICTURE HAD the same peculiarity. They had both been taken from a height two or three feet *above* the subjects. Things began to click in Quade's brain. That *might* be the motive for the murder of Herman Spiess. He had taken pictures through transoms!

He looked at his watch, saw that it was almost midnight. Clearing the photographs off the bed, he undressed and retired.

Quade had breakfast in a coffee shop near Times Square, the next morning. While he ate he mulled over the events of the night before. Herman Spiess had evidently been killed because of his candid camera—rather, a picture he had snapped with it. The chief suspect seemed to be Frenchy Renard, who was fighting a losing battle with the Federal Government.

There didn't seem to be much use in Quade's trying to pin a murder charge on a man like Renard. But his mind had been made up the minute he had seen Spiess' dead face, and realized that he had been killed because of the camera he had entrusted to Quade. Quade was that sort of a man.

That Spiess had taken snooping, indiscreet pictures did not matter. He had accepted Spiess' friendship in good faith, had been given a charge and Quade would not feel that his duty had been done, until he had apprehended Spiess' murderer, or murderers. Snapping an unwanted picture was not justification for murder, in Quade's opinion. Nothing was.

AFTER BREAKFAST HE strolled north on Seventh Avenue. Inside of a block a roving photographer snapped him. Quade took the printed card the man handed him and read:

An action picture has been made of you. Send this card with 25 cents (coin) to Acme Studios and receive a full postcard-size photograph of yourself in action—

Quade stopped before the photographer. He drew his notebook from his pocket, poised a pencil over it.

"I'm Sully Chadwick," he said, giving the name of a famous columnist of a morning tabloid. "I'm writing a piece about you boys."

"Yeah? What you gonna say?" The roving photographer's eyes lit up.

"Just some human interest stuff about your business," Quade shrugged. "Tell me, what percentage of the people you snap send in m quarter for the picture?"

"Less'n one in ten. The trouble is there's too many boys in this racket now. It used to be good, but now a guy can't make more'n coffee and cake money." The man looked disgusted.

"It's a commission proposition then?"

"Sure and I gotta pay for my own film."

"Is that so?" Quade was becoming really interested. "That means you have to size up people pretty well—figure out which are most likely to send in their quarters."

"Oh sure, guys out with their dames are best. After that, the hicks from the sticks."

"How about the old playboys out with their girl friends? Don't they spend a quarter for a picture?"

"Yeah, they're pretty good and so are the middle-aged dames with their gigolos, but take it all around, the kids about twenty or twenty-two, out with their girls, are the best."

"Thanks," said Quade, moving on. "Read about yourself in *The Globe*."

In the next block he was snapped again, this time by a man working for the Peerless Studios—the company for which Herman Spiess had worked. Quade asked the same questions, but received somewhat different answers.

"I dunno," the man said, "seems to me the young fellows are

the best bets, but the boss thinks different. He tells me to snap more old guys out with dames. It's a lousy racket anyway you take it, though. I wish I'd stayed on the W.P.A. job."

Quade talked to four more roving photographers in the next half hour; only one seemed satisfied with his work and earnings. He was a Manhattan Studios man. There were two more Acme men and another Peerless. The Peerless man preferred middle-aged men with girls, the others, young ones; one of the Acme men said he saved film by snapping only sailors and foreigners, finding that they were his best customers.

Returning to the Times Square subway station, Quade took a shuttle train to Grand Central. He emerged from the Chanin Building, and walked briskly to his lodging house in the Murray Hill district. It was a down-at-the-heels neighborhood, retaining only a remnant of its onetime glory. But Quade had an affection for Mrs. Peebles and had been coming to her place during his trips to New York, for more than a dozen years.

A surprise awaited him in Mrs. Peebles' living room in the form of a lean, hungry looking man of about thirty-five. He was being entertained by Mrs. Peebles, who called to Quade as he passed the door.

"Oh, Mr. Quade, this is Mr. Kellerman, He's been waiting more than an hour to see you." She smiled fondly at her star roomer and hurried out of the room.

Quade looked at Mr, Kellerman and drew in a soft breath of air; for Kellerman was the hungry looking man in the photo Spiess had snapped, the one giving—or taking an envelope from a woman.

"Joe Kellerman's the name, Mr. Quade." Kellerman held out

a limp hand. "I'm manager of the Peerless Studios—the outfit for which Herman Spiess worked."

QUADE HAD EXPECTED this man to be anyone but Spiess' boss.

"Too bad about Herman," he sympathized. "He was a nice lad."

"No, no," said Kellerman hurriedly. "He wasn't so nice. That is, ah, he quit his job two or three days ago—and he didn't bring back the camera."

"What of it?" Quade snapped. He was nettled by the slurring reference to the dead Spiess. "I imagine you got a deposit on it when he started working. Your sort usually does."

"Sure, but only twenty-five bucks. The camera is worth a hundred and fifty, second-hand. It's a real Leica with the new high-speed lens."

"What'd Herman have on you?" Quade shot out suddenly.

Kellerman gave a start and a flush spread over his face.

"So he told you, huh? The damn crook tried to shake me down. A girl applied for a stenographic job at the office and Herman snapped me and her together. Said he'd show the picture to my wife."

So it had been a transom shot that Herman had made of Kellerman and the woman.

"You mean he tried to blackmail you?" Quade asked.

"Blackmail me?" Kellerman said. "I hadn't done anything wrong. Well, maybe the girl was kinda close to me when I shook hands or somethin'. Herman tried to make somethin' of it. Wanted a bigger percentage on the pictures he took. That's what we had the argument about. The damn crook! He ran off with my camera."

"Well, what do you want me to do about it?"

"The camera—that's all I want." Kellerman dry-washed his hands nervously. "Mrs. Peebles told me she saw Herman take it to your room last night—just before he got killed."

A thought struck Quade. He'd left his room last night because he had figured that the big thug would return later in the night—when he was sleeping.

"Come along," he said shortly to Kellerman, and strode toward his room. The door was locked, but when Quade unlocked it and looked in, he was not disappointed. Someone had searched the room during the night and made a thorough job of it. His books were torn from shelves, drawers were emptied to the floor and his clothing from the closet was scattered everywhere.

"Someone's been in here!" He pretended surprise.

"The camera—maybe it's stolen!" said Kellerman, bleating in horror.

"If you can find it in here, I'll let you take my picture," Quade said grimly.

Kellerman almost wept tears. It took Quade ten minutes to get rid of him. Then he took a large leather grip from the closet, filled it with a big stack of books. From a corner he picked up a folding wooden stand about two feet wide. Then with the bag and bench, he left the house. Herman Spiess had worked on the corner of Madison and Forty-third the day before. He must have spotted Frenchy Renard somewhere around there, followed him to the room where he'd snapped the picture.

Perhaps lightning would strike twice in the same place, perhaps Renard would pass the same corner again today. If he came anywhere within a block Quade would see him. With his sales pitch, Quade drew everyone within that distance close to him for a few minutes at least. He was that sort of salesman.

At Madison and Forty-second Quade stepped into a cigar store. He looked up a number in the telephone directory and stepped into a booth.

"Mr. Kellerman, please," he said to the girl who answered.

"Kellerman talking," a voice said a moment later.

It was Kellerman; Quade had called the Peerless Studios just to make sure.

"I called to ask how you were feeling," he said dryly.

"Hey—is that you, Mr. Quade?" Kellerman exclaimed. "I've just been talking to my lawyer. He tells me that inasmuch as Herman loaned you that camera you are responsible for it. So if you don't come across with it I'm gonna sue—"

"Nuts!" said Quade, and banged the receiver on the hook.

In front of the American Central Bank on the next corner Quade opened his high pitch. He looked around, held up both hands and began talking in his booming voice that was famous from coast to coast.

"I'm Oliver Quade, the Human Encyclopedia! I know the answers to all questions—every subject under the sun—history, science, mathematics. Ask me a question, someone. I'll answer it correctly."

A few skeptics gathered and looked sly. Quade went on, giving himself a buildup. The sound of his voice stopped people. In sixty seconds close to a hundred persons had blocked the sidewalk.

Then Quade went to work.

"You, sir," he pointed to a man in the front of the crowd. "Ask me a question—anything at all."

The man reddened at being picked out of the crowd. He grinned foolishly and fidgeted.

"Don't be afraid," Quade coaxed. "Any question at all—any subject."

"When was Texas admitted into the Union?" the man ventured.

"That's the stuff." Quade's eyes lit up. "Texas was admitted into the Union in 1845, after having existed for nine years as an independent republic. Next question."

"How far is Mars from the earth?"

"That is hard to say, as it varies." Quade grimaced. "At intervals of fifteen to seventeen years it approaches to within 35,000,000 miles. But then it recedes to a distance of 63,000,000. Next!"

"How many roadside stands are there in this country?"

"Department of Commerce figures report approximately 200,000, which does not include gasoline filling stations, only those purveying food to the public."

THE AUDIENCE MURMURED. Trivial questions came fast and furious. Quade disposed of them all, without the slightest hesitation. Then suddenly he called a halt and produced a thick book from his heavy grip.

"And now," he boomed, "I'm going to make it possible for every one of you to be able to answer all the questions your friends can put to you. They're all in here, *The Compendium of Human Knowledge*. The knowledge of the ages, condensed, abbreviated, classified."

A nondescript looking man who had edged his way up tugged at Quade's coat. Quade looked down.

"You want to buy a book, friend?"

"No, but my boss across the street heard your spiel and he wants you to bring one across to him," said the man, who looked like an office clerk.

"Eh? I should stop my pitch to deliver a book across the street? Nothing doing. Tell your boss if he wants one to come over here and get it." Quade waved the man away and resumed his sales talk.

Five minutes later, when Quade's leather bag was almost empty, the traffic cop came charging through the crowd.

"Break it up!" he yelled. "You're blockin' traffic."

"I've got a license," Quade said indignantly.

"Not to block traffic, you ain't," retorted the cop. "Now break it up or you'll take a ride in the wagon."

Eyes slitted, Quade stepped down from his stand. He began putting it together, while the cop dispersed the crowd with considerable enthusiasm.

THE FOLDED STAND under his arm and the grip in his hand, Quade turned to the cop.

"Who made the beef?"

"How'd you know?" The policeman's eyes went wide.

"I know that you were minding your own business, then all of a sudden you got ambitious. So someone must have complained!" Quade laughed shortly.

"Well, what of it?" said the law.

Waiting at the curb behind the policeman was the nondescript man who a few minutes ago had wanted Quade to deliver a book across the street. Quade nodded in understanding.

"I get it." He brushed past the cop and stepped up to the man. "Lead on, Perkins."

The man turned and began dodging traffic through to the other side of the street. Quade followed with reckless abandon. The little man ducked into the office building entrance and Quade followed. They rode up in the elevator to the fourteenth floor. There they entered an office door on which was the name of Anthony Middleton, but no business.

None was required. The name of Anthony Middleton was familiar to Quade. He was a politician, an important one even though his picture seldom appeared in the newspapers. He held no office, but he sat behind the scenes and pulled strings while officeholders danced.

There were two desks in the outer office. At one sat a girl. The man who had led Quade up here pointed to the door of a private office.

"Go right in, sir," he said. "Mr. Middleton is expecting you."

Quade pushed open the door, noting as he did so that there was a transom over it. Anthony Middleton was the smiling man who had been snapped by Herman Spiess with Frenchy Renard—and Renard was seated right now in an armchair beside Mr. Middleton's modernistic desk.

"I'm glad you decided to come over, Mr. Quade. I want to buy one of your books—provided you're willing to give a small premium with it." The politician rose to his feet.

"Yeah," Renard joined in. "He'll even pay extra for the premium."

A slight chill ran down Quade's spine. He'd never met Renard before, but through the newspapers he was familiar with the racketeer's career. He was bad medicine.

"All right," said Quade. "We'll assume we've gone through the preliminaries; what's the proposition?"

"You come right to the point," Middleton smiled. "I like that. Well, yesterday afternoon after my secretaries had left, a snooping photographer snapped a picture of Mr. Renard and myself through the transom. He got away, but in his haste dropped some cards which showed that he was one of the roving photographers employed by the Peerless Studios. I called up there this morning and learned that he had been mysteriously killed late last night and the camera containing the films stolen. Your name was mentioned, so I'll give you one thousand dollars for the camera."

"I developed the films," Quade said. "So—you want just the film of you and Mr. Renard. Right?"

"That's all," said Middleton, deprecatingly. "I just want to know that no indiscreet use will be made of that picture. Some, ah, people might get the impression that I—" He coughed and Renard finished for him.

"The idea is that some smart prosecuting attorney might get the idea that Middleton is the 'big shot' behind me." He laughed shortly.

"Well, isn't he?" Quade asked quietly.

"Why, you—" Frenchy Renard leaped to his feet.

Middleton reached out a hand and caught hold of Renard's sleeve.

"Easy," he cautioned. He turned an ingratiating smile upon Quade. "As a matter of fact, I lived on the same street with Frenchy twenty years ago. His business has nothing to do with our friendship. But with Frenchy's affairs as they are now, it wouldn't help either of us for the newspapers to get the wrong idea about our relationship. That's why I want to buy that picture."

"An' if you know what's good for yuh, you'll come across!" snarled Renard.

"Renard." Quade took a deep breath, then looked steadily at Renard. "Before that photographer was killed last night he put that camera into my possession. He begged me not to give it to anyone. I promised I wouldn't—and I have never broken a promise.

"A promise is a promise, Mr. Quade." Middleton's nostrils flared. "You can keep the *camera*—I want only that *one* piece of film. I'll give five thousand dollars for it!"

"Mr. Middleton," Quade said steadily, "you've underestimated me. I'm Oliver Quade, the greatest book salesman in this country. I make twenty thousand a year—honestly!"

He stooped and gathered up his things. Renard took a couple of swift steps forward.

"What you gonna do?" he cried. "Give that picture to the cops?"

"First I'm going to find the murderer of Herman Spiess. After that—" Quade shrugged and walked past Frenchy to the door. Renard let him go.

As Quade stepped out of the building entrance, a big, hulking man who had been loitering there, turned away hurriedly and began looking intently into the bank window. But Quade had gotten a quick glance at him. It was the bruiser who had drawn the blackjack on him in his own room at Mrs. Peebles' boarding house the night before.

He hesitated. The man was an accomplice to the killing of Spiess. He undoubtedly knew the killer and was the link between him and Quade. The man wasn't here by accident; he was waiting here for Quade—to follow him. Well, it was easier to be followed by the quarry than to follow it. Quade started briskly toward Forty-second Street, whistling softly as he walked. He did not look back.

At the corner he turned west to the Grand Central Depot. Out of the corner of his eye he saw the big man, thirty or forty feet in the rear.

THEN SUDDENLY QUADE stopped dead in his tracks. Like a flash of lightning the missing piece in the puzzle which had eluded him all day, fell into place.

He had the solution. He knew who had murdered Herman Spiess. All he had to do now was make the man admit his guilt. And he could do that.

He dashed into the big chain drug store in the depot, worked his way to the prescription department and there wrote out a list of materials he wanted. While he waited he cast a cautious look toward the soda fountain and saw the bruiser toying with soft drinks.

A few minutes later Quade left the drug store. In five minutes he reached his hotel. He grinned. It would be a bit difficult for the trailer now. He couldn't come too close for fear Quade would recognize him, and yet he couldn't let Quade go to his room without knowing where he went. Quade decided to help out. He approached the desk and asked in a loud voice for the key to Room 821.

Reaching his room, Quade locked the door and bolted it on the inside. Then he stripped off his coat and went to work. He scooped together all the prints and films and dumped them into a large manila envelope he had purchased for that use.

Then he adjourned to the bathroom, where he remained for

twenty minutes. When he came out his eyes were smarting. He busied himself for another five minutes in the bedroom, then finally, nodding in satisfaction, sat down in an armchair.

HE DIDN'T HAVE long to wait. In less than five minutes someone rapped sharply on the door.

"Who's there?" Quade called.

"Telegram."

The trap was about to be sprung. No one knew that Quade was registered here, so no one could have sent him a telegram. It had to be the quarry.

Quade opened the door. An automatic was poked into his stomach. Two men pushed into the room, the big bruiser and— Joe Kellerman, manager of the Peerless Studios. The gun was in Kellerman's hand. He shot the bolt in the door and stood with his back toward it.

"Hello, Cull," the bruiser said as he advanced, grinning widely. "Remember me?"

"Sure. You're the dumb cluck I threw out of my place last night." Quade looked at him calmly.

"That's right," agreed the big man. "But here's somethin' I forgot to give you." And he clouted Quade on the side of the face with a huge fist. It was a cruel blow and smashed Quade half across the bed. He rose to his feet, blood dripping from his mouth, his eyes blazing.

The big man stepped forward, but Kellerman interfered.

"Later, Knucks," he said. "When I get through."

"So you're admitting you killed Spiess?" Quade snapped. His good humor was gone.

"He had it comin' to him." Kellerman sneered.

"What's the matter—was he spoiling your blackmail racket?"

"He was trying to cut in on it. The dumb cluck." Kellerman's eyes flashed. "By fool luck he happened to get a picture of Frenchy Renard and said if I didn't come through he'd get Frenchy after me."

It was as Quade had figured it Spiess had learned of Kellerman's racket. The candid photographers from the Peerless Studios with whom he had talked that morning, had really given him the tip-off. They'd said that they'd been instructed by the office to snap mainly pictures of elderly men with young women and elderly women with young men.

When the subjects foolishly sent in their quarters for the snap, Kellerman would look them up. If the person with them was not the husband or wife, Kellerman would approach them with a threat to expose them. It was small blackmail stuff, probably not good for more than fifty dollars at a crack, but anyway Herman had guessed the secret, had spied on his boss, taken a picture in the office, over the transom, of Spiess accepting blackmail money.

"That picture he got of you and the woman," Quade prodded. "He went to the woman and she said she was going to put you behind the bars. The picture was the evidence."

"He tried to play it too many ways and was too dumb to get away with it." Kellerman glowered. "He went to the dame, but then he figured he could get more from me. With the picture he had of Frenchy he knew he could get Frenchy to back him and collect heavy dough from me. That's why I knocked him off. And now I need that camera with the picture of me. That's the only proof anyone could get against me. With it burned up, I'm in the clear all around. Get the idea?"

"Sure," said Quade, "what can I do for you?"

"The camera," growled Kellerman.

"Help yourself." Quade sat down on the bed.

"Look around, Knucks," Kellerman ordered as his eyes became thin slits. "It ain't so small."

Knucks started swearing and searching the room. He looked under the bed, in the bathroom and then at last in the most logical place—the closet. He let out a bellow of triumph and emerged holding the camera.

"Your intelligence is amazing, Knucks," said Quade, dryly.

"Watch him," commanded Kellerman. He took the camera from the bruiser, snapped open the film case, then exclaimed in chagrin: "It's empty!"

"Of course," said Quade. "I developed the films. That's how I learned about the pictures. Herman didn't tell me. Maybe Knucks can find the films now. But he'd better hurry."

"I'll work him over, Boss," growled Knucks.

"In a minute." Kellerman cocked his head to one side. "What did you mean by that crack—we better hurry?"

"You didn't really expect to fool me with that telegram gag, did you? I was expecting you—and the cops'll be here any minute." Quade laughed shortly.

"Why, you—" Kellerman raised his gun and for a moment Quade held his breath. But even though his knuckles were white from tightening about the butt of the gun, Kellerman held his fire. Quade, relieved, pretended fright, however.

"Wait!" he cried. "You win. The films are in a manila envelope, taped to the back of the bureau."

"Get them, Knucks!" ordered Kellerman sharply.

Knucks lumbered to the cheap hotel dresser, dragged it out.

He gave a yelp of satisfaction as he found the big envelope and ripped it loose. He trotted to his employer with it.

Kellerman's eyes glittered. He took the envelope from Knucks, put a finger nail under the edge of the tightly sealed flap—and ripped.

A CLOUD OF white smoke puffed out of the envelope, welled up into the faces of both Kellerman and Knucks, who was hovering by.

Quade, who had been tensed, put everything he had into a punch that he swung on Knucks, who was choking, coughing and swearing in a cloud of acrid, stinging vapor.

The blow landed high on Knucks' jaw, and smashed him into Kellerman, just as the latter was trying to find Quade through the blinding gas to shoot at him. Both men crashed to the floor. The automatic exploded harmlessly and Knucks sank into oblivion, unconscious from Quade's punch. Kellerman rebounded from the floor into Quade's swinging left fist.

Then Quade whirled and bounded into the bathroom. He stuck his head out of the open window, gasping in great lungfuls of air. He had tried to hold his breath out in the bedroom, but some of the gas had got into his eyes and he was almost blinded by streaming tears.

But in a moment or two he drew in his head and doused it in the wash basin. Then, holding a wet handkerchief over his face, he reentered the bedroom and turned on an electric fan. In sixty seconds the gas was cleared out of the room.

Three minutes later as Quade was putting the finishing touches on trussing up Kellerman, the latter groaned and opened his eyes.

"What was that damn stuff?" he gasped.

"Tear gas," replied Quade, giving a yank to a knot.

"Tear gas?" exclaimed Kellerman. "How the hell could you get tear gas into an envelope?"

"By sealing the envelope tightly with paste, except for a tiny hole and by blowing the gas in through that hole with a bellows." Quade grinned impishly.

"Damn, what a stunt." Kellerman shook his head in chagrin.

"I'm the Human Encyclopedia," Quade chuckled. "I can do all kinds of stunts. Such as make tear gas. Want to know how? All you have to do is go to a good drug store and buy some bromoacetone, benxyl bromide, ethyl iodoacetate and chloropicrin. Oh, I forgot! You won't be able to go to any drug stores when you're in jail—waiting for the chair. That gun of yours will match up with the slugs in Spiess and be the final link of evidence to send you there."

Trailer Town

Oliver Quade Looks on Crime from
Behind Bars, While Two Lives Depend
on His Encyclopedic Knowledge!

OLIVER QUADE, THE Human Encyclopedia, drove into the Palm Grove Trailer Town late in the afternoon, parked his trailer in a lot assigned to him and fifteen minutes later was preparing to cook his dinner.

He whistled an aria from *Il Trovatore* as he dropped the veal chops into the frying pan.

But suddenly a discordant note broke into his harmony. He stopped whistling and then he heard it again—the voice of a woman in distress. Quade darted to the screened door of the trailer.

Outside was an indistinct knot of struggling figures. A squat, immensely thick man had one arm encircled about a young, slender chap and was cuffing him with his free hand. Behind him a girl was belaboring the squat man with futile fists.

Quade knew none of the trio involved in the fracas and it was his rule to avoid butting into affairs that did not concern him. But the thick man was plainly hurting the frail one and Quade had a passionate sympathy for any underdog.

"What's all this?" he demanded.

The thick man only continued to wallop his helpless victim. But the girl rushed to Quade. "Help!" she cried. "He's hurting my brother!"

Quade's right hand darted out, caught the squat man's thick wrist. There was strength in Quade's grip. He was a lean man, weighing only a hundred and sixty pounds, although five-feet-ten, but every ounce of his weight was bone and muscle.

The thick man yelped as Quade caught his wrist.

"What the hell!" he snarled.

"Let go of this man!" snapped Quade.

The heavy-set man was an ugly chap. His features reminded Quade of the Neanderthal restoration he had seen in the Field Museum in Chicago.

"Yeah, I'll let go!" the fellow gritted. He whirled and struck Quade a blow on the forehead.

Quade reeled back but caught himself quickly and leaped forward. He struck out with his right hand. He held it stiff and horizontal and it chopped straight at the thick-bodied man's Adam's apple. The man let out a scream that could have been heard a quarter of a mile away. He bent over and clawed at his throat, choking in agony.

Quade turned his back and walked to one side. He frowned when he saw the crowd of trailer folk that had collected to watch the fight.

The girl came up, her eyes shining. "Thank you," she said, softly.

Quade looked into her blue eyes and drew in a quick breath of surprise. He'd caught only a flash of her before, but looking at her now he saw that she was a real beauty. Tall and slender, her lithe figure was frankly revealed in the costume she wore. She wore khaki shorts, a soft tan silk shirt, stout flat-heeled and woolen socks. Her smooth, satiny legs were bare, and she wore no hat—only a ribbon tied around her blond, bobbed hair. But it was her face, aristocratic and intelligent, rather than her figure that attracted Quade. Her features were even and her skin was a smooth, light tan.

The man beside her—she had called him her brother—was

The thick man yelped as Quade caught his wrist

about six feet tall, but slender and ascetic-looking. Except for the fact that he was dark and his sister light, the family resemblance was striking.

"Thanks, old man," he said to Quade, smiling weakly. "That brute tried to annoy Mavis and when she ignored him he became insulting. I tried to chase him away, but—" He broke off, his eyes widening.

Quade whirled. The squat man was over his choking spell, but there were tears in his eyes and he was still in pain. He was glaring at Quade. "I'll fix you for this, guy," he said sourly, "or my name ain't Joe Piper."

"Any time, pal," said Quade, easily. "This is my trailer. I'll be here until tomorrow if you want satisfaction."

His eyes filled with hate the thick-bodied man pushed his

way through the crowd. Quade saw him enter the trailer on the other side of his own. Then he turned back to the girl and her brother. A slight frown was on the girl's forehead.

"I'm worried about him," she said. "He looks pretty mean."

"I can be mean, too, when I have to be," grinned Quade.

She smiled wanly. Her brother cleared his throat. "Sorry, I almost forgot," the tall young man said. "I'm Robert Webster and this is my sister, Mavis."

Quade acknowledged the introduction, gave his own name.

"This is our trailer right here," said the girl, pointing to the one next to Quade's. The smell of burning food suddenly reached Quade's nostrils. He whirled toward his trailer. Smoke was pouring out of a window.

"My veal chops!" he yelped and bounded to the trailer.

The chops were burned to a crisp. Quade threw them into the refuse can and opened wide all the windows of the trailer.

"You'd better come over to our trailer and have dinner," called Mavis Webster from the screen door. "It's our fault your chops burned."

Quade grinned. "Think you can feed another mouth?"

"We certainly can!" she laughed.

"All right, I'll be over soon's I put some adhesive tape on this scratch."

Quade had discovered blood on his forehead where the thick man's fist had bruised him. It smarted a little, so he washed the wound, put antiseptic on it and finished it up with a piece of adhesive tape.

The dinner was delightful and Quade enjoyed it immensely. The Websters, he learned, were traveling because of Bob Webster's poor health. He had been a broker in New York, but had been compelled to give up the work. Quade gathered that they had an income.

MAVIS TALKED SO well on every topic that came up that Quade was astonished. Talk was his stock in trade, and knowledge—a smattering of it on every subject under the sun—was his hobby. But this girl was able to hold her own in every subject they touched.

Quade saw her frown several times, though, and finally Bob Webster told him, chuckling: "Mavis saw that sign—Human Encyclopedia—on your trailer. She's testing you."

Quade grinned. "The name is part of the show," he explained. "You'll see after dinner."

"You have read extensively, haven't you?" Mavis asked him.

"I've read the Encyclopedia Americana from cover to cover, not once, but four times."

Mavis was amazed. "Why—why, there are twenty-five large volumes. How long—"

That was a question that Quade was often asked. "Fifteen years," he said. "I'm now on the 'Rs' on the fifth trip through—But it's getting late. Come out and listen to my pitch. It might amuse you."

Ten minutes later Quade climbed up on a two-foot wooden stand he had set up in the middle of a trailer street.

Trailer travelers, idling nearby, suddenly came to attention when Quade, spreading out his hands began talking in a stentorian voice that reached to the farthest trailer on the ten-acre trailer town.

"I'm Oliver Quade, the Human Encyclopedia," he boomed. "I know the answers to all questions. I can answer accurately any question anyone on these grounds can ask me—on any *subject!* History, science, mathematics, sports, general interest. I'll give a five dollar bill to the person who can ask a question I can't answer accurately!"

Quade reached into his pocket and brought out a huge roll of bills. He peeled off a five dollar note and waved it aloft. The trailer folk converged on his pitch. That money lure never failed. When Quade shouted in his spell-binding voice everyone within hearing came closer.

"Five dollars to anyone who can ask me a question I can't answer!" he repeated. "On any subject under the sun. Try me, someone!"

"I will," said a paunchy man in shirt sleeves. "How many trailers are in this camp right now?"

It should have been a stunner, but Quade, an authority on mass psychology, knew that the average mind runs in similar channels. When he'd joined the nomadic trailer tribe a month ago he'd crammed up on the subject of trailers, knowing that in every trailer audience there'd be some persons who'd ask questions peculiar to this subject. The particular question was one asked almost every day and just before setting up his pitch Quade had asked Mason, the proprietor of the camp, that very thing. Mason was standing to one side of the group now, his mouth agape at the uncanniness of Quade's foresight.

"There are five hundred and sixty-eight trailers inside the grounds of the Palm Grove Trailer Town right now. There! Ask Mr. Mason if I'm not right."

The bewildered Mason nodded as people turned his way. "Yeah—he's right. He asked me that same question five minutes ago and I looked it up in my register."

A roar of laughter greeted Mason's statement and the crowd began to gather closer about Quade.

"Mr. Mason's quite right," Quade chuckled. "I took the precaution of familiarizing myself with everything about this camp. I even know within ten how many people there are on the grounds, because in every large trailer camp the average is three and one-half persons to the trailer. And I can identify every different type of commercial trailer here, tell you the retail price of each. So don't waste your time. Ask me some really hard questions. And remember—five dollars for every one I can't answer accurately!"

"Who was the Confederate general at the Battle of Shiloh?" someone cried.

"Now we're getting somewhere," Quade replied, his eyes gleaming. "The Confederate general at the Battle of Shiloh was Albert Sidney Johnston. Next question."

"What's the population of Duluth, Minnesota?"

"One hundred and one thousand," Quade shot back. "The city takes its name from *Sieur* Du Lhut who built a trading post on the site in Sixteen-seventy-eight. Next!"

A man, evidently a laborer, asked, "What is chrome leather?"

"Leather treated with chromium hydroxide," replied Quade. "It toughens the leather and makes it waterproof. It has a greenish appearance and is used mainly on boots and work shoes."

"What is foxglove?" asked a man with a brown beard.

"Ah," said Quade, delighted. "We're getting into something interesting. Foxglove is a plant that grows in parts of Europe and Asia. Digitalis, the heart stimulant, is made from its leaves. Am I right?"

The bearded man nodded. "You are— And after that one I guess you can answer anything."

But others weren't content. Everyone seemed suddenly to have a question.

"Who was the heavyweight champion in Nineteen-one?"

"What's the distance from Denver, Colorado, to El Paso, Texas?"

"How can I get rid of red ants?"

QUADE ANSWERED THE questions, rapidly and accurately. But after ten minutes of it he suddenly brought the thing to a dramatic halt.

"That's all for this time, folks. I could go on all night and never miss. But that wouldn't help you, you'd forget the answers by tomorrow. I want to tell you how you can learn the answers to every question asked tonight and ten thousand more—in the same way I learned them. It's all here, folks!" He stooped suddenly and brought forth a thick volume from the leather bag at his feet.

"*The Compendium of Human Knowledge!* The knowledge of the ages, condensed, classified, abbreviated and crammed into this one volume. Twelve hundred pages of facts, facts and more facts. A complete high school education in one volume. Many of you folks travel from town to town, you don't get the opportunity to pick up knowledge, your children don't get the educations they should. But with this one book and ten minutes a day your children can stand at the head of their classes wherever they go to school. Only two dollars and ninety-five cents—"

A half hour later Quade finished his pitch, wealthier by more than fifty dollars. Lights had appeared in the trailers all over the grounds. Quade looked hopefully toward the trailer of the Websters. There was a light in it, but the door was closed. Regretfully he retired to his own trailer.

Quade awoke the next morning to a bedlam of noise. He lay for a moment wondering if all large trailer towns were as noisy in the early morning as this particular one and then he realized that there was an excited, hysterical note to the voices that were chattering outside.

He leaped from his bed, pulled aside the window shade and looked out. At least a hundred people were massed out in the trailer street. Quickly Quade slipped out of his pajamas and donned his clothing. Then he unlatched the door of his trailer and stepped out. Almost the first person he encountered was Bob Webster.

"What's up?" he asked.

Webster shook his head. "Joe Piper was found—dead—this morning. In bed. Abe Crosby, the man with whom he's traveling found him."

Quade drew in a sharp breath. "Dead? How?"

"No one seems to know. It *looks* like heart failure but Crosby says— Well, there's a doctor in the trailer now, looking at the body."

Quade turned away and began pushing through the crowd. People gave way reluctantly at first, but when they saw who it was they stepped aside nimbly. Reaching the door of Piper's elaborate trailer Quade pushed it open.

Two cots were inside, one near the door and another across the small floor. Three men were crowded around the farther cot; Mason, the proprietor of the camp, the bearded man who had asked the question about foxglove the evening before, and Abe Crosby, a rat-faced little man.

Quade came directly to the question uppermost, it seemed, in everybody's mind. "You suspect Piper was murdered?"

"It surer'n hell looks like it!" snapped Abe Crosby.

Quade did not even look at him. Instead he turned to the bearded man.

"This is Dr. Thorndyke," Mason volunteered. "He's stopping at the camp."

Quade nodded. "What do you think of it, sir?"

Dr. Thorndyke shrugged and sighed. "Frankly, I'm not sure. The symptoms indicate death by inhaling carbon monoxide gas—but in view of the circumstances, that is impossible."

EYES NARROWED, QUADE stepped forward. "Mind if I look?"

No one objected so Quade stooped over the dead body of Joe Piper. He examined it quickly and thoroughly, touching the arms and legs, sniffing carefully, and looking into the open mouth of the dead man. Then he straightened.

"It is carbon monoxide poisoning," he declared. "The lips, ears and fingernails are red, indicating that the red corpuscles of the blood have been broken down—haemoglobin is the medical term for it. The paralysis of the limbs proves, too, that the nervous system was also affected. Carbon monoxide gas produces those effects."

Dr. Thorndyke's mouth was slightly open when Quade finished his diagnosis. "Why, I didn't know you were a doctor!" he exclaimed.

"I'm not, but knowledge has been my hobby for many years

and I've tried to learn as much as I could."

"Considering your able diagnosis," said Thorndyke, "perhaps you can also tell us how Piper could have died from carbon monoxide—here?"

"That's simple. There are more than five hundred automobiles on the grounds. The exhaust from any one of them would in three minutes produce enough carbon monoxide gas to kill a man."

"Quite so," pursued Dr. Thorndyke, "but you're forgetting one thing—that Piper and Crosby both slept in here, and only Piper was affected by the gas!"

"That's impossible!" cried Quade. "If both were here and there was enough poison in here to kill a strong man like Piper it most certainly would have killed Crosby."

"Naturally, and that's why I'm reluctant to say that Piper died of carbon monoxide?"

"It is carbon monoxide," insisted Quade. "There's only one explanation for Crosby not being killed, too—and that is that he wasn't in the trailer at the time the gas seeped in."

"You callin' me a liar?" cried Crosby, belligerently.

Quade's lips peeled back slightly from his teeth. "If you said you were in here when your partner died—yes!"

Crosby yelped and started toward Quade, but suddenly stopped. "I won't stand for him callin' me a liar," he declared loudly. "If you're askin' me I'm callin' it murder—and only one person here had it in for poor Joe."

Quade grinned icily. "He means me. I had some trouble with Piper last night."

"I know about that," said Dr. Thorndyke, quickly, "but it didn't amount to anything."

"The hell it didn't!" cried Crosby. "Joe was tellin' me about it before we went to bed and he was sorer'n a boil. Said this guy swore he'd get Joe."

"It was Piper who promised to get me," retorted Quade. But the silence of Thorndyke and Mason quickly reminded him that they did suspect him.

"There ain't no use to argy about it, now," put in Mason, the camp owner. "Chief Kellerman of the city police is comin' out. This place is under his jurisdiction. He'll have to decide what's what."

Quade looked thoughtfully through the window screen just over Joe Piper's head. He let out a small sigh. "I think," he observed softly, "I'm going to send a telegram to a lawyer friend of mine in New York."

"Yeah, you'll be needin' a mouthpiece," sneered Abe Crosby meaningly.

Quade pulled a notebook from his pocket, felt around for a pencil, but couldn't find one. Dr. Thorndyke smilingly handed him a mechanical pencil, Quade wrote, broke the point and frowning, screwed out more lead. Then he finished his brief message:

IN JAM. COME TO PALM GROVE AT ONCE. OLIVER QUADE.

He handed the note with a dollar bill to Mason. "Will you please see that this telegram is sent at once?" he asked.

"Of course. But if I was you, Mr. Quade, I wouldn't leave the camp for a while."

Quade stepped out of the trailer. Outside the crowd parted for him. He returned to his own trailer, made breakfast. He had just finished eating it when someone knocked on the screen door.

Quade turned and saw Bob Webster and his sister, Mavis. Mavis wore slacks this morning but she was even more attractive in them than in the shorts she'd worn the day before.

HE QUICKLY OPENED the door and motioned for them to sit down on the couch.

"Isn't it awful about that Piper person?" began Mavis. "They're saying it's murder."

"I know," said Quade. "I'm Suspect Number One."

"That's ridiculous!" exclaimed Mavis. "If it is murder I'd say that shifty-eyed partner of Piper's is the guilty one. He and Piper probably quarreled over 'divvying the swag' I guess you call it. They're both crooks, I'm sure."

"I wouldn't be a bit surprised," replied Quade. "Anyway, Piper died of carbon monoxide poisoning. Abe Crosby claims to have been in the trailer with him all night—but the poison didn't affect him."

"What do you make of that?" asked Bob Webster.

"That Crosby lied. He couldn't possibly have been in the trailer at the time of Piper's death."

"You mean that he killed Piper?"

"I don't know. I've a hunch too, that Piper and this Crosby were mixed up in some kind of crooked business. Money might have been the motive for the killing."

"It was," said a voice at the door. Quade whirled toward the screen door and saw a heavy-set stranger in the doorway. Behind him were Dr. Thorndyke and Mason.

"I'm Chief Kellerman of the Palm Grove Police Department,"

announced the heavy-set man. "You're right about robbery being the motive. Crosby, Piper's partner, claims Piper had two thousand dollars in cash on him yesterday—and it's gone today!"

"Yes?" Quade said softly.

Kellerman cleared his throat. "I've talked with some of the folks and they tell me you were this Piper's chief enemy hereabouts. You had a bout with him yesterday. So—"

THE POLICE CHIEF had leaped into the trailer as he spoke. He took two swift strides toward Quade, jerked his arm up quickly and for a moment keenly surveyed Quade's coat sleeve. Then he looked at the other sleeve and snorted as he saw the dangling thread from which a button had been recently lost.

"When did you lose this button off your sleeve. Quade?" he shot out. "And where?"

Quade shrugged. "Who knows?" he said. "That's the answer to both questions, Chief. Does a man ever know when and where he loses buttons?"

"Then I'll tell you," said Kellerman grimly. "You lost this button in Piper's trailer last night—when you were dosing him with carbon monoxide."

Sharp exclamations came from those inside the trailer, and growls from the men outside. But Quade was not disturbed.

"You know, of course, Chief, that you are making a statement you can't prove," he said. "And aren't you rather jumping to conclusions? Has it occurred to you that I might have dropped that button in the Piper trailer just a few minutes ago—when I was in there examining the dead man? That could have been— as easily as the reason you give."

"Jumping to conclusions or not," snapped the chief, "I know one thing: If I could tie you up with that missing dough, then this button—and where it was found—would tell the whole story. So— Well, I'd like to search your trailer, and—"

Quade bit his lip. "You're welcome to search, even without a warrant," he told the chief, "but I'll save you the trouble. It happens that I have twenty-five hundred dollars in cash, five hundred of which I carry in my pocket and which the whole camp saw last night; two thousand I keep cached here in the trailer. Inasmuch as I bank in New York I always carry a large sum with me."

"Let's see it," said the chief, his eyes narrowed to slits.

Quade reached under the couch on which Mavis and her brother sat and brought out a small tin box. "Here it is," he said.

"I guess this just about clinches it," said the chief, triumphantly. He glanced at Abe Crosby who stood in the doorway. "Know the denominations of Piper's roll, Crosby?"

"Tens, twenties and hundreds," said Crosby promptly.

"Tens, twenties and hundreds," repeated the police chief, as his fingers flipped through Quade's sheaf of bills.

"A marvelous coincidence," murmured Quade satirically, but Chief Kellerman did not notice him. The police chief's eyes were glittering. It was plain he had made up his mind. Quade was the guilty man, the murderer he sought, and he did not mean to be swayed from that idea.

He nodded emphatically, slapping the bills with a big hand. "This sure clinches it," he repeated.

Mavis Webster rose to her feet. "It doesn't, at all!" she declared. "Just because people live in trailers doesn't necessarily mean they're paupers. My brother and I also have more than twenty-five hundred dollars with us. We carry it with us because we don't stay long enough in one place to open a bank account, and anyhow, it isn't convenient to bank—"

"Miss Webster!" cut in Quade. "Please!"

Mavis turned to him, flushed. "I want you to know that I believe this charge is absurd. If it hadn't been for Bob and me you never would have incurred the enmity of this—Piper man—in the first place. So—"

"So he's coming to jail with me," declared Chief Kellerman.

"I'll employ an attorney in Palm Grove for you, Mr. Quade!" cried Mavis.

Quade shook his head. "Thanks, but it won't be necessary. You see, I anticipated being arrested—even before I knew of the great mystery of the disappearing button. I knew at once that I would be suspected, being the last known person to have punched Piper in the nose, so I've already sent a telegram. Or hasn't it gone, Mr. Mason?"

The proprietor of Trailer Town bobbed his head. "Yeah, I telephoned it in."

"Good. Winters, the attorney for whom I sent, will be here tomorrow morning then. He'll probably collect heavy damages for me, for false arrest."

Palm Grove was a city of about ten thousand. Its jail was a one-story annex to the police station. It consisted merely of a double row of cells with a wide corridor in between. There were four cells on each side, but only two were occupied when Quade was brought in.

After being booked Quade was locked into one of the cells against the far wall, a place about eight by six feet, with an iron cot and mattress, a chair and a washbowl.

Quade dropped down on the mattress of the cot and let his mind speculate on the Piper affair. He wasn't greatly worried. Winters would put the local police through the hoops. He'd smash the robbery motive thing first of all, by proving that Quade had in a trust fund in New York City, fifty times the amount involved. For though he was a book agent, Quade had for years earned in excess of twenty thousand a year. He wasn't an ordinary book agent. Many people called him the greatest book salesman in the country.

Shortly before twelve a uniformed policeman brought Quade a telegram. It read simply:

COMING. WINTERS.

"Thanks," said Quade. "Now I guess I'm ready for my lunch."

"What'll it be?" asked the policeman. "The regular prison stew or some vittles from the restaurant?"

"Which would you recommend?"

"The restaurant vittles," grinned the policeman. "We don't aim to encourage prisoners to want to stick in jail by overfeedin' em. But if you can pay for it, I'll be glad to get you some real good food."

QUADE REACHED INTO a pocket and drew out the roll of bills he carried on his person and which the chief had not taken from him. There still was five hundred dollars in the roll. He pulled off a five dollar bill and handed it to the pop-eyed policeman.

"Get lunches for the boys in the other cells, too," he said. "Bring me a newspaper and get yourself some cigars with the change."

"Gosh—thanks!" exclaimed the policeman.

He returned twenty minutes later with three lunches. He brought Quade's to his cell first of all, then distributed the others. Quade heard him explaining to the other prisoners.

"Tanks, podner!" called one of the prisoners.

"Me, too!" cried the other. "Hope you stay here awhile."

The policeman came back to Quade's cell, smoking a huge cigar. "Anything you want just holler. My name's Dick Purcell. I'm in the next room and I'm on duty until six o'clock. Dan Dorgan who's on at night—he ain't so obligin' about things."

"Thanks for tipping me off," said Quade. "If I want anything, else I'll ask before six."

Quade ate his lunch, then dropped back on the couch and began reading the newspaper, the Palm Grove Daily News. It was an eight-page newspaper but Quade didn't get beyond the first page. For almost immediately he found an item that set him to thinking. It read:

BURGLARS ROB SAFE OF LOCAL PRODUCE COMPANY

A daring burglar robbed the safe of the Palm Grove Produce Company last night and got away with more than three hundred dollars in cash and seven hundred in checks. Hearing a noise shortly after 1:00 A.M., Watchman Jeff Sievers went to investigate and was struck on the head from behind. When he recovered consciousness he was bound and gagged. By a strenuous effort, Sievers was able to knock the telephone from a desk and call the police. When they arrived at 2:30 they found the safe open and the money and checks gone. Chief of Police Kellerman believes that the job was the work of a professional gang of cracksmen who have in recent weeks pulled similar jobs in neighboring cities.

"Hey!" cried Quade springing to the door. "Hey—Purcell! Come in here!"

Officer Dick Purcell ambled up a minute later. "What's wrong?"

"Listen," said Quade, "how would you like to get the credit of nabbing the burglar who cracked the safe at the produce company last night?"

"Why, fine, Mr. Quade," said the cop, his eyes gleaming. "I'm in line for promotion anyway and that would cinch it, but how?"

"Have you got a fingerprint man in this town?"

"Sure, I'm him. I took one of those courses a couple of years ago and I got an outfit—"

"Good, then run down to the produce company and see if you can get any prints from the safe that was robbed last night. If you can, I think you can nab the crook."

"I don't have to do that," exclaimed Purcell. "I already did it. First thing this morning. I found a couple of beauties."

"Fine. Then run out to the Palm Grove Trailer Town and get the prints of one Abe Crosby you'll find there. Mason, the owner, will point him out to you. I think you'll know what to do after that."

The cop brightened. "I sure hope he's the guy. I'll get someone to watch the desk and run right out there."

Exactly forty minutes later, Officer Dick Purcell returned. But his face was gloomy. "It was him all right," he said, "I got his prints from some stuff in the trailer, but Crosby—he's skipped!"

"Skipped?" echoed Quade. "They let him go?"

"No, but he wasn't under arrest and he just left the trailer and lit out."

Quade turned away wearily and Purcell went out to his desk in front. Crosby's skipping didn't make sense. If he'd killed Joe Piper why had he waited around until morning to skip? The whole affair made Quade bitterly resentful. Especially was he resentful of a bull-headed police chief who jumped at a few coincidences and insisted they were facts. Such being the case, however, there seemed no way out for Quade except to solve this thing for Kellerman.

AS HE THOUGHT, something in the back of Quade's mind bothered him. It was a stray bit of information that refused to fall into the well regimented channels in his brain— something that had to do with the problem on his mind.

He went back over the entire day, beginning with his awakening and hearing the noise outside his trailer. He thought of every bit of conversation he'd heard since morning, of every movement he'd made, every movement he'd observed others make.

He visualized Joe Piper's trailer. Crosby's bed had been just beside the door. He could have slipped out and back easily enough without waking Piper. And someone else could have slipped in just as easily. But would they have dared to? No, that was why Piper had been poisoned. The murderer had wanted something that Piper had on his person, but was afraid to tackle him—until after he was dead. That accounted for the poison. How had it been administered?

Ah! Quade remembered now. The screen directly over Piper's bed. Hadn't there been a small hole in it—a hole about a half inch in diameter? A small rubber nozzle could have been pushed through that almost into Piper's face. The other end of the hose attached to an automobile exhaust—a softly purring motor—and death.

But still Quade was worried. That wasn't the small bit of information that refused to jail into its proper slot in his brain—the slot that would co-ordinate things and make everything clear.

He pulled his notebook from his vest pocket, opened it. Sometimes it helped to write down the facts he knew and concentrated upon each in turn. But he found he had no pencil. He swore, started to shut the notebook—and stopped. Blankly he stared down at the ruled paper. He could see the faint impressions of the message he'd written to his friend Winters in New York on the first sheet. But he was looking at a tiny bit of rusted metal—less than a sixteenth of an inch long.

HE CLOSED THE book, put it back into his pocket. He knew who had killed Joe Piper!

But to prove it. The bit of evidence was so slight, so vague that it wouldn't mean a thing to anyone but Oliver Quade, who had an encyclopedic brain.

Then another thought struck him. Mavis and Bob Webster. They were in danger! Mavis had announced publicly that she and her brother had over two thousand dollars with them. The man who had killed Joe Piper for money had heard them—and tonight he would try to get the Websters' money.

A chill ran through Quade. He had to get out of here before one in the morning, for some time around that hour the murderer of Trailer Town would strike again.

But how could he get out of jail? Winters wouldn't be here until morning. Chief Kellerman was convinced that Quade was the murderer. He wouldn't listen to bail. And Quade couldn't tell his suspicions to anyone. They were too inconclusive at present. No one but Quade himself could *prove* the guilt of the murderer.

He looked around his cell. The cell bars were an inch thick, as were those at the window. Quade stepped over to the window. The bars were old and rusty, but they'd last for years more. Nothing but a crowbar or dynamite would loosen them.

Quade paced the short floor of his cell. "I've got to get out," he repeated over and over. Then suddenly he smacked his hands together. He turned to the barred door and yelled loudly: "Hey—Purcell!"

A few moments later Officer Purcell came up. "What's the trouble?" he asked.

Quade put a hand to his forehead, where the adhesive tape covered the bruise Joe Piper's fist had made the evening before. "This sore on my head has given me a terrific headache," he complained.

"Like for me to get you some aspirin?" Purcell asked, hopefully.

"Aspirin wouldn't help. I've got a bad cut and I'm afraid it's become infected. But—if you'd get me some things from the drug store I'd appreciate it greatly."

"What you want—some iodine?"

"No. I'd like about two ounces of absorbent cotton, a couple of ounces of saltpeter and some glycerin."

"Saltpeter? Ain't that the stuff they used to put in our coffee in the army?"

Quade grinned. "Yes, but when it's mixed with glycerin it's the best disinfectant there is. Here's another five. The stuff will cost you less than a dollar. Keep the change."

"Thanks," said the delighted turnkey.

He returned ten minutes later with the purchases and shoved them through the bars. Quade thanked him and Purcell returned to the police station up front.

Then Quade got busy. He washed out the aluminum cup which had held his lunch coffee, and poured in some of the glycerin. Then he slashed a hole in the bottom of the mattress on the bed and took out some of the straw. He put it in the washbowl and lit it with a match. He bent a fork and hooked it through the handle of the aluminum cup and held the cup over the tiny blaze. As the fire burned Quade fed it fresh straw.

The glycerin began bubbling in a minute. Then Quade added the saltpeter to it. The mixture let off an acrid smell that caused Quade's eyes to smart, but he persisted until the mixture was ready.

Then he took about half of the absorbent cotton and dipped it into the aluminum cup. The stuff quickly absorbed the hot liquid, swelling the cotton to several times its original size.

Quade let the mass lie in the sink to cool off and turned to the bed. With the aid of the blunt knife that the turnkey had left behind with the lunch, he loosened the screws that fastened one of the legs of the bed to the cross pieces. Quade's eyes gleamed. Yes, the thing was hollow; regular piping as he'd expected. Most of these cheap cots were made of piping.

Then he began the most intricate task of all. He squeezed all the moisture he could out of the cotton, then began tamping it into the iron pipe. He plugged the bottom end with soap, placed it down on the concrete floor, so it could not be forced out, then tamped the damp cotton into the pipe, about half full. On top of it he tamped more soap.

Finished, he fastened the loaded pipe back to the bed and removed all traces of his work, washing the ashes from the fire down into the washbowl drainpipe. Then he threw himself upon the bed again.

Purcell removed the dishes from his lunch and brought his dinner. At six o'clock the new turnkey came on duty. At nine the lights went out. Quade pretended to go to sleep.

Midnight came at last, heralded by an hourly tour of inspection on the part of the turnkey. The minute he was gone Quade rose from his cot. He unfastened his loaded pipe-leg and upended the cot, facing the spring side toward the outer wall. The mattress, a good thick one, he held up with his hands while he climbed under it.

He let the thing fall over his head so part of it was covering his head and back, protecting his back from the iron bars. Then he gripped the length of loaded pipe in his right hand.

If his encyclopedic memory had not failed him, he held a very deadly bomb; a bomb that had in it the equivalent of nitro-glycerin. Almost pure nitrate from the Chilean saltpeter, mixed with glycerin and soaked in absorbent cotton, the equivalent of guncotton. Each ingredient harmless by itself—but mixed together and confined, a deadly explosive.

IF HE HAD guessed wrong at the proportions the bomb might kill Quade. Again it might not be powerful enough to blow out the iron window bars.

But two lives depended on Quade's getting out of this jail—

and he had to take the chance. The murderer of Trailer Town would strike again tonight. Of that Quade was sure.

He drew a deep breath, then hurled the pipe-bomb straight at the steel barred window.

The room rocked to a thundering explosion. Quade was hurled back against the iron bars of the door with terrific force. It was fortunate that he'd taken the precaution of padding his back with part of the mattress. Even so he was stunned for a moment. But he recovered quickly and pushed forward against the bed. It fell with a crash and then Quade saw the gaping hole in the wall and knew that the bomb had been successful. It had torn away the bricks from the bottom of the iron bars, leaving a hole of more than two feet in diameter.

Stumbling over fragments of bricks on the floor Quade sprang to the hole. He grasped a couple of iron bars and found them so loose that he was able to bend them upward without any effort.

Instantly he started clambering through the hole. He was almost through when he heard a yell in the jail behind him. The night turnkey, no doubt. But Quade didn't stop to look around. He dropped to the grounds outside and came up running.

He made the street, tore up it a block, then turned a corner. He dashed halfway down the street, cut through a yard to the alley and continued up that. Five minutes later he was at the edge of town.

FIFTEEN MINUTES AFTER that he slipped stealthily into the grounds of the Palm Grove trailer town.

The ten-acre tract was quiet. It was close to one o'clock and the trailer folk had mostly retired. Only here and there was a light burning in a trailer. Quade kept to the shadows, but made his way quickly to the street where his own trailer was parked.

If the police had not found it there was a gun in his own trailer. Quade decided that he had better get it. Anything might happen when he tackled the killer. He reached the street where he had left his trailer. He saw the gleam of the Websters' metal trailer in a bit of moonlight that shone through the trees and was able to make out his own trailer next to it.

His eyes traveled over the shadowy-trailers for a moment, but he saw nothing out of the way. He started swiftly across the dark street, then suddenly tripped on something and pitched headlong to the ground. His fate struck a sharp stone and he could not quite stifle an exclamation.

But fortunately the exclamation was muffled by an automobile motor nearby being started up at that moment. Quade rolled over and sat up. For a fraction of a second his mind did not take things in. Then he held back his almost unconscious exclamation. After the first grinding as the motor was started it had settled into a smooth purring.

Purring—creating carbon monoxide gas!

Quade sprang to his feet and something brushed his ankles. He kicked at something that looked like a rope. That was what had tripped him.

But it wasn't a rope. It was a thin, flexible rubber hose. A shudder ran through Quade. Quickly he snatched up the hose and pinched it tightly, praying that he had stopped the flow of carbon monoxide gas soon enough. For he knew where the end of that hose was!

Clutching the hose tightly, Quade began pulling on it. It

dragged snakily on the ground toward him, from the direction of the Websters' trailer!

It took thirty seconds or more to pull the end of the hose to him, for it was a long one. But then he let go his first grip on the hose and pinched the end of it, shutting it off.

An orange flame spat suddenly out of the darkness; it was followed instantly by a thunder clap. A puff of wind shot past Quade's face. He made a tremendous leap for the protection of the closest trailer.

Thunder split the darkness again and a sharp sudden pain seared Quade's side. He gasped, stumbled.

Feet pounded the ground, coming toward Quade; the feet of the murderer, determined to kill him. Quade whirled the loose end of the rubber hose around his head, swung out with it, just as a shadow swooped down on him. The hose smacked the shadowy figure, bringing a startled cry. At the same instant the gun spat flame again and a bullet smashed into the trailer beside Quade, driving a splinter into his face.

Then Quade had hurled himself upon the shadow. He hit out fiercely in the semi-dark, drove the killer backward. Desperately he tried to get the gun from the man's hand, but missed it in the first reach.

The gun found him, however. It lashed out of the darkness and smashed against the side of his head. The blow knocked Quade to his knees. A red haze exploded in his head, threatening to envelop him. But he fought it down and lunged forward. His arms shot out, circled—and enfolded a pair of stout legs. Wildly he pulled the legs toward him. His shadowy assailant crashed to the ground, swearing furiously.

Quade expected a bullet to crash into his head, but none

came, and he suddenly realized that the gun must have been knocked from the killer's hand as he was thrown to the ground.

But the man was strong and Quade was half dazed and weak from the bullet that had seared his side and the blow on his head. It was all he could do to keep his encircling grip on the man's legs. And the man had both hands free to swing at Quade's head.

He pummeled Quade with fists. Every blow sent screaming pain shooting through Quade's whole body, but he merely buried his face deeper against the man's legs and hugged them for dear life.

Suddenly a whiff of gasoline penetrated Quade's nostrils, even though his face was forced against the man's trouser legs. Nausea gripped him, too. He almost released his antagonist's legs as he realized that he had dropped the end of that rubber hose close by and the automobile motor was still running and pouring forth carbon monoxide gas.

What a spot! Except for its being mixed with gasoline fumes, the carbon monoxide gas was odorless. Tasteless, too. It would overcome him—*and* his antagonist—before either of them realized it. They were too close to the spouting nozzle.

A tremendous blow on the top of his head made Quade gasp out in agony. In that infinitesimal fraction of a second he knew he could not hold out much longer. Not against the blows of his attacker and the carbon monoxide gas.

He suddenly released one hand from about the man's legs and groped out with it. The fingers brushed sand and gravel—and something long and soft and smooth. Hot air blew on his fingers.

He tightened his fingers about the thing and suddenly stabbed his hand up into his antagonist's face. Then he held his breath and buried his face as tightly as he could against the man's legs.

The blows on his head were renewed in intensity, but Quade was beyond caring. He had shot his bolt and if it failed—

And then suddenly the blows stopped. Quade, gasping for air, gathered together the last remnant of his strength and rolled away quickly. Into a beam of white light.

"What's going on here?" a voice that seemed a mile away said.

Then Quade let go and blackness swooped down on him. When he came to he was bathed in white light and people were moving about him. He took a deep breath of fresh air and suddenly sat up.

"What happened?" he asked.

"Mr. Quade!" That was Mavis Webster's voice. She was dropping to her knees beside him. "Thank the Lord you're all right!" She was dressed in pajamas and a dressing gown.

A COUGHING FIT seized Quade. But in a minute he was able to say: "I'll be okay, I guess. But—how's Thorndyke?"

"You knew he was the murderer?" exclaimed Bob Webster.

Quade nodded weakly, but it was not until an hour later that, seated in his trailer, he explained the whole thing to Mavis and her brother. That was after Chief Kellerman had taken a very sick Dr. Thorndyke to the hospital in Palm Grove and apologized to Quade for arresting him. Quade said he wouldn't sue for false arrest if the city didn't sue him for a damaged jail.

"The thing was almost a perfect crime," Quade told the Websters, as he'd earlier explained the thing to Chief Kellerman. "Thorndyke could have made it one, too, if he hadn't overlooked some few small things.

"The plan of attaching that rubber tubing to the exhaust of his car was all to the good for his purpose. The motor was a quiet one and anyone unsuspicious would pay no attention to it. Automobiles are apt to be running at any time of the day and night in a place like this.

"Sticking that metal pencil of his into the screen and making a hole large enough to stick in the end of the soft tubing was all right, too—but Thorndyke's mistake was in not throwing that pencil away. I borrowed it from him to write that telegram to Winters, my lawyer friend in New York. The lead broke and I had to screw out some more. At least I thought it was the lead that broke off, but it turned out to be a tiny piece of rusted wire from the screen, caught in the end of the pencil when he'd pushed the point of it against the screen to enlarge a hole for the tubing.

"That little bit of rusted metal was the tip-off to me that Thorndyke was the guilty man. It took some proving, of course, but I was finally able to do that, even to Chief Kellerman's satisfaction. He'd poked that same pencil through your own screen and again a bit of rusty wire stuck in the pencil point. That and the scratches around the pencil from making the holes—and the tubing running to his own car exhaust, are enough to send Dr. Thorndyke to the gallows."

Mavis Webster's eyes sparkled. "That gas pipe bomb you made in the jail is the most amazing thing I ever heard of!" she exclaimed. "You risked your life with that!"

"Speaking of pipes," cut in Bob Webster, "reminds me I think I'll smoke a pipeful of tobacco before turning in. I'll just run over to our trailer and get it."

He barged through the screen door. Quade looked at Mavis,

sitting on the couch. Her long lashes drooped over half-closed eyes. For a moment there was silence in the trailer, then Mavis spoke.

"For a Human Encyclopedia you are pretty dumb," she said softly.

"What?" Quade exclaimed.

"My brother is smart," she said. "He'll take at least five minutes to find that pipe, and—and—don't you think a man clever enough to solve such a crime—and save a girl's life, too—deserves at least one kiss?"

A delighted look spread across Quade's face. "Well, why didn't you say so?" he exclaimed, and started toward her, his arms out eagerly.

Ask Me Another

No one saw how a man locked in an incubator could be killed by poison, but Oliver Quade found the guilty one with the aid of a bent piece of wire

OLIVER QUADE WAS reading the morning paper, his bare feet on the bed and his chair tilted back against the radiator. Charlie Boston was on the bed, wrapped to his chin in a blanket and reading a copy of Exciting Confessions.

It was just a usual, peaceful, after-breakfast interlude in the lives of Oliver Quade, the Human Encyclopedia, and Charlie Boston, his friend and assistant.

And then Life intruded itself upon the bit of Utopia. Life in the form of the manager of the Eagle Hotel. He beat a tattoo upon the thin panels of the door. Quade put down his newspaper and sighed.

"Charles, will you please open the door and let in the wolf?"

Charlie Boston unrolled himself from the blanket. He scowled at Quade. "You think it's the manager about the room rent?"

"Of course it is. Let him in before he breaks down the door."

It was the manager. In his right fist he held a ruled form on which were scrawled some unpleasant figures. "About your rent, Mr. Quade," he said severely. "We must have the money today!"

Quade looked at the manager of the Eagle Hotel, a puzzled expression on his face. "Rent? Money?"

"Of course," snapped the manager. "This is the third time this week I've asked for it."

A light came into Quade's eyes. He made a quick movement and his feet and the front legs of the chair hit the carpeted floor simultaneously.

"Charles!" he roared in a voice that shook the room and caused the hotel manager to cringe. "Did you forget to get that money from the bank and pay this little bill?"

Charlie Boston took up Quade's cue.

"Gosh, I'm awful sorry. On my way to the bank yesterday afternoon I ran into our old friend John Belmont of New York and he dragged me into the Palmer House Bar for a cocktail. By the time I could tear myself away, the bank was closed."

Quade raised his hands and let them fall hopelessly. "You see, Mr. Creighton, I just can't trust him to do anything. Now I've got to go out into the cold this morning and get it myself."

The hotel manager's eyes glinted. "Listen, you've stalled—" he began, but Quade suddenly stabbed out a hand toward him.

"That reminds me, Mr. Creighton, I've a couple of complaints to make. We're not getting enough heat here and last night the damfool next door kept us awake half the night with his radio. I want you to see that he keeps quiet tonight. And do something about the heat. I can't stand drafty, cold rooms."

The manager let out a weary sigh. "All right, I'll look after it. But about that rent—"

"Yes, of course," cut in Quade, "and your maid left only two towels this morning. Please see that a couple more are sent up. Immediately!"

The manager closed the door behind him with a bang. Oliver Quade chuckled and lifted his newspaper again. But Charlie Boston wouldn't let him read.

"You got away with it, Ollie," he said, "but it's the last time. I know it. I'll bet we get locked out before tonight." He shook his head sadly. "You, Oliver Quade, with the greatest brain in

captivity, are you going to walk the streets tonight in ten below zero weather?"

"Of course not, Charles," sighed Quade. "I was just about to tell you that we're going out to make some money today. Look, it's here in this paper. The Great Chicago Auditorium Poultry Show."

Boston's eyes lit up for a moment, but then dimmed again. "Can we raise three weeks' rent at a poultry show?"

Quade slipped his feet into his socks and shoes. "That

remains to be seen. This paper mentions twenty thousand paid admissions. Among that many people there ought to be a few who are interested in higher learning. Well, are you ready?"

Boston went to the clothes closet and brought out their overcoats and a heavy suitcase. Boston was of middle height and burly. He could bend iron bars with his muscular hands. Quade was taller and leaner. His face was hawk-like, his nose a little too pointed and lengthy, but few ever noticed that. They saw only his piercing, sparkling eyes and felt his dominant personality.

The auditorium was almost two miles from their hotel, but lacking carfare, Quade and Boston walked. When they reached their destination, Quade cautioned Boston:

"Be sharp now, Charlie. Act like we belonged."

Quade opened the outer door and walked blithely past the ticket windows to the door leading into the auditorium proper. A uniformed man at the door held out his hand for the tickets.

"Hello," Quade said, heartily. "How're you today?"

"Uh, all right, I guess," replied the ticket-taker. "You boys got passes?"

"Oh, sure. We're just taking in some supplies for the breeders. Brr! It's cold today. Well, be seeing you." And with that he breezed past the ticket-taker.

"H'are ya, pal," Boston said, treading on Quade's heels.

The auditorium was a huge place but even so, it was almost completely filled with row upon row of wire exhibition coops, each coop containing a feathered fowl of some sort.

"What a lot of gumps!" Boston observed.

"Don't use that word around here," Quade cautioned. "These poultry folks take their chickens seriously. Refer to the chick-

ens as 'fine birds' or 'elegant fowls' or something like that...
Damn these publicity men!"

"Huh?"

Quade waved a hand about the auditorium. "The paper said twenty thousand paid admissions. How many people do you see in here?"

Boston craned his head around. "If there's fifty I'm countin' some of 'em twice. How the hell can they pay the nut with such a small attendance?"

"The entry fees. There must be around two thousand chickens in here and the entry fee for each chicken is at least a dollar and a half. The prize money doesn't amount to much and I guess the paid admissions are velvet—if they get any, which I doubt."

"Twenty thousand, bah!" snorted Boston. "Well, do we go back?"

"Where? Our only chance was to stay in our room. I'll bet the manager changed the lock the minute we left it."

"So what?"

"So I get to work. For the dear old Eagle Hotel."

Quade ploughed through an aisle to the far end of the auditorium. Commercial exhibits were contained in booths all around the four sides of the huge room, but Quade found a small spot that had been overlooked and pushed a couple of chicken coops into the space.

Then he climbed up on the coops and began talking.

THE HUMAN ENCYCLOPEDIA'S voice was an amazing one. People who heard it always marveled that such a tremendous voice could come from so lean a man. Speaking without noticeable effort, his voice rolled out across the chicken coops.

"I'm Oliver Quade, the Human Encyclopedia," he boomed. "I have the greatest brain in the entire country. I know the answers to all questions, what came first, the chicken or the egg, every historical date since the beginning of time, the population of every city in the country, how to eradicate mice in your poultry yards, how to mix feeds to make your chickens lay more eggs. Everything. Everything under the sun. On any subject: history, science, agriculture, and mathematics."

The scattered persons in the auditorium began to converge upon Quade's stand. Inside of two minutes three-fourths of the people in the building were gathered before Quade and the rest were on their way. He continued his preliminary build-up in his rich, powerful voice.

"Ask me a question, someone. Let me prove that I'm the Human Encyclopedia, the man who knows the answers to all questions. Try me out, someone, on any subject: history, science, mathematics, agriculture—anything at all!"

Quade stabbed out his lean forefinger at a middle-aged, sawed-off man wearing a tan smock. "You, sir, ask me a question?"

The man flushed at being singled out of the crowd. "Why, uh, I don't know of any… Yes, I do. What's the highest official egg record ever made by a hen?"

"That's the stuff," smiled Quade. He held out his hand dramatically. "That's a good question, but an easy one to answer. The highest record ever made by a hen in an American official egg-laying contest is three hundred and forty-two eggs. It was made in 1930 at the Athens, Georgia, Egg-Laying Contest, by a Single-Comb White Leghorn. Am I right, mister?"

The sawed-off man nodded grudgingly. "Yeah, but I don't see how you knew it. Most poultry folks don't even remember it."

"Oh, but you forget I told you I had the greatest brain in the country. I know the answer to all questions on any subject. Don't bother to ask me simple poultry questions. Try me on something hard. You—" He picked out a lean, dour looking man. "Ask me something hard."

The man bit his lip a moment, then said:

"All right, what state has the longest coastline?"

Quade grinned. "Ah, you're trying the tricky stuff. But you can't fool me. Most folks would say California or Florida. But the correct answer is Michigan. And to head off the rest of you on the trick geography questions let me say right away that Kentucky has the largest number of other states touching it and Minnesota has the farthest northern point of any state. Next question!"

A young fellow wearing pince-nez put his tongue into his cheek and asked, "Why and how does a cat purr?"

"Oh-oh!" Quade craned his neck to stare at the young fellow. "I see we have a student with us. Well, young man, you've asked a question so difficult that practically every university professor in this country would be stumped by it. But I'm not. It so happens that I read a recent paper by Professor E.L. Gibbs of the Harvard Medical School in which he gave the results of his experiments on four hundred cats to learn the answer to that very same question. The first part of the question is simple enough—the cat purrs when it is contented, but to explain the actual act of purring is a little more difficult. Contentment in a cat relaxes the infundibular nerve in the brain, which reacts upon the pituitary and bronchial organs and makes the purring sound issue from the cat's throat... Try that one on your friends, sometime. Someone else try me on a question."

"I'd like to ask one," said a clear, feminine voice. Quade's eyes lit up. He had already noticed the girl, the only female in his audience. She was amazingly pretty, the type of a girl he would scarcely have expected to find at a poultry show. She was young, not more than twenty-one, and she had the finest chiseled features Quade had ever seen. She was a blonde and the rakish green hat and green coat she wore, although inexpensive, looked exceedingly well on her.

"Yes, what is the question?" he asked, leaning forward a bit.

The girl's chin came up defiantly. "I just want to know why certain poultry judges allow dyed birds to be judged for prizes!"

A sudden rumble went up in the crowd and Quade saw the sawed-off man in the tan smock whirl and glare angrily at the girl.

"Oh-oh," Quade said. "You seem to have asked a delicate question. Well, I'll answer it just the same. Any judge who allows a dyed Rhode Island Red to stay in the class is either an ignorant fool—or a crook!"

"Damn you!" roared the little man, turning back to Quade. "You can't say that to me. I'll—I'll have you thrown out of here." He started pushing his way through the crowd, heading in the direction of the front office.

"If the shoe fits, put it on," Quade called after him. Then to the girl, "Who's he?"

"A judge here. Stone's his name."

"Well, let's get on with the show," Quade said to the crowd. "Next question?"

Quade had lost nothing by his bold answer to the girl's question. The audience warmed to him and the questions came fast and furious.

"Who was the eleventh president of the United States?"

"What is the Magna Charta?"

"Who was the 1896 Olympic 220-meter champion?"

"How do you cure scaly legs in chickens?"

"How far is Saturn from the Earth?"

Quade answered all the questions put to him, with lightning rapidity. But suddenly he called a dramatic halt. "That's all the questions, folks. Now let me show you how you can learn all the answers yourselves to every question that has just been asked—and ten thousand more."

He held out his hands and Charlie Boston tossed a thick book into them which he had taken from the suitcase they had brought with them. Quade began ruffling the pages.

"They're all in here. This, my friends, is *The Compendium of Human Knowledge,* the greatest book of its kind ever published. Twelve hundred pages, crammed with facts, information every one of you should know. The knowledge of the ages, condensed, classified, abbreviated. A complete high-school education in one volume. Ten minutes a day and this book will make you the most learned person in your community!"

Quade lowered his voice to a confidential pitch. "Friends, I'm going to astonish you by telling you the most ridiculous thing you've ever heard: The price of this book. What do you think I'm asking for it? Twenty-five dollars? No, not even twenty… or fifteen. In fact, not even ten or five dollars. Just a mere, paltry, insignificant two dollars and ninety-five cents. But I'm only going to offer these books once at that price. Two-ninety-five, and here I come!"

Quade leaped down from his platform to attack his audience, supposedly built up to the buying pitch. But he was destined not to sell any books just then. Charlie Boston tugged at his coat sleeve.

"Look, Ollie!" he whispered hoarsely. "He got the cops!"

Quade raised himself to his toes to look over the chicken coops. He groaned. For the short man in the tan smock was coming up the center aisle leading a small procession of policemen.

Quade sighed. "Put the books back into the suitcase, Charlie." He leaned against a poultry coop and waited to submit quietly to the arrest.

But the policemen did not come toward him. Reaching the center aisle, the man in the tan smock wheeled to the left, away from Quade, and the police followed him.

Quade's audience saw the police. Two or three persons broke away and started toward the other side of the building. The movement started a stampede and in a moment Charlie Boston and Quade were left alone.

"Something seems to have happened over there," Quade observed. "Wonder what?"

"From the mob of cops I'd say a murder," Boston replied dryly.

The word "murder" was scarcely out of Boston's mouth than it was hurled back at them from across the auditorium.

"It is a murder!" Quade gasped.

"This is no place for us, then," cried Boston. "Let's scram!"

He caught up the suitcase containing the books and started off. But Quade called him back. "That's no good. There's a cop at the door. We'll have to stick."

"Chickens!" howled Boston. "The minute you mentioned them at the hotel I had a hunch that something was going to happen. And I'll bet a plugged dime, which I haven't got, that we get mixed up in it."

"Maybe so, Charlie. But if I know cops there's going to be a lot of questioning and my hunch is that we'll be better off if we're not too upstage. Let's go over and find out what's what."

He started toward the other side of the auditorium. Boston followed, lugging the suitcase and grumbling.

ALL OF THE crowd was gathered in front of a huge, mahogany cabinet—a mammoth incubator. The door of the machine was standing open and two or three men were moving around inside.

Quade drew in his breath sharply when he saw the huddled body lying on the floor just inside the door of the incubator. Gently he began working his way through the crowd until he stood in front of the open incubator door.

The small group came out of the incubator and a beetle-browed man in a camel's hair overcoat and Homburg hat squared himself off before the girl in the green hat and coat. The man in the tan smock, his head coming scarcely up to the armpits of the big man, hopped around like a bantam rooster.

"I understand you had a quarrel with him yesterday," the big man said to the girl. "What about?"

The girl drew herself up to her full height. "Because his birds were dyed and the judge—the man behind you—refused to throw them out. That's why!"

The bantam sputtered. "She—why, that's a damn lie!"

The big detective turned abruptly, put a ham-like hand

against the chest of the runt and shoved him back against the incubator with so much force that the little man gasped in pain.

"Listen, squirt," the detective said. "Nothing's been proved against this girl and until it is, she's a lady. Up here we don't call ladies liars."

He turned back to the girl and said with gruff kindness, "Now, miss, let's have the story."

"There's no story," declared the girl. "I did quarrel with him, just like I did with Judge Stone. But—but I haven't seen Mr. Tupper since yesterday evening. That's all I can tell you because it's all I know."

"Yesterday, huh." The detective looked around the circle. "Anybody see him here today?"

"Yes, of course," said a stocky man of about forty-five. "I was talking to him early this morning, before the place was opened to the public. There were a dozen or more of us around then."

"You're the boss of this shebang?"

"Not exactly. Our poultry association operates this show. I'm Leo Cassmer, the secretary, and I'm in charge of the exhibits, if that's what you mean."

"Yeah, that's what I mean," replied the detective. "You're the boss. You know the exhibitors then. All right, who was here early this morning when this Tupper fellow was around?"

Cassmer, the show secretary, rubbed his chin. "Why, there was myself, Judge Stone, Ralph Conway, the Wyandotte man, Judge Welheimer and several of the men who work around here."

"And Miss Martin—was she here?"

"She came in before the place was officially opened, but she wasn't around the last time I saw Tupper."

"Who're Welheimer and Conway?"

A tall, silver-haired man stepped out of the crowd. "Conway's my name."

"And the judge?" persisted the detective.

A long-nosed man with a protruding lower lip came grudgingly out of the crowd. "I'm Judge Welheimer."

"You a real judge or just a chicken judge?"

"Why, uh, just a poultry judge. Licensed by the National Poultry Association."

"And you don't hold any public office at all? You're not even a justice of the peace?"

The long-nosed chicken judge reddened. He shook his head.

The detective's eyes sparkled. "That's fine. All that talk about judges had me worried for a bit. But listen, you chicken judges and the rest of you. I'm Sergeant Dickinson of the Homicide Squad of this town. There's been a murder committed here and I'm investigating it. Which means I'm boss around here. Get me?"

Quade couldn't quite restrain a snicker. The sergeant's sharp ears heard it and he singled out Quade.

"And who the hell are you?"

"Oliver Quade, the Human Encyclopedia," Quade replied glibly. "I know the answers to all questions—"

Sergeant Dickinson's face twisted. "Ribbing me, ha? Step up here where I can get a good look at you."

Quade remained where he was. "There's a dead man in there. I don't like to get too close to dead people."

The sergeant took a half step toward Quade, but then stopped himself. He tried to smooth out his face, but it was still dark with anger.

"I'll get around to you in a minute, fella." He turned belligerently to the show secretary. "You, who found the body?"

Cassmer pointed to a pasty-faced young fellow of about thirty. The man grinned sickly.

"Yeah, I got in kinda late and started straightening things around. Then I saw that someone had stuck that long staple in the door latch. I didn't think much about it and opened the door and there—there he was lying on the floor. Deader'n a mackerel!"

"You work for this incubator company?" the sergeant asked.

The young fellow nodded. *"I'm* the regional sales manager. Charge of this exhibit. It's the finest incubator on the market. Used by the best breeders and hatcherymen."

"Can the sales talk," growled the detective. "I'm not going to buy one. Let's go back on your story. What made you say this man was murdered?"

"What else could it be? He was dead and the door was locked on the outside."

"I know that. But couldn't he have died of heart failure? There's plenty of air in that thing, and besides there's a ventilator hole up there."

"He was murdered," said Quade.

Sergeant Dickinson whirled. "And how do *you* know?"

"By looking at the body. Anyone could tell it was murder."

"Oh yeah? Maybe you'll tell me how he was killed. There ain't a mark on his body."

"No marks of violence, because he wasn't killed that way. He was killed with a poison gas. Something containing cyanogen."

The sergeant clamped his jaws together. "Go on! Who killed him?"

Quade shook his head. "No, that's your job. I've given you enough to start with."

"You've been very helpful," said the sergeant. "So much so that I'm going to arrest you!"

Charlie Boston groaned into Quade's ears. "Won't you ever learn to keep your mouth shut?"

But Quade merely grinned insolently. "If you arrest me I'll sue you for false arrest."

"I'll take a chance on that," said the detective. "No one could know as much as you do and not have had something to do with the murder."

"You're being very stupid, Sergeant," Quade said. "These men told you they hadn't seen Tupper alive for several hours. He's been dead at least three. And I just came into this building fifteen minutes ago."

"He's right," declared Anne Martin. "I saw him come in. He and his friend. They went straight over to the other side of the building and started that sales talk."

"What sales talk?"

The little poultry judge hopped in again. "He's a damn pitchman. Pulls some phony question and answer stuff and insults people. Claims he's the smartest man in the world. Bah!"

"Bah to you!" said Quade.

"Cut it," cried Sergeant Dickinson. "I want to get the straight of this. You." He turned to Cassmer. "Did he really come in fifteen minutes ago?"

Cassmer shrugged. "I never saw him until a few minutes ago. But there's the ticket-taker. He'd know."

The ticket-taker, whose post had been taken over by a policeman, frowned. "Yeah, he came in just a little while ago. I got plenty reason to remember. Him and his pal crashed the gate. On me! First time anyone crashed the gate on me in eight years. But he was damn slick. He—"

"Never mind the details," sighed Sergeant Dickinson. "I can imagine he was slick about it. Well, mister, you didn't kill him. But tell me—how the hell do you know he was gassed with cy—cyanide?"

"Cyanogen. It's got prussic acid in it. All right, the body was found inside the incubator, the door locked on the outside. That means someone locked him inside the incubator. The person who killed him. Right so far?"

"I'm listening." There was a thoughtful look in the sergeant's eyes.

"There's broken glass inside the incubator. The killer heaved in a bottle containing the stuff and slammed the door shut and locked it. The man inside was killed inside of a minute."

"Wait a minute. The glass is there all right, but how d'you know it contained cyanogen? There's no smell in there."

"No, because the killer opened the ventilator hole and turned on the electric fans inside the incubator. All that can be done from the outside. The fans cleared out the fumes. Simple."

"Not so simple. You still haven't said how you know it was cyanogen."

"Because he's got all the symptoms. Look at the body—pupils dilated, eyes wide, froth on the mouth, face livid, body twisted and stiff. That means he had convulsions. Well, if those symptoms don't mean cyanogen, I don't know what it's all about."

"Mister," said the detective. "Who did you say you were?"

"Oliver Quade, the Human Encyclopedia. I know everything."

"You know, I'm beginning to believe you. Well, then, who did the killing?"

"That's against the union rules. I told you how the man was killed. Finding who did it is your job."

"All right, but tell me one thing more. If this cyanogen has prussic acid in it, it's a deadly poison. Folks can't usually buy it."

"City folks, you mean. Cyanogen is the base for several insecticides. I don't think this was pure cyanogen. I'm inclined to believe it was a diluted form, probably a gas used to kill rats on poultry farms. Any poultry raiser could buy that."

"Here comes the coroner's man," announced Detective Dickinson. "Now, we'll get a check on you, Mr. Quade."

DR. BOGLE, THE coroner's physician, made a rapid, but thorough, examination of the body. His announcement coincided startlingly with Quade's diagnosis.

"Prussic acid or cyanide. He inhaled it. Died inside of five minutes. About three and a half hours ago."

Quade's face was twisted in a queer smile. He walked off from the group. Charlie Boston and Anne Martin, the girl, followed.

"Do you mind my saying that you just performed some remarkable work?" the girl said admiringly.

"No, I don't mind your saying so." Quade grinned. "I *was* rather colossal."

"He pulls those things out of a hat," groused Boston. "He's a very smart man. Only one thing he can't do."

"What's that?"

Boston started to reply, but Quade's fierce look silenced him. Quade coughed. "Well, look—a hot dog stand. Reminds me, it's about lunch time. Feel like a hot dog and orangeade, Anne?"

The girl smiled at his familiarity. "I don't mind. I'm rather hungry."

Boston sidled up to Quade. "Hey, you forgot!" he whispered. "You haven't got any money."

Quade said, "Three dogs and orangeades!"

A minute later they were munching hot dogs. Quade finished his orangeade and half-way through the sandwich suddenly snapped his fingers.

"That reminds me, I forgot something. Excuse me a moment..." He started off suddenly toward the group around the incubator, ignoring Charlie Boston's startled protest.

Boston suddenly had no appetite. He chewed the food in his mouth as long as he could. The girl finished her sandwich and smiled at him.

"That went pretty good. Guess I'll have another. How about you?"

Boston almost choked. "Uh, no, I ain't hungry."

The girl ordered another hot dog and orangeade and finished them while Boston still fooled with the tail end of his first sandwich.

The concessionaire mopped up the counter all around Boston and Anne Martin and finally said, "That's eighty cents, mister!"

Boston put the last of the sandwich in his mouth and began going through his pockets. The girl watched him curiously. Boston went through his pockets a second time. "That's funny," he finally said. "I must have left my wallet in the hotel. Quade...."

"Let me pay for it," said the girl, snapping open her purse.

Boston's face was as red as a Harvard beet. Such things weren't embarrassing to Quade, but they were to Boston.

"There's Mr. Quade," said Anne Martin. "Shall we join him?"

Boston was glad to get away from the hot dog stand.

The investigation was still going on. Sergeant Dickinson was on his hands and knees inside the incubator. A policeman stood at the door of it and a couple more were going over the exterior.

Quade saluted them with a piece of wire. "They're looking for clues," he said.

The girl shivered. "I'd like it much better if they'd take away Exhibit A."

"Can't. Not until they take pictures. I hear the photographers and the fingerprint boys are coming down. It's not really necessary either. Because I know who the murderer is."

The girl gasped: "Who?"

Quade did not reply. He looked at the piece of wire in his hands. It was evidently a spoke from a wire poultry coop, but it had been twisted into an elongated question mark. He tapped Dickinson's shoulder with the wire.

The sergeant looked up and scowled. "Huh?"

"Want this?" Quade asked.

"What the hell is it?"

"Just a piece of wire I picked up."

"What're you trying to do, rib me?"

Quade shrugged. "No, but I saw you on your hands and knees and thought you were looking for something. Thought this might be it."

Dickinson snorted. "What the hell, if you're not going to tell me who did the killing, let me alone."

"O.K." Quade flipped the piece of wire over a row of chicken coops. "Come," he said to Boston and Anne Martin. "Let's go look at the turkeys at the other end of the building."

Boston shuffled up beside Quade as the three walked through an aisle. "Who did it, Ollie?"

"Can't tell now, because I couldn't prove it. In a little while, perhaps."

Boston let out his pent-up breath. "If you ain't the damnedest guy ever!"

Anne Martin said, "You mean you're not going to tell Sergeant Dickinson?"

"Oh yes, but I'm going to wait a while. Maybe he'll tumble himself and I'd hate to deprive him of that pleasure... What time is it?"

"I don't know," Boston said. "I lost my watch in Kansas City. You remember that, don't you, Ollie?"

Quade winced. Boston had "lost" his watch in Uncle Ben's Three Gold Ball Shop. Quade's had gone to Uncle Moe in St. Louis.

"It's twelve-thirty," the girl said, looking at her wristwatch.

Quade nodded. "That's fine. The early afternoon editions of the papers will have accounts of the murder and a lot of morbid folk will flock around here later on. That means I can put on a good pitch and sell some of my books."

"I wanted to ask you about that," said Anne Martin. "You answered some really remarkable questions this morning. I don't for the life of me see how you do it."

"Forsaking modesty for the moment, I do it because I really know all the answers."

"All?"

"Uh-huh. You see, I've read an entire encyclopedia from cover to cover four times."

Anne looked at him in astonishment. "An entire encyclopedia?"

"Twenty-five volumes… Well, let's go back now. Charlie, keep your eyes open."

"Ah!" Charlie Boston said.

DR. BOGLE'S MEN were just taking away the body of the murdered man. Sergeant Dickinson, a disgusted look on his face, had rounded up his men and was on the verge of leaving.

"Not going, Captain Dickinson?" Quade asked.

"What good will it do me to hang around?" snorted the sergeant. "Everyone and his brother has some phony alibi."

"But your clues, man?"

"What clues?"

Quade shook his head in exasperation. "I told you how the murder was committed, didn't I?"

"Yeah, sure, the guy locked the bloke in the incubator and tossed in the bottle of poison gas, then opened the ventilator and turned on the fans. But there were more than a dozen guys around and almost any one of them could have done it, without any of the others even noticing what he was doing."

"No, you're wrong. Only one person could have done it."

A hush suddenly fell upon the crowd. Charlie Boston, tensed and crouching, was breathing heavily. The police sergeant's face became bleak. Quade had demonstrated his remarkable deductive ability a while ago and Dickinson was willing to believe anything of him, now.

Quade stepped lazily to a poultry coop, took hold of a wire bar and with a sudden twist tore it off. Then he stepped to the side of the incubator.

"Look at this ventilator," he said. "Notice that I can reach it easily enough. So could you, Lieutenant. We're about the same height—five feet ten. But a man only five-two couldn't reach it even by standing on his toes. Do you follow me?"

"Go on," said Sergeant Dickinson.

Quade twisted the piece of wire into an elongated question mark. "To move a box or chair up here and climb up on it would be to attract attention," he went on, "so the killer used a piece of wire to open the ventilator. Like this!" Quade caught the hook in the ventilator and pulled it open easily.

"That's good enough for me!" said Sergeant Dickinson. "You practically forced that wire on me a while ago and I couldn't see it. Well—*Judge Stone, you're under arrest!*"

"He's a liar!" roared the bantam poultry judge. "He can't prove anything like that on me. He just tore that piece of wire from that coop!"

"That's right," said Quade. "You saw me pick up the original piece of wire and when I threw it away after trying to give it to the sergeant you got it and disposed of it."

"You didn't *see* me!"

"No, I purposely walked away to give you a chance to get rid of the wire. But I laid a trap for you. While I had that wire I smeared some ink on it to prove you handled it. Look at your hands, Judge Stone!"

Judge Stone raised both palms upward. His right thumb and fingers were smeared with a black stain.

Sergeant Dickinson started toward the little poultry judge. But the bantam uttered a cry of fright and darted away.

"Ha!" cried Charlie Boston, and lunged for him. He wrapped his thick arms around the little man and tried to hold on to him. But the judge was suddenly fighting for his life. He clawed at Boston's face and kicked his shins furiously.

Boston howled and released his grip to defend himself with his fists.

The poultry judge promptly butted Boston in the stomach and darted under his flailing arms.

It was Anne Martin who stopped him. As the judge scrambled around Boston she stepped forward and thrust out her right foot. The little man tripped over it and plunged headlong to the concrete floor of the auditorium. Before he could get up Charlie Boston was on him. Sergeant Dickinson swooped down, a Police Positive in one hand and a pair of handcuffs in the other. The killer was secured.

Stone quit then. "Yes, I killed him, the damned lousy blackmailer. For years I judged his chickens at the shows and always gave him the edge. Then he double-crossed me, got me fired."

"What job?" asked Dickinson.

"My job as district manager for the Sibley Feed Company," replied Stone.

"Why'd he have you fired?" asked Quade. "Because you were short-weighing him on his feed? Is that it?"

"I gave him prizes his lousy chickens should never have had," snapped the killer. "What if I did short-weigh him twenty or thirty percent? I more than made up for it."

"Twenty or thirty percent," said Quade, "would amount to quite a bit of money in the course of a year. In his advertising in the poultry papers Tupper claimed he raised over eight thousand chickens a year."

"I don't need any more," said Sergeant Dickinson. "Well, Mr. Quade, you certainly delivered the goods."

"Not me, I only told you who the murderer was. If it hadn't been for Miss Martin he'd have got away."

Quade turned away. "Anne," he said, "Charlie and I are flat broke. But this afternoon a flock of rubbernecks are going to storm this place and I'm going to take quite a chunk of money from them. But in the meantime… That hot dog wasn't very filling and I wonder if you'd stake us to a lunch?"

Anne Martin's eyes twinkled. "Listen, Mr. Quade, if you asked me for every cent I've got I'd give it to you right away— because you'd get it from me anyway, if you really wanted it. You're the world's greatest salesman. You even sold Judge Stone into confessing."

Quade grinned. "Yes? How?"

She pointed at Quade's hands. "You handled that first wire hook with your bare hands. How come *your* hands didn't get black?"

Quade chuckled. "Smart girl. Even the sergeant didn't notice that. Well, I'll confess. I saw the smudge on Judge Stone's hands away back when I was putting on my pitch. He must have used a leaky fountain pen or something."

"Then you didn't put anything on it?"

"No. But *I* knew he was the murderer and *he* knew it… only he didn't know his hands were dirty. So…."

The girl drew a deep breath. "Oliver Quade, the lunches are on me."

"And the dinner and show tonight are on me," grinned Oliver Quade.

Rain, the Killer

*The Human Encyclopedia borrows
a trick from the Ancients*

RAIN PADDED ON the roof with sodden, maddening intensity; it swished on the leaf-barren trees outside the window and pelted the water-gorged earth with deadly monotony. It had rained for three days. Inside the bedroom it had seeped into the soul of the schizophrenic, the man with the dual personality; had filled him with sadistic despair until there was only one outlet for him.

Murder.

The schizophrenic rose from the bed on which he had been lying, went to the desk beside the rain-swept window and took from a drawer a long, pointed paper-knife. This was later to be called The Murder Weapon.

At the door of his room he halted. He had never killed a human being before and the all but vanquished normal half of his split personality made one last struggle. It screamed to the soul of the schizophrenic not to pass through this door, for once it did, it was damned forever.

The face of the man twisted from the struggle within him; a sob was torn from his racked body... and then he opened the door. The victory, temporarily at least, was won by the destructive personality that had been nurtured to full strength by the three-day downpour from the heavens.

The man with the paper-knife walked to another door in the corridor, opened it and stepped into the room.

A man lay on the bed, his form a darker shadow in the semi-dark of the room. The schizophrenic moved to the side of the bed. He stood there looking down at the sleeping man.

The intensity of his thoughts may have transmitted themselves to the subconscious brain of the sleeper, for suddenly he stirred and his eyes opened.

"Hello," he said, startled. "What is it?"

"I am going to kill you," said the standing man and raised his right hand over his head.

The man in the bed, shocked awake, saw death in the killer's eyes. He gasped:

"Don't! Don't! Please, I'll—"

The slender paper-knife came down with terrific force. It struck the throat of the man on the bed, went clear through as if it had been soft butter.

The man on the bed choked horribly and his body thrashed about for a moment. It made a wrestler's arch and the killer stepped back in alarm. Then the body collapsed.

The killer came forward again. In the semi-gloom he groped for the knife handle, found it and pulled it out of the dead man's throat. The blood, rushing out, made a soft, gurgling sound.

Methodically, the murderer took hold of the edge of the bedspread. He wrapped the knife in it and wiped it thoroughly, removing from it blood as well as finger prints. Then he let the knife drop to the floor and walked out of the room. He went to his own room, closed the door and entered the bathroom.

He switched on the light above the wash-bowl and washed his hands. He dried them on a towel, hung the towel up neatly on the rack, then looked at his reflection in the mirror over the medicine chest.

The face that looked back at him did not look like the face of a killer.

Rain splashed against the bathroom window. Slowly the monotonous wet sound of it penetrated the consciousness of the killer. A frown creased his forehead. He spoke to the face in the mirror; a half whisper with a trace of returning doubt in it:

"You are a murderer."

Schizophrenics are unhappy persons. Their dual personalities are constantly at war with one another. In moments of depression, stress or mental anguish, the element without inhibitions gains the ascendancy and the schizophrenic will do things for which he will later suffer untold remorse. But having won once, the uninhibited element wins again… and again… and in time will rule.

Remorse was already wrapping its cold fingers around the heart of the man in the bathroom. The merciless rain beat against the window.

The rain was the real murderer.

OLIVER QUADE, THE Human Encyclopedia, had debated with himself about taking the detour and after he'd gone a mile on it he wished he'd decided against it. The only thing that kept him on the narrow, winding road now was that the road shoulders were too soft and muddy for him to risk turning around.

The road was graveled, but wherever there was a depression in the gravel there was a muddy pond. The ditches on each side of the road were miniature torrents. And the rain still came down in sheets. Jupiter Pluvius had a real mad against the world.

It was six o'clock in the afternoon and dark as the inside of an inkwell. Quade cursed dispassionately and wished he'd been content to remain in drowsy idleness back there in the city. He'd come too far, though, to turn back; it would be easier to continue to the next town. There had to be one soon, despite the detour.

The headlights of his little coupé picked out a car on the road ahead. It was a touring car with side curtains, a large machine but not too comfortable for such sodden weather. Its head-lights were silhouetting a framework ahead of it. It wasn't until Quade had come up within fifty feet that he could make out that the framework was a bridge.

Quade braked his car to a stop a few yards behind the touring car and then he saw something else; water was rushing over the flooring of the bridge.

He rolled down the window at his left elbow, stuck his head out into the downpour and yelled, "Bridge go out?"

A man wearing a glistening raincoat sloshed up to Quade's car. "Naw," he said. "She ain't out yet, but she's creaking and won't stand much more."

"You going to cross?" Quade asked.

The man shrugged. "We gotta make it across, but we're scared to take a chance. The current's pretty swift. We'd be carried right away."

Another man in a dripping slicker came up. "Mister, your car's a lot lighter than ours," he said. "You might make it." Quade pursed his lips. "Well, the road's too narrow to turn around and go back so I guess I'll have to chance it."

The man who had come up first, said, "Mind if we ride across with you? We got to get over there."

"Hop in," Quade invited. "Three hundred and fifty pounds more won't make enough difference."

He opened the door on the far side of him and the two men trudged around. They squeezed into the front seat, the closest man's slicker wetting Quade clear through to the skin.

He gunned the motor and the wheels swished on the soaked gravel. For a moment Quade thought his car was already stuck, but then the little motor jerked the car out of the rut and it went back. Quade stopped it fifty yards from the bridge.

"Hang on," he said, grimly. "I'm going to take it full speed."

"In high?" asked the man beside him.

"No, the water's too deep for that and if I should kill the motor I doubt whether I could start it again. I'll take it in low, but I'm not stopping for anything."

"I thought I heard the bridge creak," said the second man. "Think we ought to try it?"

Quade thought that he saw the bridge skeleton move. The car was insured and could be replaced. His life wasn't insured and couldn't be replaced. He asked:

"How important is it for you to get across?"

The man beside Quade sighed. "Very important. I'm Dave

Starkey, the sheriff of this county. And this is Lou Higgin-botham, my deputy. A murder has been committed over on that island. That's why we want to get over."

"Then," said Quade, "Hold tight… and pray!"

He shifted into low, kept his foot on the clutch and raced the motor. Then suddenly he let out the clutch. The car leaped forward and Quade pushed the gas throttle to the floorboards. He gripped the steering wheel firmly and missed the lawmen's car by inches. The coupé hit the water covering the bridge floor and splashed it mightily.

Quade felt the wheels grip the bridge planking. Water splashed up through the floor-boards, soaked his trousers to his knees, but he kept his foot down on the throttle.

Half-way across! The bridge creaked ominously and for a giddy moment Quade thought it was going out. He heard the sheriff beside him gasp.

Three-quarters across and the bridge swayed so that Quade had to fight the wheel. Higginbotham, the deputy, whimpered.

And then, miraculously, the coupé leaped clear of the water and climbed the steep, graveled road on the other side. Quade continued to the crest of the ridge before he lifted his foot from the throttle. He stopped the car then, and a tremor ran through him. He knew that there was a fine film of perspiration on his forehead.

"We made it," the sheriff said and there was a catch in his voice.

"Do you think your own car can make it?" Quade asked.

The sheriff shook his head. "No, not a chance in the world. That bridge is going out of its own accord inside of a half hour."

"Then perhaps you'd better not walk back after it. I'll drive you to where you're going."

The sheriff nodded. "Thanks. It's the Olcott place. 'Bout a quarter mile ahead, then a driveway to the left."

There was a stone arch over the driveway leading into the Olcott place. That told Quade that he was entering the grounds of a rich man's estate.

The house, two hundred yards from the highway, was built on a hilltop. It was ablaze with lights and had, Quade estimated, at least twenty rooms. A smaller house nearby was evidently the servants' quarters.

Quade braked the coupé to a stop before the big house. The raincoated officers climbed out.

"Thanks a lot, mister," the sheriff said. "If you ever get arrested in Spurling I'll see that you get treated better than usual."

Quade said, "That's very generous of you. But how the devil am I going to get away from here? You said this was an island?"

"Yeah, I'd forgot." The sheriff frowned. "There's another bridge a quarter-mile beyond, but I've a notion that it's gone out already. It was lower than the one we crossed."

"Fine," said Quade. "I was just looking for an excuse not to drive any more tonight. And I've always wanted to spend a day or two on a swell estate like this."

"You forget why we're here," said the sheriff. "A murder—"

"Dead ones don't scare me," Quade replied. "Only live ones. I don't imagine Mr. Murderer hung around here to wait for the cops. Let's go inside."

Someone inside the big house must have heard the car stop for before the three men reached the front door it was thrown wide open. A butler in livery peered out. He asked:

"Are you the police?"

"We are," said the sheriff. "And we had one sweet time getting here."

Quade and the officers entered the house and began taking off their dripping coats. The butler took them.

A white-haired man came out of the living room on the right.

"Sheriff Starkey!" he exclaimed. "I'm glad you made it. I— well, you know why we sent for you."

"Yes, Mr. Olcott. You said your brother was killed."

The man called Olcott shook his head. "It—it was frightful. Allison went to call him for dinner and there—there he was."

"Lead the way, Mr. Olcott," the sheriff said.

The white-haired man grimaced and turned to a staircase. The sheriff, the deputy and Quade followed.

A wide corridor split the second floor. On the side where the staircase was, five doors opened onto the corridor; on the unbroken side, six doors. All the doors except the last one to the left of the stairs were open. Ferdinand Olcott led the way to the closed door.

The sheriff pushed open the door. The light was on in the bedroom.

"Ah," said the sheriff. The deputy cleared his throat hoarsely.

The dead man was about fifty; in life he had been an athletic, heavy-set man. His hair was iron-gray and his face tanned as if he had lived in the open.

There was much blood on the bed. Quade felt his insides tighten and wished that he had stayed in the city, back there fifty miles or so.

The sheriff drew a breath and approached the bed. He examined the body, then said, "It's just a little hole. He must have bled to death."

"No," said Quade. "He died almost instantly. The blade went through the spinal cord at the back of his neck. If he hadn't died instantly, he would have screamed."

The sheriff looked sharply at Quade. "Maybe he did scream; what makes you think he didn't?"

"Mr. Olcott said the butler came to call him for dinner. If he'd screamed, someone in the house would have heard him."

"Mmm." The sheriff looked suspiciously at Oliver Quade. "What about the knife hitting his spinal cord? How'd you figure that? Are you a doctor?"

"No, not at all. I'm Oliver Quade, the Human Encyclopedia."

Sheriff Starkey's eyes widened. "The Human what?"

"Human Encyclopedia."

"I don't get you. Why should you be a Human Encyclopedia?"

"Well, because I sell encyclopedias."

"You're a book agent? I'll be damned."

Mr. Olcott, standing just inside the door, said anxiously: "He—he was killed? It's not suicide?"

The sheriff looked at the paper-knife lying on the floor, near the foot of the bed, then at the edge of the sheet where the killer had wiped off the blade.

"It couldn't have been suicide," he said. "The blade was obviously wiped off and a man killing himself wouldn't do that."

"He was your brother?" Quade asked, turning to Olcott.

Olcott nodded. "Yes, but I hadn't seen him in six years until he came to visit here last week."

The sheriff looked disapprovingly at Quade. Then he said to the old man, "Then you don't know very much about your brother?"

"As much as anyone, I guess. He wrote me often. He owns a tremendously large cattle ranch down in the Argentine."

Quade saw the sheriff's eyes light up and knew the question of inheritance had popped into his mind. But the sheriff didn't ask it. Instead he examined his finger nails.

"I'd like to use your phone now, Mr. Olcott," he said.

"Of course. Downstairs."

"Yes. I'm through here, for the time being."

The upper corridor was strangely devoid of servants. The dead man in the end bedroom had frightened them down-stairs, Quade reasoned.

He and the lawmen and Ferdinand Olcott descended to the entrance hall. There the sheriff picked up a phone from a stand. He jiggled the hook, then replaced the receiver on it.

"It's dead. I've been expecting that." He looked at his deputy. Higginbotham was a big man, standing over six feet, and weighing close to two hundred pounds. He was a young fellow, not over twenty-five. His forehead wrinkled as soon as the sheriff looked at him.

"Lou," the sheriff said. "You'd better go and see if either of the bridges are still in. With the telephone wire down…" He left the sentence unfinished.

The deputy coughed awkwardly. "You mean I should walk?"

The sheriff looked at Quade, then at Olcott. He said, "Isn't your chauffeur here, Mr. Olcott?"

"Yes, of course, he's in the kitchen with the rest of the servants. I'll have him get out one of the small cars and drive your man."

Allison, the butler, came out of a door. "Allison," said Mr. Olcott, "tell Charles to take this deputy where he wants to go. In the smallest car."

The butler and the deputy went through a door at the end of the hall. Olcott turned to the sheriff then. "I suppose you will want to talk to the family—and the guests?"

"Yes, of course."

FERDINAND OLCOTT LED the way into a living room that ran the width of the house, more than forty feet. There were seven or eight people in it. Quade wondered that none had been curious enough to come out into the hallway when he and the police officers had arrived.

There was one woman. She was young, beautiful; a rather tall, blonde girl with a boyish figure and classic features. Oliver Quade liked her intelligent expression. She was Martha Olcott, the daughter of the house.

The men interested Quade most. His sharp eyes studied them carefully. Movie-goers would instantly have picked the swarthy man as the villain of the play. He was of middle height, slightly stout, used pomade on his hair, and had a pointed, waxed mustache. This was Arturo Nogales and he was, Ferdinand Olcott explained, the dead man's business manager.

The second man, from the way he kept his eyes on Martha Olcott, was her sweetheart. He was a well-built, dark young man of about twenty-five or twenty-six. He had probably played football at college and played it well, Quade thought. His name was Lynn Crosby.

The last man came rightly last. He was that sort of man; he was probably five feet six, had sandy hair, wore tortoise-shell rimmed glasses and would have walked around an impudent cat on the sidewalk, rather than dispute the right-of-way. He was Clarence Olcott, Ferdinand Olcott's son.

The introductions over, Sheriff Starkey got down to business.

"As sorry as I am about everything, I'm still the sheriff of this county and it's my duty to make an investigation. I must determine first of all where everyone was in the house at the time the murder was committed."

His bluntness drew a couple of gasps. Ferdinand Olcott protested. "Why, Sheriff, you talk as if you suspect someone in *this* house killed my brother."

The sheriff's eyes popped wide open. "Isn't that what you think?"

"Of course not," replied Olcott, indignantly. "The thought never occurred to me that it was done by anyone but an intruder, some second-story man who entered the house for nefarious purposes."

The sheriff gulped. "In daylight, during the kind of weather we had today? Oh, come now, Mr. Olcott, does it sound reasonable that a sneak thief or burglar would try to come into a house during a rainstorm when he knows that more than a dozen people are in it?"

Olcott frowned and shook his head. "But it's preposterous to think that anyone in this house committed the—crime. The servants have all been with us for years and surely you don't think—"

"He means just that," the mousy Clarence surprised everyone by saying. "And I believe he's justified in that contention. I've been giving some thought to the matter and I can see only one logical explanation: Someone in this house killed Uncle Walter."

There was some rumbling about that. Quade decided then that he had been silent long enough. He said, "Mr. Olcott's right. No outsider would have used a paper-knife as a weapon for killing someone in this house. A pocket knife or blackjack would have been a more likely weapon for an outsider. Sheriff, I know you intended to do it, but don't you think it's time to find out from whose room the murder weapon came?"

The sheriff glared at Quade. At that moment the outer door slammed and Higginbotham, the deputy, came into the big living room. "Both bridges are out and the river's gone up more than six feet."

"Six feet!" cried the sheriff. "It couldn't go up that much in such a little time."

"It could if the dam went out up the river," said Lynn Crosby with his eyes still on Martha.

Ferdinand Olcott exclaimed in consternation. "Fourteen years ago, before that dam was built, we had a flood here and the water came up almost to the spot where this house is built. I never thought that dam would go out."

"You mean, Father," interposed Martha Olcott, "that there's actual danger from the flood?"

Olcott looked frankly worried. "Why, I—I'd hate to think that, but if the dam's broken, the water's going to get pretty high. I don't think it'll quite reach the house, but, with the bridges out and the telephone wires down, we may be isolated for several days."

"There's enough food in the house for a month," said Martha Olcott.

Nogales, the Argentinian, showed white teeth. "Good! Then there is nothing to worry about."

"Nothing," said Quade, "except that a man has been murdered in this house, that the murderer is still here, and that we're on an island, cut off from the rest of the world. There's going to be a flood out there and people are going to be too busy for a while to think about this little group here. We may be here a week... with a dead man in the house."

The sheriff took a deep breath. "Then we may as well get some things straight. I'm the law here and I'm conducting a murder investigation. Mr. Human Encyclopedia, you did a good job in getting us over here, but, just to avoid trouble in the future, keep in mind that I'm running things here. Understand?"

Quade looked sardonically at the sheriff. "It so happens that I'm one of the three people here not under suspicion. I've violated no laws and I'm probably the most intelligent person here."

Clarence Olcott took up the challenge. "I'm a Harvard man, mister," he said. "I've got an A.B. and M.A. and I'm working for an LL.D. I think my educational qualifications are the equal of anyone here."

"I guess I spoke out of turn," said Quade. "But, Mr. Olcott, can you tell me in what direction Reno, Nevada, is from San Diego, California?"

Clarence Olcott looked superciliously at Quade. "Any schoolboy could tell you that. Reno is northeast of San Diego."

"I'm afraid the schoolboy who'd say that would flunk," Quade replied. "It so happens that Reno is northwest of San Diego. Look it up on the map."

Clarence strode to a bookcase and took out an atlas. After a moment he grunted. "I'll be damned. You're right. But that was a trick question. All right, it's my turn. I'll ask you something. Hmm. Who invented the principle of the door lock?"

Clarence Olcott had evidently asked the first question to come to his mind, without realizing the magnitude of it. Quade screwed up his mouth. "That," he said, "is a very good question. Only about six persons in this country could answer it. I'm one of the six. The ancient Egyptians invented the door lock. The principle of it died with the decline of Egypt, and in medieval days an inferior lock was evolved by Europeans. The first real lock of modern times was invented by Robert Barron in 1774. In 1848 Linus Yale invented the modern tumbler lock, using the principle of the ancient Egyptian lock, patterned after one found in the ruins of Nineveh."

Almost everyone in the room was staring at Quade by this time. He chuckled and went on: "With the Yale lock and key, 32,768 combinations are possible... Do you want to ask me another question, Mr. Olcott?"

Sheriff Starkey interrupted: "This is no time for games, Quade. A murder has been committed here and there's work to be done."

"Quite so," said Quade. "Well, what about the paper-knife?"

The sheriff turned to his deputy. "Lou, run upstairs and bring down that knife with which Walter Olcott was killed."

The big deputy's eyes rolled as he left the room. Quade heard him take the stairs two at a time. He was in the upper corridor less than a half-minute, then came tearing down the stairs.

He brought the knife into the room, holding it gingerly between thumb and forefinger. The sheriff took it from him and held it aloft. "This paper-knife belonged to someone in this room, didn't it?"

"It's mine," said Martha Olcott.

Her father gasped. "Martha!"

"There's no point in denying it," said Martha. "It's from that desk set you got me for my birthday two years ago. The shears to match are in my desk right now. But this—haven't seen it for a couple of days."

"It's yours, though, you're sure of that?" persisted the sheriff. "Yes."

"That doesn't prove a thing," cut in Lynn Crosby. "Any of the servants here could have taken it from Martha's room. Or, for that matter, anyone else here."

"As a matter of fact," cut in Clarence Olcott, "I saw that paper-knife on the hall table only this morning."

Allison, the butler, cleared his throat. "Beg pardon, but Mr. Clarence is right. I found it in this room and meant to take it back to Miss Martha's room. Then the mail came and I used it to open some of the house mail. I'm sorry; I forgot all about it after that."

"And no finger prints on it," murmured Quade. "There goes your only clue, Sheriff."

"Perhaps," said the sheriff sarcastically, "you could conduct this investigation better."

"Yes, I believe I could."

The sheriff showed his teeth. "And just what would you do?"

"Well, first of all, I'd establish a motive for the killing. There's always a motive for murder, you know. Usually it's for financial gain, although sometimes it's for jealousy or hate. Establish your motive and you may point the finger at the murderer."

The glare went out of Starkey's eyes. "I was about to start along those lines... Mr. Olcott, you said upstairs that your brother was a very wealthy man."

"Arturo can tell you more about that," said Olcott Senior.

"Quite so," said the swarthy dandy. "I was associated with Mr. Walter Olcott for eight years. He was, in my country, a very important man and, I am happy to say, one of the wealthiest men in Argentina."

"How wealthy?" asked Starkey.

Nogales shrugged. "How wealthy is a man who owns two million acres of land, more than a hundred thousand cattle, several mines, a few factories and a railroad or two?"

Sheriff Starkey looked intently at Ferdinand Olcott. "Mr. Olcott," he said, trying to make his voice sound casual. "Do you happen to know to whom your brother was leaving his money?"

"Of course I don't," snapped the old man. "My brother was here on a brief visit. He was a comparatively young man. No reason at all for me to ask him about his will. I'm not exactly a pauper myself, you know."

The sheriff was thwarted on that line of questioning. But he persisted for another hour. He even summoned all the servants and put them through a verbal third degree. He learned nothing.

The schizophrenic looked at the people in the room around him. He saw in their faces doubt of one another... and fear. And it filled him with gloating. "They're afraid of me; they don't know which one of them I'll kill next."

But then he looked at Oliver Quade, the Human Encyclopedia, and he was not so sure of himself. "He's the most dangerous man here. He has brains! He is almost as smart as I am. Almost! Well, if he guesses too much I'll give him what I gave Walter Olcott!"

The sheriff declared that he and Deputy Higginbotham

would remain down in the living room for the night. He advised the others to go to sleep.

Quade was shown to the room directly opposite the one in which lay the dead body of Walter Olcott. He grimaced as he looked at the closed door. "I'm the one who wasn't afraid of dead ones," he reminded himself.

AFTER LOCKING HIS bedroom door, Quade threw himself on the bed and smoked a cigarette. He was tired, but the monotonous patter of the rain on the window kept him awake. That, and thinking about the events of the evening. Somewhere in this house was a murderer and Quade had an uneasy feeling that he was not yet through.

The knowledge that a flood had cut the island off from the rest of the world, that the people on the island could not escape, could not appeal for help from the outside, would give the murderer a feeling of security. The killer had plenty of time to figure things out.

Quade dozed after a while. Something woke him. Voices. Loud voices; some of them outside the house and a bellowing one inside, downstairs. Quade stepped quickly to the window and raised the lower half. Rain beat in on him.

He saw moving figures down in the gloom and then a light went on downstairs and shed its rays out into the yard. Quade gasped. The yard was full of water!

The figures were servants, splashing in the water to the main house which was on higher ground.

Quade unlocked the door of his room and stepped out into the hallway. He almost collided with Martha Olcott, clad in a dressing gown.

"Something's happened!" Martha Olcott cried out when she saw Quade.

He nodded. "The servants are coming to the house. The water's risen and driven them out of their place."

"Do you think," Martha asked, "the water'll come—here?"

Quade shook his head. "I don't know. I haven't seen the topography of this country in the day time. But the way it's been raining and the condition of the river and all, I'm afraid…."

While they talked, they descended the stairs. The servants, dripping from the rain and their wading, were streaming into the house. Sheriff Starkey and Higginbotham were dashing about.

Inside of a minute everyone on the island was gathered in the big living room. The place was a bedlam of noise. A couple of the maids were wailing and the men were chattering excitedly.

In the midst of it all, Oliver Quade sniffed the close air in the room and a sudden chill struck at his vitals. He edged away and stepped out into the kitchen.

Black smoke was puffing through the cracks of a door. Quade sprang to the door, tore it open and a huge cloud of smoke gushed out into his face. He retreated before it, then advanced again and looked through the smoke, down the staircase, into the cellar.

Flames flickered through the black smoke. Quade sprang back into the living room. "The place is on fire!" he announced.

Pandemonium broke loose. Everyone yelled and cried out at the same time and for a moment people rushed about bumping and jostling one another. Then Quade took command of the situation. "The fire's beyond control. The best thing we can do is get out of the house."

Smoke was coming into the living room now. With it came the roar and crackle of flames. "We've got to fight the fire!" thundered Lynn Crosby. He dashed toward the kitchen. Arturo Nogales and Sheriff Starkey dashed after him.

"It's no use," said Quade. "A couple of hundred gallons of oil have been spilled down there. That's what makes the smoke so black. And you can smell the oil. Let's get out."

There was a sudden explosion in the cellar and the men from the kitchen came reeling back. "It's too late!" cried Sheriff Starkey. "The house is a goner!"

Then there was a stampede for the doors. By the time they got outside, flames were shooting through the windows of the kitchen.

"Where can we go?" someone cried in the semidark.

"The other house," directed Quade. "The floors will be wet but it's the best there is!"

There were two feet of water on the main floor of the servants' quarters. Only half of the handful of survivors on Olcott's Island were in the servants' house when the electric light went out. Ferdinand Olcott cried out in agony: "That was the light plant. Now what?"

Now what, indeed! The water was rising. The big house was burning. The servants' quarters weren't much protection. The water was swirling around in it.

Quade stood by a window watching the roaring holocaust that had been the Olcott mansion. In the room behind him, people were talking, some sobbing, some whimpering. All were restless and afraid.

Then the small-town sheriff, Starkey, voiced the thing that had been in Oliver Quade's mind the past ten minutes and which he hadn't wanted to express aloud.

"That fire seemed to me as if someone'd set it," the sheriff said. "It makes a crematory for the dead one. A regular funeral pyre. If the flood hadn't wakened the servants, it would have been one for us all."

Then there was near panic. It took the combined efforts of Oliver Quade, Lynn Crosby, Arturo Nogales and Ferdinand Olcott to soothe the others. And by that time the water had risen two inches. A creak and groan of straining timbers suddenly shook the house.

"I think," Quade suggested then, "we had better leave this house."

"Leave the house!" cried Clarence Olcott. "Why, it's raining cats and dogs outside."

There was a terrific wrench and the house joggled heavily. "The foundations are going," said Quade. "The water's loosened them. In a few minutes this house will wash away."

Again there was a mad rush for the door and again the servants and family charged out into the torrent of water.

The big Olcott mansion was a glowing skeleton of fire. Quade sloshed ahead of the others, the water above his knees. He circled the house to the right, found himself going up. "The ground's higher back here," he called out.

"Of course it is!" cried Ferdinand Olcott. "There's a ridge behind the house. Ten feet or more. We'll be safe there. It'll never reach that high."

Quade wasn't so sure of that, but he led the way to the ridge. And there they huddled, thirteen wet, cold, and miserable people.

One of them was a murderer.

"I burned the house down," the schizophrenic said to himself. "I'm going to die... but it's fun watching these weaklings. They'll die a thousand deaths each. They're afraid to die."

He was afraid, too, but his egotism refused to admit the fear.

It was a nightmare, there on the promontory behind the ruined house. The fire sputtered and hissed for several hours. It gave some light and a small amount of heat to those crouching on the wet ground. It was a blessing to them; without it, some of them would have gone into hysterics. Some of the women folk were already near it.

The butler and a couple of the maids knelt on the wet ground and prayed. None of the others joined, but neither did they scoff. And perhaps they would join in the praying when the water rose higher.

Quade sat on the muddy side of the promontory. Twice in three hours he moved higher as the water came up and licked at his feet. Around midnight he gave his coat to Martha Olcott.

"Thanks!" she shivered. Lynn Crosby scowled for not having thought of the chivalrous gesture himself. He came down and sat beside Quade then.

"How high do you think the water'll get?" he asked.

"It can't go much higher," Quade replied. "Wouldn't have come this high if the dam hadn't gone out. The water doesn't worry me."

"What does?"

"Exposure. Everybody soaked to the skin, sitting on this wet ground. All of us will have colds by morning and some—worse. We can't stay here like this. Not long."

"But we can't leave. I know this island. The river'll be a quarter-mile wide and too strong to swim. I'd try it now if I thought it'd be any use."

"You couldn't swim fifty feet in it," said Quade. "There's got to be some other way."

"Maybe we can build a raft?" suggested Crosby eagerly.

"We'll see when morning comes… There goes the servants' house!"

It went with a violent wrenching and screeching. The rush of water tore it bodily from its moorings, swept it to the burning mansion and then carried it down into the valley below, turning it over and over like a toy.

IT WAS THE longest night anyone had ever gone through. No one slept. When the black sky turned to gray Quade waded down in the water, closer to the smoldering ruins of the mansion.

He found a branch of a tree and poked around for a while. Deputy Higginbotham joined him. His teeth chattered. "Gawd, if I only had a stiff drink of gin," he muttered. "The water's got into my bones."

"A drink or two apiece wouldn't hurt any of us," said Quade. He continued poking in the débris.

Sheriff Starkey joined them, cursing under his breath. "Who's your idea of the killer?" he asked.

"There are things more important right now than arresting a murderer."

"You mean you know who the killer is?" exclaimed the sheriff.

"Of course," replied Quade. "I knew last night after he set fire to the house."

"Who is it?" asked the sheriff hoarsely. "The South American?"

"I'm more interested right now in saving the lives of thirteen people than arresting one murderer," said Quade. "Martha Olcott already has a cold. She can't stand another night here. A couple of the maids are coughing pretty hard too."

The sheriff muttered under his breath. "We're stuck here until the water goes down."

"It won't go down for a week. The rain's letting up now, but even so, we can't stay here a week. We've got to get away—today!"

"How?"

Quade shrugged. "Go away and let me think!"

The sheriff cursed under his breath, but retreated. Higginbotham went with him.

The rain lessened considerably in the next fifteen minutes and dawn broke grudgingly over the island. Quade's vision was lengthened then and what he saw disheartened him. A sea of water stretched out as far as he could see. The tops of trees stuck out of the water, like lonely sentinels. The water moved south and west in a steady sweep. It was another quarter-hour before Quade could see the river and then his spirits dropped even lower. The river was a raging torrent, a visible swift current in the sea of water sweeping over the island.

The entire island except the promontory on which the refugees crouched was under water. There was land on the other side of the river, quite a bit, and most of it high out of the water. But it was a half-mile away, too far for anyone to swim in the rushing water.

But there lay safety. If someone over there saw them on the island here and if they had a powerful boat....

Quade turned to the others. "Anyone live over there?" he asked, pointing.

Ferdinand Olcott shook his head sadly. "No one lives within five miles of this island."

"And I imagine those out there are having their own troubles."

"If someone could get over there and get help…" Quade thought aloud.

Arturo Nogales, the swarthy South American, began peeling off his soggy coat. "I am a strong swimmer," he said.

"If you were the strongest swimmer in the world you couldn't swim across that current out there. There's a low valley to the south and you'd be swept out before you could reach the high land."

Martha Olcott came up. "Are we—finished?" she asked.

Quade looked bleakly at her. "All my life I've been a resourceful person, but somehow I can't think of anything to do now."

She bit her lip. "If we could only build a fire here…"

"Everything's water-logged," said Quade. "Perhaps if the rain stops we can gather some wood and get it dried. Or—I'll be damned! Look at that garage there. It's still on its foundations."

"Yes, it's built on concrete. But there's nothing there except some tools and things."

"Tools?" Quade's eyes flashed. He turned around and called to Lynn Crosby. "Crosby, mind coming with me to the garage?"

Crosby came over. "What good'll that do? The cars are under water."

"I know," said Quade. "I wasn't counting on them. But there are tools over there, I understand. Perhaps we can do something with them."

"You said last night a raft couldn't make it."

"Chances are almost negligible, but we might figure out something else."

Higginbotham and the chauffeur, a stocky man named McCarthy, joined Quade and Crosby. They waded in water to their armpits to the garage.

"Look for saws, hammers and nails," Quade instructed.

They found a keg of thirty-penny spikes, a couple of saws and several hammers, as well as a hand-ax. Quade himself discovered something that filled him with glee. It was about fifty feet of two-inch rope hawser. He carried it to the promontory.

"What's the rope for?" asked Clarence Olcott, when the four men deposited their spoils on the wet ground.

Quade did not reply. He looked at the telephone poles which stuck out above the water. He bit his lips and scowled for several moments. The others had by this time conceded Quade the leadership and they waited anxiously for him to arrive at some decision.

"That telephone wire," Quade said after a while. "There are two strands of it. If we could get a thousand yards, I think—I think we would have a chance. The wires are broken somewhere along the line because the phone was dead. I could put that wire to work for us, I believe. Will you get it?"

Sheriff Starkey snorted. "What good would wire do you?"

Quade pointed toward the promontory on the far side of the river. "If we could get this wire there we could rig up a sort of breeches buoy and I think we could all get away."

"Yeah, but how you going to get the wire there?" demanded Lynn Crosby.

Quade said with more confidence than he felt: "If the rest of you will get the wire I'll get it across the river."

"How? You said no one could swim that current," exclaimed Clarence, the mousy one.

"Get the wire," said Quade. "I promise to get it over there."

There was some grumbling but finally the men went out to get the wire from the telegraph poles.

Quade trotted down to the ruins of the Olcott house. He began pulling at some beams and two-by-fours. He dragged out several sizable timbers that had not been burned too much.

"Just what are you going to build?" asked Martha Olcott after watching him for some time.

Quade wiped the excess moisture from one of the saws on his trousers. He grinned, the first grin that had been seen on the little island since the night before.

"I'm going to make a catapult," he said.

Martha Olcott looked at him as if he had suddenly gone insane. "A catapult?" she repeated. "What—what for?"

"To throw that wire over to the mainland. You remember your history?"

She nodded. "Yes, I know that the Ancients used catapults in their warfare. They threw stones and things with them. But—"

"They threw stones big enough to batter down walls distances of twelve to fifteen hundred feet," said Quade. "So why can't we throw a wire that far?"

"Have you ever built a catapult before?"

He shook his head. "No. As a matter of fact, I've never even seen one."

She drew in her breath. "Then how do you know you can build one?"

He grinned at her. "You forget I'm the Human Encyclopedia."

She grimaced impatiently. "Yes, yes, I heard you arguing with the men last night. I'll admit that you seem to know an amazing number of things. But is building a catapult one of those things?"

"I know everything, Miss Olcott. Everything that man has ever known… or that got into print. I've read the Encyclopedia from cover to cover four times."

She gasped. "You're joking!"

"No. I sell encyclopedias because I believe in them. I practice what I preach. Fifteen years ago I started reading the set I sold and I've been reading it ever since. The Encyclopedia contains all the knowledge of the ages. That stuff I pulled last night was on the level. I've an unusual memory. I remember everything I read and therefore I know everything that's in the encyclopedia. And there's a very fine drawing of a catapult the Crusaders used at the siege of Acre. They battered down the best fortifications of Saladin with it. I'm going to build a catapult like it."

She looked strangely at him for a moment. Then she said, "Mr. Quade, I really believe you can do it. Let me help you."

"Fine," he said. "Go down there then and poke around in those ruins. Find the spears that were hanging on the walls of the living room last night. The heads, I mean. The shafts are burned, I imagine."

Quade sawed and hammered. After an hour the men began trooping back with long lengths of dead telephone wire they had cut from the telephone poles. They complained of exhaustion, but after resting a while and seeing Quade working without stopping, they went back for more wire.

They had fourteen hundred feet of wire by noon. That was all that was obtainable. The poles beyond that distance were too close to the raging river.

By that time Quade had the framework of the catapult built. It was a massive structure, resting on solid eight-inch beams.

AT TWO O'CLOCK they had twisted the rope hawser into place, and the other men had spliced the wire and coiled it in a neat pile beside the makeshift catapult.

Martha Olcott had found two spear heads and Quade spent a half-hour fashioning shafts for them and attaching the end of one to the telephone wire.

At last everything was finished. The rain was a mere drizzle then, but the water had risen a couple of inches more.

The recent college graduates, Clarence Olcott and Lynn Crosby, examined the catapult with extreme skepticism. "It won't work," Clarence declared. "You need some sort of spring attachment to throw that thing."

"My friend," said Quade, "did the ancient Greeks have springs? They did not. This rope twisted in here is all the spring that's necessary. Here, we'll try it out with a stone first."

There was a narrow slot running down the back of the catapult. Quade adjusted things and dropped the stone into the slot. Everyone on the tiny island gathered around.

Quade took a deep breath. Up to now he'd bolstered up his confidence. He remembered the details of the plans in the encyclopedia, accurately, but suppose—suppose the artist who had drawn them had made an error?

"All right," he said. He touched a wooden lever with his foot. The lever released the trigger and there was a swish and twang and the stone was hurtled out of the catapult. It sailed up in a swift arc, so fast that the eye could hardly follow it. Then it disappeared out of sight. But Quade watched the water and saw no splash. He knew that the stone had gone beyond the water.

Exclamations of awe went up all around Quade. "It worked!" Lynn Crosby cried.

Quade was adjusting the spear which was attached to the wire when Clarence, the scoffer, voiced another doubt. "How you going to make the spear stick over there?"

That was the thing that had worried Quade most. "There are plenty of thick trees over there. I'm hoping it will hit one of them squarely."

"Suppose it does. Will it have enough force to stick hard enough for the wire to hold up a person?"

"If the spear hits a twelve-inch tree there's sufficient force to drive it clear *through* the tree!"

Quade dropped to the soggy ground and looked out along the slot of the catapult. He had aimed the thing high to give the spear a trajectory but still it shouldn't go too high or too low.

The ropes were twisted tight again. The threaded spear was laid in the slot. Quade shot the trigger.

The spear hurtled out of the slot, drawing the wire with it. It sailed high in the air, went far out and then began dropping. Quade held his breath as the spear began falling—and his spirits fell with the spear.

"It didn't make it!" cried Lynn Crosby.

It was true. The spear had fallen a hundred feet short. The disappointment of all was heavy. Quade began hauling in the wire.

"What are you going to do now?" scoffed Sheriff Starkey.

"Try again."

It took a half hour to haul in the wire, coil it carefully and get the catapult ready for another trial. Quade moved the machine back a few inches and elevated it slightly and twisted the rope hawsers until they couldn't be twisted another sixty-fourth of an inch.

He was as taut as the twisted rope, when he placed the spear into the slot for the second trial. He knew if the catapult didn't have enough power now, there was no use trying any more. The fault lay in the hawser; it wasn't thick enough.

"If it doesn't go this time," he said grimly to those around him, "figure on spending a week or so here; without food or shelter."

A couple of the women servants began sobbing and two or three of the men on the island cleared their throats.

"He knows," said the schizophrenic to himself. "He knows I'm the killer. The man's smart. If this thing works he must stay here... dead!"

Twang!

The spear was catapulted out again. It seemed to those around that it left the slot with increased force. Quade knew it had. He watched the flight of the spear with a prayer on his lips and his jaws crunched.

The spear began falling....

It disappeared into the woods on the far side of the wide river and the wire suddenly stopped playing out.

"It made it!" cried Lynn Crosby.

Quade gripped the wire. "Now, let's hope that it landed true."

He pulled up the slack of the wire, tugged hard. It refused to give.

"I think it's stuck," he said grimly. "Here, help me pull, Crosby."

Crosby stepped up beside Quade and pulled with him. The two of them could not pull the wire more than a couple of inches.

Perspiration broke out on Quade's forehead. "We're safe!" he exclaimed.

Cheers and sobs of joy went up.

The breeches buoy was fixed on to the wire and the wire securely lashed around a telephone pole some distance behind the catapult.

"The women will go first," Quade said.

Lynn Crosby stepped up behind Sheriff Starkey and jerked the sheriff's gun out of his holster. "No," he said. "I'm going first!"

"Lynn!" That was Martha Olcott. Her face showed terrible anguish. Quade, looking at her, knew that she'd been guessing the truth, but hadn't wanted to believe it before.

He cursed himself silently. He should have been alert at the critical moment for just some such move on Crosby's part. He'd known since the night before that Lynn Crosby was the schizophrenic, the killer who had brutally murdered Martha's uncle and set fire to the big house and put them all in this predicament. But Quade's mind had been too filled with the bigger problem. Even if they had subdued the murderer, they would still have to face the problem of getting off the island. Now Crosby had suddenly revealed himself.

"Stand back, everyone!" he commanded, steadying the gun on them.

Deputy Lou Higginbotham, who until then had been a

nonentity, reached for a piece of glory. He went for his gun. He got his hand on it, had it half out of the holster and then Lynn Crosby shot him through the face. Higginbotham pitched to the ground.

"I'll kill every one of you if you try to stop me," Crosby snarled. His face revealed the soul behind it. He had a split personality no longer. He was absolutely and completely insane now. No more moments of sanity, no more fighting between the two personalities. Lynn Crosby was completely mad.

"Do as he says," Quade ordered, knowing what Crosby would do if someone crossed him.

Crosby scooped up Higginbotham's gun and stuck it into the waistband of his trousers. He brandished the sheriff's gun and his face broke into a huge grin as the group of men and women retreated before him. He laughed raucously. "The flood! Ha-ha! The flood got all of you poor people. All except me. My story will be you wanted me to go over first to test the wire and I did. Then it broke. Too bad. Too bad." He laughed again, uproariously.

"Lynn!" said Ferdinand Olcott, "you're insane!"

Lynn Crosby cursed in sudden frenzy. "You—you're the cause of all this! You thought I wasn't good enough for your daughter. You told me to get a job and make a name for myself and then you'd think about letting me marry her. That's what you told me, isn't it? Well, ask Martha—did we wait for you?"

Ferdinand Olcott staggered back. "Martha—did you—"

Martha could hardly raise her head. "We—were married two weeks ago."

"Secretly," sneered Lynn Crosby. "You forced us to get married secretly."

"But we never lived together," said Martha Olcott. "That—I am glad of that, anyway."

Crosby showed his fangs. "You get satisfaction out of that, do you? Well, then think over this: I never loved you at all. I married you for your money, your uncle's money. He told me he was leaving everything to you. That's why I killed him. To get his money, through you. And now, as your husband, I'll get your father's too."

Crosby turned toward Quade. "How did you know it was me?"

"The salt," said Quade. "You went down into the cellar and started that oil fire. You'd heard somewhere that salt killed the odor of oil so you washed your hands with it after setting the fire. I didn't smell oil on your hands, but you got salt over your clothes. That's how I knew."

Crosby nodded. "You're a smart guy, Quade. Much too smart to stay alive. You might figure out some other way of getting across. So—"

The gun in his hand thundered. Almost at the instant Crosby squeezed the trigger Quade started to throw himself to one side. The bullet went through his left shoulder. He fell limply to the ground. He was fully conscious but to show that he wasn't mortally hit would only invite another bullet. His face fell into three inches of water and he kept it there.

He held his breath as long as he could, then slowly turned his head sidewise and brought his mouth out of the water. He drew in air sharply and looked toward the catapult.

Lynn Crosby was already in the crude breeches buoy, working his way out over the water, hand over hand.

Quade watched him for a moment, then rose to his knees.

"Mr. Quade!" cried Martha Olcott. "You're not—" then she saw the blood mixing with the water on his shoulder and sprang to his side.

"It's all right," Quade cried out grimly.

The others gathered around. "He'll cut the wire when he gets almost there," said Clarence Olcott. "He can pull himself to the other side with what's left but we—the wire'll be too short then."

Quade said to Martha Olcott, "Take the women back a way and don't look. We've got only one chance, but it won't be pretty to see."

She understood him immediately. Her face tightened but she quickly herded the maids to the rear.

Quade picked up the spear. Lynn Crosby was out two hundred feet and moving at the rate of fifty feet a minute, out of revolver range. There was only one spear—it had to kill—to save twelve lives.

Quade placed the spear in the slot of the catapult and then the others understood. "You're going to kill him!" gasped Clarence.

Quade did not reply. He adjusted the catapult quickly, depressing it in front. He dropped down beside the slot, sighted through it, then made some more adjustments.

"All right," he said then. "He's three hundred feet out. We've got one shot. If it misses, we stay here."

He kicked the trigger.

Twang!

The spear whanged out of the slot, shot out through space in a low arc—and landed in flesh.

The schizophrenic lived two seconds. In those two seconds the part of him that had been suppressed since the day before screamed: "You were wrong! Wrong!"

And then it, too, died. Finally and definitely.

Death on Eagle's Crag

Oliver Quade finds a murder clue in money

MRS. MATTIE EGAN, proprietor of Eagle's Crag, was the toughest prospect Oliver Quade had worked on in many months. For ten minutes he had extolled the merits of the set of encyclopedias. He had painted glorious pictures for Mrs. Egan, had told her of marvelous benefits she would derive from owning the books. He had told her all those things in a voice that could be heard half-way down the mountain.

But Mrs. Egan was unmoved by it all. Her resistance was summed up in the stubborn, unyielding statement: "I'm fifty-six years old, come next January, and I ain't never owned no books of my own and I don't intend to start buying none now."

The word "quit" was not in Oliver Quade's lexicon. He was the best book salesman in the country. He admitted it himself; his rivals conceded it. Mrs. Egan may never have bought books from any other salesman, but she was going to buy from Oliver Quade.

He told her: "Mrs. Egan, I'm not trying to sell you *books*. I'm trying to sell you knowledge. In these twenty-five volumes is the knowledge of the ages; everything that the human race has learned since the dawn of time. Everything, Mrs. Egan. Do you know how far the sun is from the earth? Do you know that a certain condiment in your kitchen is a better fire extinguisher than any chemical?"

"No," replied Mrs. Egan. "I don't know them things but I've lived fifty-six years without knowin' 'em and I guess I can struggle along a little longer without any encyclepeedies."

Behind Mrs. Egan, on the broad porch of the lodge which was the main building on Eagle's Crag, several people were listening with various expressions of interest. Oliver Quade appealed to them. "Folks, I'm asking you, haven't I made all of you want to own these marvelous books of knowledge?"

It was a trick on Oliver Quade's part. He'd made his sales talk to the proprietor, Mrs. Egan. The summer guests had heard it merely incidentally. Not being canvassed directly, they were wide open. They didn't know that the moment they expressed their interest Quade would shift the weight of his sales attack to them, and then carry Mrs. Egan along on the buying tide.

A bespectacled youth of nineteen or twenty made an opening

sally. "I wouldn't want your books, Mister. I already know all the things you've asked. The mean average distance-to the sun is 92,900,000 miles. And baking soda is the fire extinguisher you referred to."

Quade pretended to be disconcerted. Actually, he was delighted. He hadn't counted on the good fortune of having an intellectual in his audience. The youth would be a perfect stooge.

"Ah," he chuckled. "We have a student with us. Tell me, sir, who was the first American born president?"

The boy's forehead wrinkled. He thought quickly, then replied, "James Buchanan."

Quade shook his head. "It was Martin Van Buren. All presidents previous to him were born English subjects. Here's another: Of which are there more in this country—telephones or automobiles?"

The student scowled. "You're asking trick questions. I can ask *you* questions you can't answer."

Oliver Quade pulled a thick roll of bills from his pocket. He peeled off two ten-dollar notes. "Mister, you've bought yourself something. They call me the Human Encyclopedia because I know the answers to all questions. I've read all the encyclopedias four times and I remember all I've read. This twenty dollars is yours if you can ask me three questions I can't answer."

The challenge aroused the interest of the others on the veranda. There was a stout, middle-aged woman with a haughty look and a sleek-looking man of about forty.

"I'd like to ask one of those questions," cut in the sleek man. "If Danny Dale has no objections."

The youth shook his head. "No, go ahead, Mr. Cummings.

You ask the first one. I want to think a moment about my two."

Mr. Cummings cleared his throat. "All right, when was the half-tone process of reproducing photographs for printing invented and who is generally conceded to be the inventor?"

Quade's eyes flashed. "You're a publisher, Mr. Cummings? Well, that's a question ninety percent of the newspaper and magazine men couldn't answer. But I can. George Meisenbach, of Munich, patented, in 1882, the process by which the first practical half-tones were made, although in 1852 Fox Talbot, of England, suggested the breaking up of a photograph by means of a screen."

Cummings whistled. "Mr. Quade, you're good! I'll listen to Danny Dale's questions."

The cock-sureness had left young Dale's face. He tried, however, to look blasé. "I've got a couple of real ones for you. Number one, what is an astrolabe? Number two, what are the ingredients of gunpowder?"

"The astrolabe," Oliver Quade said, "is the oldest scientific instrument in the world. It was invented about 150 B.C. by Hipparchus. The mariner's sextant is an off-shoot of it. Gunpowder—there are many formulas, but all have the same three basic ingredients: saltpeter, sulphur and charcoal. The most commonly used formula consists of seventy-five percent saltpeter, fifteen percent charcoal and ten percent sulphur. Do I win?"

Danny Dale looked crestfallen. "Yes, I guess so."

Quade slapped his hands together. "Fine; then let's get back to business. All the things I've told you are in this set of encyclopedias. And a hundred thousand more—"

There was an interruption. Behind Quade, in the two-acre

clearing, a girl came running, her short bobbed hair tossed to the winds, her lithe figure covering the ground in long strides. Behind her a few feet, running more easily, was a tall young man of about thirty.

It was the girl's cry that had interrupted Quade. "Mother! Mrs. Egan! Mr. Thompson—he's dead!"

The stout woman on the veranda let out a frightened "eek." Cummings and Danny Dale rose from their seats and came quickly down the three-step flight of stairs.

Quade was watching Mrs. Egan's face and he saw her eyes blink behind her thick glasses. Then a shudder ran through her.

"What do you mean, Mr. Thompson's dead," she said, sharply. "I saw him only fifteen minutes ago."

The young man who had been outdistanced by the running girl was within talking distance now. "He is dead," he confirmed the girl's hysterical announcement. "He's been killed by a rattlesnake."

Quade stabbed a lean finger at the man. "He was alive fifteen minutes ago and now he's dead from a rattlesnake bite?"

The young man shrugged. "I know what you're thinking. That a rattlesnake bite seldom kills inside of two or three hours. But you see, the fang marks were plain and Thompson killed the snake with a club before he succumbed himself." He jerked his head in the direction of the roadway. "Down there."

Mrs. Mattie Egan dropped her triple chins upon her bosom. "Miss Judy," she said to the girl, "you stay here with your mother. She looks kinda sick. The rest of you can come if you like."

She started determinedly across the clearing to the road leading down the mountain. The men followed her. They descended a hundred yards down the steep slope, then rounding a turn came abruptly on the body of a man. He lay at the side of the crushed rock road, his arms flung out on either side of him, his right hand clutching a thick stick. Five or six feet away, lay a dead rattlesnake, its back broken in three or four places. The deductions of the girl and the young man were sensible—but Quade shook his head.

"This man didn't kill that snake," he said, "and the snake didn't kill him."

Gasps went up around the circle. Martin Faraday, who with the girl, Judy Vickers, had discovered the body of Harold Thompson, challenged Quade's statement. "How can you know?"

Quade pointed down at the dead man. "The stick is in the right hand. But this man—Thompson you say his name was—was left-handed!"

The amazing announcement resulted in a stunned silence. Quade broke it himself. "Mind you, I've never seen Thompson before. But I can see that his belt end is facing to the right; only a left-handed man would wear his belt like that. His tie also goes to the right, exactly opposite of the way an ordinary man ties it. And the thumb and forefinger of his left hand are ink-stained, proving that he was not only left-handed but that he wrote a great deal with pen and ink. My guess is that Mr. Thompson was a bookkeeper. No, he wouldn't have been up here on a bookkeeper's salary. Accountant, then."

"I'll be damned," swore Frederick Cummings. "He told me only yesterday that he was an accountant. Said he was from Buffalo. And I saw him writing left-handed."

Quade nodded. "Left-handed people are commoner than

the average person suspects. In fact, one of every eight people is left-handed."

"Some more encyclopedia stuff," scoffed Danny Dale.

Quade ignored the jibe. "We've got to notify the sheriff."

"The sheriff?" cried Mrs. Egan. "What for?"

"I just got through saying that this man was—murdered!"

Mrs. Egan winced. The others took the startling announcement with more fortitude.

Faraday said, "Then no one had better touch anything."

Quade turned to the proprietor of Eagle's Crag. "Mrs. Egan, you've a phone at the lodge?"

Mrs. Egan shook her head. "No, I ain't. Young man, d'you realize we're thirty-three miles from town by road, sixteen from the main highway, thirty-two hundred feet up on a mountain-top. The bloomin' phone company wanted more to run a line out than Eagle's Crag is worth."

"You can send someone to town though?"

The owner of Eagle's Crag frowned. "This is kinda early in the season and I ain't got my full crew yet. Only McClosky, the cook. Him and me been runnin' things. But I guess he can take the station wagon and run down to Hilltown."

They left the dead man where he lay and climbed back up the steep road to the lodge.

"Mac!" yelled Mrs. Egan. "Where are you?"

A bandy-legged man in bibless overalls and a patched flannel shirt came out of a shed near the lodge. "Here I am, Miz Egan," he said meekly. His long, handlebar mustaches drooped down to the receding chin.

Mrs. Egan looked suspiciously at him. "Mac, you've been drinking again!" she accused.

McClosky wiped the right side of his mustache with the back of his hand, giving the lie to his denial. "No, I ain't, Miz Egan, honest I ain't. I was fixin' up the autymobile in there, that's what I was doin'."

"You're a liar, Mac," Mrs. Egan said. "But pull out the wagon and head for town. Tell the sheriff one of my guests had been bit by a rattlesnake—only some folks here," she looked pointedly at Quade, "are tryin' to make murder out of it."

"Murder?" yelped McClosky. "Mr. Thompson's dead?"

"How'd you know it was Thompson?" Quade cried.

McClosky took a quick step back and his eyes rolled. "Why, he's the on'y one ain't here, so natcherly I figured…" his words trailed off.

"That was quick work, McClosky," said Oliver Quade.

"So was yours," cut in Cummings.

"He's right, Quade," said Martin Faraday. "If it is murder as you claim, none of us here is above suspicion. Remember, Quade, you passed us on the road coming up ten minutes before we discovered Harold Thompson's body."

"The man's a perfect stranger to me," said Quade. "He wasn't a stranger to any of you though."

"A man doesn't have to know a man to kill him," Cummings looked down at his well manicured nails. "Robbery is sometimes a mighty good motive for murder."

Quade's mouth became grim. He looked toward his battered flivver over near the lodge. "All right, I'm a suspect, too. But so is McClosky and everyone here. I don't think *anyone* should leave here. Not singly, at least."

"I know Mac better'n any of you," cut in Mrs. Egan. "Someone's gotta go to town and I vote for Mac, suspect or no suspect.

He's too dumb to make a getaway anyway. G'wan, Mac, get out the wagon."

McClosky popped into the garage and backed out an ancient looking station wagon. He whirled it around the clearing, headed toward the descending road, then suddenly braked the car to a stop.

"Car comin' up, Miz Egan," he called.

Mrs. Egan frowned. "Why, I wasn't expectin' any more guests until next week. Wonder who it could be?"

Quade could hear the automobile, coming up in second gear, grinding furiously for it was a long, steep ascent to Eagle's Crag. A moment later it nosed up onto the plateau. It was a big black touring car with side curtains. The driver slewed into the path of the station wagon and stopped.

Men began climbing out, four in all.

"Oh-oh," Quade said softly.

THE NEWCOMERS SPREAD out in fan shape and leisurely approached the summer resort crowd. One of the men walked a little ahead of the others. He was of slight build, under middle height. He wore an unmatched coat and trousers and a vest that was open. He was hatless, his eyes oddly cold and calculating and he had a two days' growth of black beard.

He said in a toneless voice: "Who runs this shebang?"

"I do, Mister," Mrs. Egan snapped.

The slight man continued to come forward. Quade could see his eyes then; they were the coldest he had ever seen in a human. They were a pale, washed-out blue, steady and unblinking under heavy, bushy eyebrows.

"Me and the boys figure on stoppin' here a while," the man said.

Mrs. Egan fidgeted. "Well, the lodge ain't rightly open for another week yet and I don't know as how I can accommodate you."

One of the other men, a giant who stood six feet five and weighed close to 250 pounds, sneered. "G'wan, chief, tell her. What the hell!"

The slight man was unmoved by his friend's urging. His voice was still toneless as he said, "You'll put us up. And you better have your man run that buggy back in the garage."

Then Mrs. Egan flared up. "Say, listen, who are you to tell me what to do around here? I said I couldn't accommodate you and I meant it."

"There's a dead man down the road," the leader of the four said. "Have you called in the law yet, or was this old coot just goin' now?"

"What'd you call me?" cried McClosky.

The newcomer turned leisurely toward McClosky, who was climbing belligerently out of the station wagon. "I said you was an old coot," he repeated. "And my name is Lou Bonniwell."

"Bonniwell!" cried Danny Dale. "You're Lou Bonniwell?"

"Yeah, sure, that's him," boasted the giant. "And me, I'm Jake Somers. Big Jake."

Quade took a deep breath. "Welcome to Eagle's Crag, boys. Me, I'm a stranger here, too."

"Who're you?" demanded Bonniwell.

"Oliver Quade, the Human Encyclopedia. The man who knows the answers to all questions. I know—"

"Do you know where the law is right now?" asked Bonniwell.

Quade cocked his head to one side. "Far from here, or you wouldn't be here. You came here to hide out, didn't you?"

"Yeah. Monk was raised hereabouts. He claims you can see seven States and six counties or something like that from this mountain-top."

A squat man with long arms grinned vacantly. "Three States and six counties, Lou. And you saw the road yourself. We could hold off an army."

Bonniwell nodded. "The layout's all right, Monk. But they'll get us sooner or later."

"Not me they won't get," boasted Big Jake Somers.

Bonniwell looked bitterly at his big henchman. "You're big, Jake, but if one forty-five slug doesn't cut you down, two will."

"A twenty-two in the right place will do it," Quade offered.

Big Jake said savagely, "Who the hell asked you?"

Quade grimaced. "Pay no attention to me. I talk too much."

"You do at that, pardner," said Bonniwell. "Jake, take one of the guns and sit down over there by the road. Monk, you and Heinie look through things here. Gather up all the artillery."

Like a general Bonniwell dispatched his forces, and like obedient soldiers his men obeyed. Jake Somers brought a vicious looking submachine gun from the touring car. He walked with it to the head of the road leading down from Eagle's Crag and seated himself upon a boulder. No one could now leave or enter Eagle's Crag without his permission.

Monk Moon, the squat man, and Heinie Krausmeyer, a roly-poly blank-faced man, frisked the Eagle's Crag guests. Then the two disappeared into the lodge.

Mrs. Egan, who had been quiet for a little while spoke then. "That Monk man," she said. "I recognize him now. He's Tim Moon's boy, Alfred. He was raised down there in the valley."

She shook her head. "I never liked him even as a boy. Too sly and sneaky. I allus said he'd come to a bad end."

"Quite right, ma'am," agreed Lou Bonniwell. "Monk'll get hanged some day, if he don't get shot first."

Danny Dale stepped forward brightly. "Say, Mr. Bonniwell, I was listening to the radio last night. That was some escape you made from the penitentiary."

Bonniwell looked at Danny. "Sonny, I was hopin' there wouldn't be no kids here. Always complicates things."

Danny Dale reddened. "I'm not a kid. I'm twenty and I'm a university graduate. I even have a master's degree."

A fleeting smile crossed Bonniwell's face. "Is that so, now? Well, bub, you just watch your p's and q's and you won't get hurt. I never went to college myself, but I been around."

Danny Dale retreated. Quade looked around at the others. Besides himself there were Frederick Cummings, Marty Faraday, Judy Vickers and her mother, Mrs. Egan and McClosky. Plus four escaped convicts and killers. And one dead man down on the road—murdered by someone on Eagle's Crag.

"Just so there won't be no mistake, folks," Bonniwell said, "we killed two guards when we made the break yesterday morning. In the afternoon we knocked off a cop when we got the guns and stuff at the police station. You can imagine what the law's gonna do to us if they catch up. Now, I got no quarrel with any of you here. I'm only here because this is a good hideout. We may be here a day or a week. Maybe, two. Until we leave you folks are gonna stay put. Understand?"

After a while Monk Moon and Heinie Krausmeyer came out of the lodge, carrying three shotguns, two rifles and a small pistol. "We found 'em here and there, boss."

"My husband was a huntin' man," said Mrs. Egan. "Them shotguns and rifles was his'n. The pea-shooter, I dunno."

"That's mine," said Cummings. "I—I always carry it with me when I'm traveling."

"I'll mind it for you, Mister," said Bonniwell. "O.K., Monk, toss 'em in the car. Then git out the glasses and kinda look out over them six States and seven counties. The rest of you," he turned to the Eagle's Crag folk, "just go about your business. Only don't get too close to Jake's machine-gun there."

Monk Moon brought a big pair of military field glasses from the car. He started toward the rear of the lodge. Quade followed him leisurely. Monk chuckled as he fondled the glasses. "I never had nothin' like this when I was a kid. Boy, I bet I see four States."

Behind the lodge the mountain fell away in a sheer precipice. Quade approached it gingerly. "A drop of over two thousand feet," he grimaced.

"On practically three sides," said Monk. "Only way up or down is by that road."

"Hey, you!" called Bonniwell, coming up.

Quade turned. "I wasn't intending shoving him over," he said.

"I know you wouldn't commit suicide by a stunt like that," Bonniwell said. "Couple of the folks back there say you said that bozo down on the road was murdered instead of bit by a snake. What's that—a bit of malarkey? You got plenty of it."

"I have at that," admitted Quade. "I wouldn't be the book salesman I am if I didn't have it. But I was telling the truth about that chap. He was murdered. Someone killed the rattlesnake with a club then put the club in this fellow's hand after killing him—only he didn't know the man was left-handed and put it in his right hand to make it look as if he'd killed the snake. Aside from that, take a look at the man's calf, where the snake was supposed to have bitten him."

"I think I will," said Bonniwell. "The thing kinda makes me curious. Come along."

They walked past Jake Somers sitting on the boulder with his machine-gun. Bonniwell casually dropped behind Quade then, keeping one hand near his waist-band in which was stuck an automatic. When they reached the body of the dead man Quade pointed to Thompson's left leg. The trouser leg was pulled up part way and two angry red spots were plainly visible. Quade pointed at them. "See how far apart the punctures are? And how deep?"

"No rattler ever did that," Bonniwell laughed shortly. "There's a murderer in your crowd. I'm kinda curious to know which of you gazabos had the nerve to pull a job like this. Offhand, I'd say it was you."

"Not me," denied Quade. "I'm just a book salesman who happened to drift up here thinking I could make a couple of sales. I never saw any of these people before today."

"Hmm," mused Bonniwell. "A while ago you were shooting off about how smart you was. You claimed to know just about everything."

"That's right. I'm the Human Encyclopedia."

"But you don't know who killed this guy?"

Quade shrugged. "I'm more interested in knowing *why* he was killed. I've been playing with an idea how to find out."

"What is it?"

"Well, Cummings, the fat play boy back there, says Thompson told him he was an accountant. Often accountants have opportunities to get their hands cn large sums. My guess is that Thompson stole a wad of money and came here to hide out until the smoke blew away."

"I think you got something there, fella. Say, ride this hunch of yours and find out how much dough this bozo had and maybe where it is."

Quade knew that the escaped convict was exceedingly eager to acquire a large sum of money. It would be mighty handy for a quick getaway once he left Eagle's Crag. It might even persuade him to leave sooner and Quade desired that very much.

They went back to the lodge and Bonniwell herded all those on Eagle's Crag, with the exception of Jake Somers, into the big livingroom.

"Folks, there's a murderer among us," Bonniwell began and Danny Dale promptly snickered. The escaped convict stared at him coldly. "Sonny," he said. "I'm trying hard to remember you're just a kid and my mother told me always to treat women folks and kids with kindness." He gestured to Quade. "You carry on."

"Have you thrown in with them?" asked Judy Vickers.

Quade looked steadily at the girl and she flushed. He said then, "Harold Thompson was murdered. I'm sure of that. I'm also pretty sure that he was a fugitive from justice, an absconder. I believe he had his loot with him and was killed for it."

The crowd began murmuring and looking at one another. Quade continued, "Mr. Cummings, you say Thompson told you he was from Buffalo. I imagine, therefore, that he was actually from the opposite direction. New York, I'd say. You're from there. Have you heard of anyone recently who ran off with a large sum of money?"

Cummings puckered up his mouth. "Mmm, in New York there's always someone stealing from his firm. The biggest one I heard of lately was a trusted employee of the Horgan Packing Company who ran off with eighty thousand dollars. But the man's name was Miller, I believe, not Thompson."

"It's him!" cut in Mrs. Mattie Egan. "I mind only last week when I was—well, sorta looking through his stuff that I found some handkerchiefs with the initial M on them. I thought it funny, seein's how his name was Thompson."

"Then Thompson was Miller," said Quade. "And he brought with him eighty thousand dollars."

"Eighty grand," Bonniwell mused. "That's a pretty good haul. Why with eighty grand I could—" He broke off, but his eyes remained speculative. After a moment he jerked his head toward Heinie and Monk. "Boys, let's start on a treasure hunt. Eighty grand makes a pretty big package and it's somewhere in this shebang."

The trio started eagerly up the stairs to the bedrooms. Quade watched them go. They would make an intensive search of everyone's room. If the money was upstairs they would certainly find it.

Judy's mother, Mrs. Vickers, broke the silence that fell on the group when Bonniwell and his men went off to make the search. "How long is this going to go on? Isn't there some way we can get aid?"

"If we had some sleeping powders or knockout drops we might put in their food—" suggested Faraday dryly.

"There's a medicine chest in the bathroom," said Mrs. Egan. "I guess it's got some chloroform or ether in it"

"Marty," said Judy Vickers. "Stop joking. This is a serious matter."

Mrs. Vickers looked coldly at Martin Faraday, then turned to Frederick Cummings. Her face softened. "Have you any *sensible* ideas, Frederick?"

Quade got the picture then. Mother Vickers favored Frederick Cummings, but the daughter preferred Faraday. It gave Quade an idea. Mrs. Vickers probably wasn't as well off as she tried to give the impression. Cummings was wealthy—or Mrs. Vickers thought he was. Faraday? Probably a clerk or some sort who had saved for a year or more to have this outing. Faraday would like a large sum of money. It would remove parental objection. Then, too, perhaps Cummings wasn't as well off as he pretended to be. He too, could use a large sum of money and he seemed to have been better acquainted with the dead accountant than any of the others.

But then the others would all do considerable for eighty thousand dollars. Mrs. Egan's entire property was worth only a fraction of that sum. She was a formidable person, had made her own way for years.

McClosky? Quade couldn't overlook the cook and handy man's original suspicious reactions to the announcement of Thompson's death. Danny Dale? A twenty-year-old intellectual, he was the equal of anyone here, excepting Quade.

AN HOUR LATER the three convicts returned to the livingroom and Bonniwell's calmness was gone. He was scowling and Quade knew that the frustration of not finding the money had made the killer a dangerous man.

"We're goin' to search down here, now," he snarled. "But I'm warnin' you all if we don't find it, I'm going to ask some questions. One of you knows where the dough is stashed and he's gonna tell me."

They ripped the furniture, tapped the walls and sounded the floors while Mrs. Egan shrieked dismay. They pried in every nook and corner, but they didn't find the eighty thousand dollars. When Bonniwell finally called off the search it was nearly dark outside and he had been compelled to turn on the electric lights. There was a portable electric light plant on Eagle's Crag.

Bonniwell postponed the inquisition, however. He was too hungry. He ordered McClosky to cook food. "And you're eatin' first from everything," he warned. "So go easy on the rat poison."

The three killers wolfed their food. Monk Moon relieved Jake Somers then and the giant came in and ate. The guests of Eagle's Crag ate sandwiches that McClosky prepared. Bonniwell herded them all together then.

"Now, folks, let's find that money. One of you here knows where it is. I'll begin with you, smart guy." He looked at Oliver Quade.

"I came up here exactly fifteen minutes before you did," said Quade. "Do you think I'd have had time to locate Thompson's money, hide it and kill him, besides trying to sell books to these folks for almost all of that time?"

"He did show up just before we found Mr. Thompson," said Judy Vickers. "He passed Marty and myself as we were walking down the road."

"And how long was I trying to sell you that marvelous set of encyclopedias, Mrs. Egan?" Quade asked.

Mrs. Egan sighed. "Too long, but actually I'd say ten or fifteen minutes."

Bonniwell growled and questioned the three women briefly.

Mrs. Vickers was haughty and indignant, Judy frank and guileless. Mrs. Egan was truculent. Finally Bonniwell threw up his hand. "You women get upstairs. Go to bed. I don't want you around."

They left and the killer turned savagely to the men. "Now, then, one of you killed that gink and swiped his money. You, Cummings, who the hell are you and why are you here?"

Cummings flushed. "I'm a publisher of trade journals in New York City. I'm here on a vacation. Mrs. Vickers invited me to come here."

"She's trying to marry you off to her daughter. Yeah, I got that."

Martin Faraday snickered. Cummings looked angrily at him. "You don't think her mother would let her marry a poor schoolteacher, do you?"

"Perhaps Judy has a mind of her own," retorted Faraday.

"And she'll use it," said Cummings, "when she discovers that her mother has already borrowed more than five thousand dollars from me."

Faraday paled with surprise.

"Ah, love!" Danny said sneeringly.

"Bub!" snapped Bonniwell. "Get to bed."

Danny Dale glared but when Bonniwell gestured to Big Jake he got up hastily and almost ran up the stairs.

"Now, listen," said Bonniwell. "You, Faraday, and you, Cummings, you're both stuck on the girl and I figure one of you two know where the dough is. I don't give a damn if you knocked off a man. I'm not a cop. But I do want that dough and one of you is going to tell me where it is. Otherwise...." He left the sentence unfinished but looked toward the stairs the women had gone up.

A chill ran up Oliver Quade's spine. Bonniwell had the Indian sign on the two men. He was quite capable of harming Judy Vickers if he thought by it he could force either Faraday or Cummings to reveal the hiding place of the money. "I'll give you until tomorrow morning to make up your minds," Bonniwell continued. "I need sleep myself. Last night was a busy night."

Bonniwell first sent Heinie out to stand guard with Monk Moon, then he and Somers followed the others upstairs. There was a series of bedrooms on both sides of the long hallway. Quade found one that was vacant and after locking the door, undressed and went to bed. He fell asleep at once.

THE SUN SHINING on his face awakened Oliver Quade. He yawned and, getting out of bed, walked to the window. Far in the distance he could see a tiny huddle of buildings, a little village. It was more than a dozen miles from Eagle's Crag though and was visible only when the sun was strongest and there was no haze in the air, as this morning.

The events of the day before crowded into Quade's mind. He shook his head and went into the bathroom, and as he looked into the mirror over the washbowl the idea struck him. He acted immediately.

Lifting up a thick water glass he smashed it into the mirror, then gingerly caught a large section of the mirror that fell out. He carried it into the bedroom and found a piece of cardboard.

He went to the window then and held the mirror, face into the sun, letting the rays flash on it. He held it steady, then covered it with the cardboard. Quickly he removed it, then covered it again. He was about to repeat the operation when there was a knock on the door. Quade laid down the piece of mirror and cardboard and, walking across the room, unlocked the door.

Danny Dale, already fully dressed, was in the doorway. "Hello," he said. "Just get up?"

Quade nodded. "Come in, Danny."

Danny came in and Quade locked the door again. Quade went back to the window and picked up the mirror and cardboard. He operated it a couple of times and Danny Dale exclaimed, "A heliograph!"

"Yep," said Quade. "I've read of them doing this in the South Sea Islands and South Africa. They say they signal fifty and sixty miles. All I want to signal is about fifteen miles. There's a little village out there and someone surely ought to know the Morse code. They ought to have a telegraph office there, at least."

"But look," said Danny. "If you get a bunch of lawmen up here aren't Bonniwell and his gang going to turn on us first?"

"Look, Bonniwell's going to want that money today so he can get away tonight. Even if he gets the money I hardly think he'll care much about leaving anyone behind here to tell he'd been here. And if he doesn't get the money he'll kill us. So...." Quade went on signaling with his home-made heliograph.

Ten minutes went by and there was no answering signal. Quade sighed, "You'd think someone would have seen the flashes."

"It's only a little after six," said Danny Dale. "Maybe they're not up yet over at that tank-town."

"That's an idea. Well, I'll try again."

He rested ten minutes, then tried again. And suddenly he caught a flash of light from the distance.

"They're answering!" Quade exclaimed excitedly. "Look, there's another flash."

"I saw it," said Danny Dale. "It came from that little town."

"Here goes the message then," said Quade grimly. He operated the heliograph swiftly and surely, spelling out the message in the Morse code of long and short flashes. At length he finished and said, "Now, we'll see if they answer."

He leaned out of the window, Danny Dale beside him, breathing hard. It came then—a bright flash of directed light. Then others.

"Y-e-s," Quade spelled out. "They got it!"

"What'd you tell them?"

"About Bonniwell and the boys. And after a while—"

There was a violent explosion outside the door. Quade, whirling, saw splinters sticking out from the panels.

"Bonni—" began Danny Dale and then a bullet smashed the lock. Danny Dale yelped, and dropped to wriggle under the bed. Quade paled but held his ground. The man outside smashed in the door with his foot. Then he stood in the doorway. It was Bonniwell, with a huge automatic in his fist and a snarl twisting his mouth.

"You sneaking double-crosser!" he said, his tone cold with intense fury.

Quade backed a couple of steps until he collided with a chair. His hands went behind his back and caught hold of it. "What do you mean, Bonniwell?" he asked thickly.

"That mirror stuff. You think I didn't see the flashes. Yah, I ain't that dumb. I know you was signaling and—" His face worked and then Quade brought the chair up and around in a violent swing. He anticipated Bonniwell by a fraction of a second, but of course he couldn't beat a bullet.

The chair was off the floor, beginning its arc when a bullet smashed against Quade's left shoulder like a giant fist and hurled him back against the wall. He ricocheted from it to the floor, landing on hands and knees. A thousand Niagaras were suddenly roaring in his ears, a red haze swirled before his eyes. Quade fought to retain his grip on things. He half lifted himself up on his hands and then one of the Niagaras burst over his head and he fell... down... down... into oblivion.

The roaring was the last thing he heard when he passed out. Water was the first thing he felt when he came to, dripping water, cool and soothing on his fevered brow.

Quade opened his eyes and looked up into the white face of Judy Vickers. He grinned. "I'm still here."

"With a bullet in your left shoulder," she replied, soberly. "And if Bonniwell discovers you're not dead he'll put another bullet in you."

Quade sat up and fought giddiness for a moment. Gingerly he felt his left shoulder with his right hand. There was a thick bandage already wrapped around it. "You did this, Miss Vickers? Thanks. Where are the rest?"

"Bonniwell and his men are getting ready for a siege."

Quade frowned. "I had hoped they'd light out instead. But out there he couldn't possibly hope to last another day or two. The mountains are swarming with posses. He figures this is as good a place as any for the last fight. And he's right, of course."

"You're very lucky, you know," said Judy Vickers. "McClosky—wasn't."

Quade exclaimed. "Bonniwell killed him?"

She shook her head. "He says not, but this morning McClosky was found in the kitchen with his head smashed in with a stove poker."

"Stove poker? Bonniwell or his men wouldn't have bothered with that. I guess the same man who got Thompson finished McClosky. He knew something. I suspected it."

"There was a hypodermic needle in his pocket."

"Ah? That's what made the rattlesnake punctures in Thompson. McClosky found the needle and knew who had thrown it away."

"Miss Vickers!" called a voice from out in the hall. "Judy Vickers!"

"Here," replied Judy.

Danny Dale bobbed into the room. He grinned when he saw Quade sitting up. "I knew it was just a shoulder wound, but I didn't tell Lou. He would have slipped you a couple more."

"That was mighty decent of you," said Quade dryly. "How come you didn't get one yourself? You were in here with me."

"Oh, I talked him out of it," said Danny Dale glibly.

"From under the bed?" Quade rose to his feet. "What's going on downstairs?"

"Lou wants everybody down there. He's plenty burned up about things and my hunch is that it's going to be an interesting session."

Judy Vickers looked at Quade, her forehead creased. "He's been after Marty and Mr. Cummings all morning."

Quade sighed. "I guess we'd better go though, or he'll be coming up here."

EVERYONE ON THE mountain-top, with the exception of Jake Somers, was gathered in the livingroom. Lou Bonniwell's eyes flashed when Oliver Quade came in with Judy and

Danny Dale. "My aim's gettin' lousy," he said, "but I'll talk the thing over with you again in a little while. Right now," his tone became brittle, "I want to find that roll!"

Frederick Cummings was jittery. Martin Faraday was trying to be calm, but not doing a good job of it. The women, even Mrs. Egan, were frightened.

"The cook," said Bonniwell. "None of my boys finished him. So it was one of you birds. I figure McClosky knew something and one of you shut him up. Now which one was it?"

"Not me," cried Frederick Cummings, trembling visibly.

Faraday looked scornfully at him. He remained quiet.

Bonniwell gestured in a frenzy. He looked suddenly like a dog gone mad. Quade could understand now why the man was such a cold-blooded killer.

"Monk, grab the girl and give her a working over. One of them will talk or else."

Mrs. Vickers shrieked. The perspiration rolled off Cummings' face, but he made no move. Faraday did. He stepped up beside Judy Vickers. "Keep your hands off her," he said to Monk who was advancing, his long gorilla-like arms swinging at his sides.

Roly-poly Heinie Krausmeyer grinned vacantly and stepped up to Marty Faraday. The gun in his hand swished up and clouted Faraday along the right side of his face. Faraday yelped in pain and went down to his knees. Heinie struck him again, on the top of his head. Faraday fell flat to the floor and lay still.

"You fool!" snarled Bonniwell. "How can he talk now?" He looked at Cummings. "You white-livered coward," he sneered. "You wouldn't talk even if I cut off her nose."

Judy Vickers dropped to her knees beside Marty Faraday. "Mother, get some water. He's hurt, badly."

It was Quade who got the water. He had to step over McClosky's body which lay in the kitchen just inside the door.

Water did not help Faraday. He revived partially but he merely moaned and cried out incoherently. "Judy!" He called her name over and over.

"His skull's fractured," Quade said. "I don't think he'll do any talking today."

Bonniwell turned toward Heinie. The roly-poly killer ducked out of the door.

"Get out your medicine chest," Quade ordered Mrs. Egan. "Otherwise there'll be one more dead man at Eagle's Crag."

Bonniwell made no objections. In fact he furthered Quade's offer of treating Faraday. "Patch him up so he can talk by tonight. I'm sure he's the guy."

They moved Faraday to the couch and Quade treated the schoolteacher's wounds. Judy Vickers hovered anxiously nearby, despite her mother's sighing and muttering. Mrs. Egan's medicine kit was a good one and Quade was able to help the injured man.

By that time Bonniwell and his men were searching outside for the hidden treasure. They ransacked the garage, the outbuildings and even moved boulders that lay here and there in the clearing.

Quade moved McClosky's body out of the kitchen and Mrs. Egan cooked for everyone. Quade spent most of his time going back and forth, examining Faraday and soothing Judy Vickers. "He'll be all right by this evening," he assured her.

"And then those killers will start all over on him," sobbed Judy. Quade couldn't assure her about that. He knew that when the posse came he would himself be in vital danger.

It happened shortly after twelve o'clock. The mountain-top was still one moment; the next the quietness was shattered by a thundering roar. Jake Somers' machine-gun. Bonniwell and the others immediately rushed to their car and began hauling out guns. They ran to join Jake who was standing up behind the boulder at the head of the road, still sending an occasional burst down the hillside.

Even before the first burst from Somers' gun had ceased Oliver Quade was down from the veranda and walking toward Bonniwell's car. He walked softly but with a determined step. He was a dozen feet from it when Bonniwell suddenly turned around and saw him.

"You!" he cried. "Your posse's here, but you're not going to welcome them."

He had picked up a twin to Somers' tommy gun from his car and he held it facing Quade, as he walked back toward him.

"Are you sure it's a posse?" Quade asked quickly. "It might be some tourists?"

"Two cars full of them," replied Bonniwell. "With rifles and tommy guns? Tourists, yeah!"

"But Jake fought them back!" cried Quade. "No harm done."

"They went back around the turn, that's all," said Bonniwell. "You know what I promised you—"

"Wait!" cried Oliver Quade desperately. "I can tell you how to get away!"

The muzzle of Bonniwell's gun did not waver. His eyes flashed though and Quade knew that he had struck a responsive note.

He said quickly, "Make a deal with them. You can't take us all along as hostages, but you can tell 'em if they don't let you go you'll kill all of us up here. They couldn't allow that."

"What makes you think I'm not going to kill all of you anyway?" asked Bonniwell.

"Because you'll die then yourself. My way you'll have a chance. The posse came a long way. There won't be any of them down below. Make them come up here and give you a head start. That's all you'll want, isn't it?"

"Yeah, that and the eighty grand. But they won't miss a lousy, double-crossing book peddler!"

Quade knew that he had never been closer to death in all his life. "The money!" he cried. "I'll find it for you!"

"Then it was you!" snapped Bonniwell.

"No, of course not. But I can find the money for you. I know I can. Give me twenty minutes—fifteen. Think of it, Bonniwell. A head start and eighty thousand dollars. What more can you want?"

"I'll bite once more," said Bonniwell. "But it's the last time. I'll make the deal with the posse and I'll give you exactly fifteen minutes to find the money. If you don't find it I'll leave without it, but you won't be alive then."

"And if I do find it?"

"Then I'll let you live."

"Give me your word?" Quade asked eagerly.

Bonniwell hesitated a moment, then shrugged. "All right. I promise. You've got fifteen minutes." He turned back to his pals and yelled down the mountain-side.

OLIVER QUADE TURNED toward the lodge and saw Judy Vickers running toward him.

"I heard!" she cried. "He'll kill you if you can't find the money."

"I made the best of a bad deal," said Quade. "But I've *got* to find that money."

"But I'm sure you—it wasn't *you!*" exclaimed Judy Vickers. "Can you find it in fifteen—thirteen minutes?"

Quade looked at his watch. "It's 11:12. I've got until 11:25. Please go back to the veranda. I've got to think—fast."

Cummings was coming down from the veranda. Judy headed him back.

Quade looked around the two-acre plateau, the house, the garage and the outbuildings. He sighed and seated himself upon the ground. Eighty thousand dollars. Did it even exist? If it did, where was it?

Harold Thompson had been at Eagle's Crag a week. He'd had ample opportunity of finding a good hiding place. The house? Bonniwell and his men had searched it thoroughly. Quade could forget it. They'd searched the other buildings, too.

The ground? Thompson could have come out one night and buried it in the ground. But if he had, Quade would never find it. Not in fifteen minutes. It would take six men many days to dig up every foot of the plateau.

Quade looked at the persons on the veranda. They were all there now—Mrs. Egan, Cummings, Judy, her mother and Danny Dale. Faraday was inside the house, injured and sleeping a drugged sleep.

One of those six was a double-killer and knew where the money was. One of them couldn't talk, the others wouldn't.

Quade shook his head. "Damn! Where would *I* hide eighty thousand dollars?"

Quade put himself in the place of Harold Thompson. Thompson was a fugitive from justice. He would be skittish. His two great concerns would be his own safety and the safety of the money. He wouldn't take any chance of anyone stumbling on the money. He'd give considerable thought to a hiding place. He'd find a safe place, one where no one would think of looking. And people seldom looked in the most obvious place. Quade leaped to his feet. Quickly he approached the veranda.

"I think I know where it is!" he announced.

"Where?" everyone on the porch cried.

Quade looked at his watch. "I've got eight minutes left. I want everyone to remain here. When I come back, you'll see the money."

Quade passed into the house. He looked at Martin Faraday and saw that he was sleeping peacefully. Then Quade picked up the medicine kit. He carried it with him to the kitchen. He opened it up and looked over the bottles in it. He picked up one labeled ether. His eyes gleaming, he opened a cupboard door. Quickly he looked over the cans and bottles and packages in it. He took down one or two, also a china mixing bowl.

He began pouring things into the bowl and biting, acrid fumes stung his nostrils. He worked with difficulty because of his wounded, bandaged shoulder, but he persisted. And finally he poured a half gill or so of a yellowish liquid into a bottle and corked it. He slipped it into his pocket and went back through the house to the veranda.

The moment he stepped out of the house he saw Lou Bonniwell out in the clearing. The escaped convict was carrying a tommy gun.

"Quade!" the killer called.

Quade descended the short flight of stairs to the ground. "Did you make a dicker with the posse?"

"I did. But—your time's up!"

"I found the money," said Quade. "At least I think I did. If I guessed wrong—"

Quade dropped to his knees beside the little three-step flight of stairs leading up to the veranda. "I figured this was the most obvious place on Eagle's Crag," he said. "So obvious that no one would look here. If I were hiding something...." He reached under the stairs, rummaged about for a moment, then brought out both hands. There was a package in them; a package wrapped in oil cloth, about five inches square. Quade rose to his feet and handed it to the outlaw chief.

Bonniwell put the gun on the ground at his feet. He ripped the oil cloth from the package. Inside the contents were wrapped in newspaper. Bonniwell tore away a corner, looked and nodded.

"You win, Quade," he said.

Feet pounded down the stairs behind Quade. It was Danny Dale and there was a .32 caliber revolver in his hand.

"Bonniwell," he said, "that's my money and I'm going with you."

Bonniwell gave a start. "Where'd you get the popgun, kid?" he asked.

"The hell with that kid stuff," snarled Danny. "I'm as tough as you are. If you don't believe it, reach for that gun." He gestured with his gun to the automatic that was stuck in Bonniwell's waistband.

Bonniwell shifted his glance from Danny to Quade. "So this—this punk is the rattlesnake killer!"

"He is," said Quade. "I figured the minute the money showed up he'd reveal himself. He's killed two men for that money already and he'd want to go where that money went."

"And I'll kill some more if I have to," sneered Danny. "I outsmarted the whole gang of you and I'd have got away with it if you hadn't found that money."

"You see," Quade said to Bonniwell. "He's a smart kid. Too smart. He finished university at the age of nineteen and found himself mentally the equal of many men years older. But physically he was still a boy, and business men offered him a boy's job and a boy's salary. I imagine Danny's father told him after he'd put him through college he'd have to shift for himself. But Danny didn't like the idea of a boy's job and boy's salary. Somehow or other, probably by accident, he got wind of Thompson and—"

"Accident, hell!" snarled Danny Dale. "I used my head. My father's a bookkeeper with the Horgan Packing Company himself. I heard all about Harold Miller and I outsmarted the cops. I went to Miller's rooming house and went through the trash bins in the basement. I found a map of this section, torn into bits. I came to Hilltown and did some asking around. I found this joint. Accident, hell. I used my brains," he bragged.

"Was it necessary to kill him, though?" asked Quade.

"Of course it was. The fool recognized me. He'd seen me only once, two years ago when I visited the old man at the office. I had to knock him off."

"Just like that, Danny?" asked Quade. "Then why the hypodermic needle? Did you just happen to have that with you? And did the snake just happen to come around conveniently when you killed Thompson—or Miller?"

"I figured it all out before I came here. Even the stuff in the needle. It's not snake poison either. Something like it but faster. McClosky, the lousy old snooper, found the hypo in my room so I had to knock him off."

"You're very handy about this knocking off business," said Quade.

Danny Dale whirled on Quade. "I've had about enough of you. I'm giving you the—"

He never got out the last word. He had made a fatal mistake. He had challenged Bonniwell to go for his gun and then had taken his eyes from him. No one could be that careless with Lou Bonniwell.

The outlaw chief dropped the package of money and in the same movement went for his automatic. Danny saw the quick movement and tried to turn his gun back on Bonniwell. He was too late. Bonniwell's gun thundered.

The big slug lifted Danny clear off his feet and hurled him back to the ground, his head almost blown off.

"He was too young to be that mean," said Bonniwell, softly.

Oliver Quade walked away from the veranda. Bonniwell fell in beside him.

"It's all fixed," he said. "The posse's coming up here with their guns in their fists. They're going to give us three minutes head start." He raised his gun in the air and fired three shots.

Almost immediately Quade could hear automobile gears grinding. A moment later the nose of a car showed around the turn in the road. It came up in second gear. Behind it came another car. Both of them came into the clearing, but drew off to one side.

Men began climbing out, all of them armed to the teeth. Bonniwell and his men gathered cautiously at the side of their touring car. Their own guns were in their hands. Quade stood beside them.

Bonniwell counted the members of the posse. "Twelve. That's right."

The leader of the posse, a stocky man with a badge on his vest, said, "After you git in your car you got three minutes head start."

"Three minutes?" Bonniwell chuckled. He reached into his coat pocket and brought out a large, egg-shaped object.

"A hand grenade!" cried the sheriff.

"Don't get your dander up, Sheriff," cut in Bonniwell. "This ain't for you. Just for the road—after we pass it. I figure we need more'n three minutes start. Wanta break the agreement?"

The sheriff looked at Bonniwell and his men, then at the resorters to one side. "No," he said thickly. "Get going!"

Monk Moon climbed in behind the wheel. Heinie slipped in beside him. Over Monk's shoulder he held a tommy gun, pointed at the posse. Jake Somers and Lou Bonniwell climbed into the rear of the car. They promptly poked out guns.

"So long, everybody," Bonniwell cried as the car began moving.

The car rolled over the little clearing and began descending. The sheriff and his men did not move until Bonniwell's car had gone around the turn in the road, out of sight. "Let's go now, boys!"

Then there was a thunderous explosion down the mountainside.

Then all of them heard what Quade had been waiting for— the screams of several men. They came from down the mountain. Almost immediately afterward there was the crash of tin and metal, silence for a moment, then another terrific crash.

"They went off the road. They're finished!"

"Went off the road?" cried the sheriff. "What kind of fool driver—"

"Not his fault," said Quade. "The road's steep and he was hurrying. One of the tires blew out."

"How do you know a tire blew out?"

"Because I poured some stuff on it. A little mixture with an ether base. Ether dissolves rubber and a couple of simple ingredients make it work faster. Lord, I was afraid you'd hold him here too long."

"Gawdalmighty!" The sheriff looked in awe at Oliver Quade. "You deliberately killed them?"

"They were killers," said Quade. "They would have killed several more people before they were killed or taken. So I had to do it. Now I can get back to the encyclopedias...."

Dog Show Murder

The Human Encyclopedia plots a suicide

THE SECRETARY OF the Westfield Kennel Show said to Oliver Quade, the Human Encyclopedia: "The price of a small booth is seventy-five."

"No," said Oliver Quade. "You misunderstood. I don't want to rent this booth for the entire year. I want it only for the duration of the dog show—four days."

"That's what I quoted you on," retorted the secretary. "Some of our larger exhibitors are paying as much as five hundred dollars. What are you exhibiting? Remedies, dog foods?"

"No," said Quade. "Nothing commercial. Mine is an educational exhibit. That's why I can't pay any fancy prices for booth space. How about five dollars?"

Ten minutes later they compromised on twenty dollars. Quade paid the money and stowed away his receipt. Then he said to a burly man who had stood by patiently during the dickering, "All right, Charlie, prepare the exhibit."

Charlie Boston picked up a heavy suitcase and started for the main part of the building. Quade followed along.

"Ollie," said Boston. "You know I'm not terribly happy. I never am around dogs. I can't for the life of me figure out why you want to work this dog show. Last week you wouldn't work the Elks' Convention in Buffalo. And now," he shuddered, "look at that whole row of English bulldogs. Gosh, if they should get loose—"

"Nothing to it. The only way to handle a dog is to let him know you're not afraid of him."

"I tried that once. That was the time I lost the seat of my pants."

The dog exhibit building had a small arena, containing about two hundred seats, built around a tanbark pit, where the dogs were put through their paces. The rest of the building was

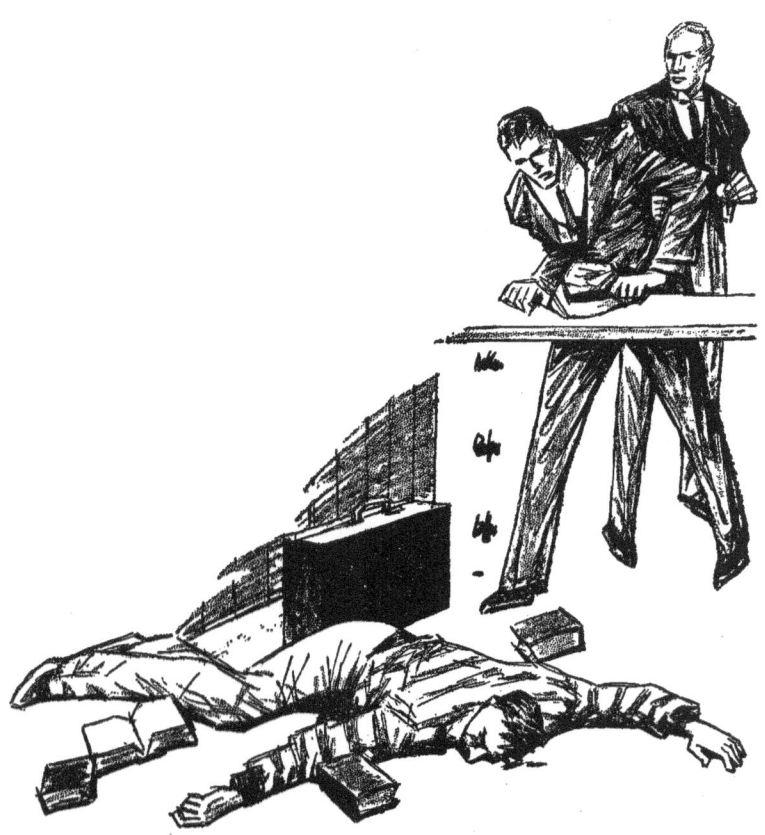

crowded with rows of stalls, separated by wooden partitions. Each stall contained a pedigreed dog. Around the outer edge of the room were commercial exhibits, dog remedies, foods, supplies, equipment.

Oliver Quade's booth was wedged in between one display-
ing dog biscuits and another featuring a line of disinfectants
and remedies.

Boston set the suitcase on the floor outside the booth.
Oliver Quade stepped on to it to the counter. Then he began
talking.

"I am Oliver Quade," he boomed in a stentorian voice that
rolled out across the auditorium and bounded back from the
far walls, "Oliver Quade, the Human Encyclopedia. I have
the greatest brain in the world. I know everything. I know the
answers to all questions: What came first, the hen or the egg;
the age of Ann; the batting and fielding average of every big
and minor league baseball player; every date in history. Everything under the sun."

A group of youths had stopped in the aisle before Quade the moment he had started to talk.

"Oh, yeah?" one of them said.

"Oh, yeah?" Quade retorted. "I can answer any question *you* can ask me. On any subject—history, science, mathematics, sports, anthropology. Go ahead, ask me a question and see."

The wise-cracking boy looked puzzled. His pals urged him on. "Go ahead. You started it."

"All right," grinned the boy. "Here's one. How does a fox rid itself of fleas?"

The other boys began tittering, but Quade threw up his hands. "That was supposed to be a brain teaser. But I can answer it correctly. Br'er Fox's reputation for cleverness is justly earned. When he's bothered with fleas he takes a piece of wool or wood into his mouth and lets himself into a pool of water, tail first. The fleas don't like to be drowned so they scramble further up on his body. Pretty soon only the fox's nose and mouth are above the water and the fleas get into the wood or wool he's got in his mouth. Then the fox drops the thing into the water and removes himself promptly from the vicinity."

A roar of laughter swept the crowd that had now gathered on the aisle. Quade's eyes gleamed and he went on: "Try me on something else. Anything, anyone!"

"What kind of dogs are these?" The interrogator was a young woman and she had them on leash; two huge animals, only a little smaller than St. Bernard dogs, and infinitely ludicrous. Long, woolly hair covered their faces, their entire bodies. They looked more like sheep than sheep themselves.

Quade chuckled as he replied, "Those, Madam, are Old English sheep dogs. Once when I was lost in a wild section of

England, near the Scottish border, I killed one of those dogs, thinking it a sheep. It was not until later that I learned of my mistake and I haven't been able to eat mutton since."

Again the crowd roared. The questions came fast and furious after that. Everyone seemed to want to play the new game.

"How far is it to the moon?"

"What is the population of Talladega, Alabama?"

"When was the Battle of Austerlitz?"

"What is ontology?"

Quade answered all the questions, promptly and accurately. The audience applauded each time he gave a prompt answer. Then, after ten minutes, Quade called a dramatic halt.

"Now," he bellowed, "I want to tell you how you can learn the answers to all the questions you've asked me. All those and ten thousand more. I'm going to give every one of you the opportunity to do what I did—have at your fingertips the answer to every single question anyone can ask you. Every one of you can be a Human Encyclopedia...."

Charlie Boston opened the suitcase at Quade's feet. He brought out a thick volume and handed it to Quade.

"Here it is, folks," Quade said. "The compendium of human knowledge of the ages. The answers to all questions. A complete college education crammed into one volume. Listen." Quade leaned forward and lowered his voice to a confidential bellow.

"I'm not asking twenty-five dollars for this marvelous twelve-hundred-page book. I'm not even asking fifteen dollars, ten or five. Just a mere, paltry, insignificant two dollars and ninety-five cents. Think of it, folks, the knowledge of the ages for a mere pittance... And here I come!"

He leaped down the from the counter and grabbed an

armful of books. Then he attacked the crowd, talking as he went through. He sold the books, twenty-two of them. Then, when the remnants of the crowd still lingered to hear more entertainment, Quade blithely walked off. There was no use wasting time on dead-heads. In a little while there'd be a new crowd and Quade would attack them. But now, he had a half-hour intermission.

He was walking through a dog aisle when a biting voice said to one side of him: "Sheep!"

It was the girl who had asked Quade to identify the sheep dogs. He grinned. She was very easy on the eyes, blonde, and with the finest chiseled features Quade had ever seen on a girl, a complexion of milk and honey and eyes that danced with blue mischief. She was not more than twenty-one or two.

"Sorry I had to embarrass you," Quade apologized. "But I ask you in all fairness, do those creatures look like dogs?"

He pointed at the one in the stall. The girl surveyed the dog critically. "Well," she conceded, "the man I got them from told me they were dogs. Sometimes I'm inclined to disbelieve him. But say, what's the trick about that question and answer stuff you pulled back there?"

"No trick at all, it's on the level."

"Oh, come now, you don't really know everything."

"But I do. I have a smattering of every subject under the sun."

"I don't understand. No one person could know everything."

"You heard my pitch. I sell small encyclopedias. They're pretty good, worth the money. But I didn't get my knowledge from them. I got it from a twenty-five volume set. I've read it from cover to cover, not once, but four times."

She looked at him in awe. "How long—"

"Fifteen years. And I remember everything I read. For example, in the premium list of the Westfield Kennel Show I remember the name of Lois Lanyard as the exhibitor of a pair of Old English Sheepdogs...."

"And you're Oliver Quade. And now we're introduced."

Quade's eyes sparkled. The friendliness of the girl delighted him. He talked for a moment more with her, then a sleek-haired young man in white flannels came up.

"Freddie," said Lois Lanyard, "this is Mr. Quade, the Human Encyclopedia. Mr. Quade, my fiancé, Mr. Bartlett."

Quade started to put out his hand but Bartlett nodded shortly and turned to Lois. "The judge is going to place the awards on the pointers in a few minutes," he said. "Shall we watch?"

Lois flashed an angry look at her fiancé but Bartlett bluntly took her arm and walked off with her. Quade shrugged and walked down the aisle containing the English bulldogs. He made friends with a couple of the dogs, although he had some uneasy moments while doing so.

"Maybe," Quade said to himself, "they'll judge the pointers today. Then again maybe they won't!"

When he walked away, the snap fastening the biggest bull-dog to the wall was loose. The dog, however, didn't know it yet. Later, instinct and nature would take its course.

Quade went quickly back to his booth, climbed up on his stand and began his pitch. And if he had talked loud before he shook the rafters now. The noise was too much for the dogs and they set up a terrific racket. Inside of thirty seconds bedlam reigned in the building. Men and women began rushing about. That excited the dogs even more. And then, Quade, on his perch, saw a big bulldog leap out of his stall. He went no further than the neighboring one, which contained a bulldog almost as big as himself. Also a male.

The fight created a riot in the building. A hundred people clamored, screamed and yelled. A half dozen dog handlers had to use water and burning newspaper to get the dogs apart.

Quade watched the fight, but Charlie Boston was conspicuous by his absence. He had taken flight outside the building the moment he'd heard one of the bulldogs was loose.

When the dogs were back in their stalls and the crowd began dispersing, Quade strolled into the pointer aisle. "Going to judge the pointers today?" he asked Freddie Bartlett.

Bartlett glared at him, "No, some damn fool let one of the bulls loose and it'll take two hours for the dogs to quiet down."

"Next time," Quade said to himself, "maybe Freddie will be more particular who he snubs."

Charlie Boston dashed up, wild-eyed. "Oliver," he croaked. "Come over here a minute. I gotta tell you...."

Quade followed Boston to one side. "In your booth," gasped Boston. "Gawd, a dead man!"

"Hell, I just left that booth five minutes ago."

"Maybe so, but there's a stiff there now."

Quade's lips tightened. He distanced his partner, reaching the small booth a dozen steps ahead of him. He leaned over the four-foot counter, looked down into the small space behind— and caught his breath.

A man wearing white flannels, white doeskin shoes and a black and white striped sweater was lying there in the tan-bark. And a dark brown liquid had trickled from a spot over his left eye down over the bridge of his nose.

Quade turned. "Call the show secretary and the police."

"But he's in *our* booth."

"Call the cops," Quade repeated sharply.

CHARLIE BOSTON HAD a policeman at his side and, in their wake, coat-tails flapping, the dog show secretary.

"Murder!" bleated the secretary. "Murder, here! Oh, my God!"

The dogs started barking again and Quade slumped in disgust. The fool secretary was starting another riot. It lasted for a full ten minutes, then a dozen Westfield police arrived and herded everyone in the building into the aisle before Quade's booth.

Chief Costello of the Westfield Police Department was in command. "This is your booth, I understand," he began on Quade.

"Yes, it's my booth and you want to know what I know. The answer is, nothing. There was a dog fight and I joined the crowd to watch it. My assistant here, Charlie Boston, found the body and told me about it. That's all I know."

"Zat so?" The chief turned on Boston and put him through a bad few minutes. But Boston defended himself ably. He had left the building when the dog fight started because he didn't like dog fights. When the dogs had quieted he'd returned and found the body here in the booth. He'd gone to tell Quade immediately. He stuck stoutly to that story.

The coroner come and examined the body inside the booth. He came out in a few minutes. "Shot with a .32 caliber bullet, I'd say."

"And no one heard the shot?" the chief said sarcastically. "A hundred people in here, too."

"And five hundred dogs," added Quade. "All of them barking. You couldn't have heard a machine gun."

The chief glared at him. "I'll talk to you some more." He turned to the coroner. "S'pose you'd better take him to town. We'll give the notice to the papers and someone may come down and identify him."

"That's not necessary," said the coroner. "I know him. His name is Wesley Peters."

"Wesley! My God!"

The scream came from a gorgeously blonde young woman in the front of the crowd. Quade stepped quickly toward her, but couldn't quite catch her as she sank to the tanbark. He dropped to his knees and bumped into a slender, dark-haired chap who was also stooping to pick her up.

"I beg your pardon!" the man exclaimed. "It's my wife."

Quade pushed a path through the crowd to a booth with a long table in it. The young fellow brought his wife behind Quade, deposited her gently on the table. The coroner came through but the woman had already revived and was struggling to sit up. She moaned. "Wesley! He's dead… dead!"

Lois Lanyard came up, put her arm around the girl and spoke soothingly.

"I'll take her home," said the young husband.

"Hmm. Guess it's all right," grunted the chief of police. "I know both of you."

But the woman who had fainted protested at being taken home and after a moment insisted she was quite recovered.

"Thanks for trying to help," the young fellow told Quade.

"Quite all right."

"My brother, Bob," Lois Lanyard said. "And his wife, Jessie."

Quade had already guessed the relationship. The family resemblance between Bob and Lois Lanyard was striking, but whereas Lois was wholesome and vital, her brother seemed to be the ascetic, brooding type. His wife was dressed expensively, her hair was burnished gold and her coiffure marvelous. Lois' clothes had probably cost as much as Jessie Lanyard's but didn't look it. Which was the difference between them. Lois was born to money, Jessie had married it.

The chief of police became brusque. "All right, we know who he is. Now let's see if we can't find out who killed him. You," pointing at Quade, "you say this is your booth. I don't see nothin' in it."

"I do not display samples."

"Naw? What's your racket?"

The show secretary stretched up on his toes and whispered to the chief. There was a light in the chief's eyes when he tackled Quade again. "A book agent, huh!" he snapped in glee. "So you're the bloke who's been making all the racket around here today. Come on now, talk and talk fast."

"Why would I want to kill this man? I never saw him before in my life."

"So what? Does every robber and thug have to be introduced first to the people he robs?"

"Has he been robbed?"

A startled look came into the chief's eyes. He turned away hurriedly and pulled the coroner into the booth. He emerged a moment later, crestfallen.

"He wasn't robbed."

"Ah, his money is still on him, eh? How much?"

"Over a thousand dollars," admitted the chief. "And there's a watch and stickpin. But—maybe you didn't have time."

"No? You forget that I was the one who sent for the police?"

The chief swore roundly. "Say, who's the policeman here? You or me?"

"Don't you know?"

"Why you—!" The chief started to swing a punch at Quade, but caught himself with an effort. "Enough of that stuff now. We've got to find the gun."

He signaled to a couple of policemen and barked orders at them. They scattered through the neighboring booths. And inside of two minutes one of them yelled in discovery. He came back carrying a nickel-plated .32 caliber revolver in a handkerchief. The chief's eyes gleamed.

He sent policemen scurrying about getting the name of everyone present. Then he allowed everyone to depart. He dispersed the exhibitors too and posted policemen at each door.

"No one'll be allowed in here until we've had time to go over the building," he announced. "Three o'clock in the afternoon anyway."

OLIVER QUADE AND Charlie Boston strolled toward a restaurant a short distance from the dog building. "Don't look now," said Boston as they entered. "But there's a flatfoot shadowing us."

"Naturally. The chief hasn't forgotten that it's my booth."

Lois Lanyard, her brother and his wife and Freddie Bartlett were in the restaurant, seated at a large table. The only vacant spot was at a small table next to theirs. Quade and Boston sat down at it.

Lois introduced them all around.

A waitress came to take their order, then Quade leaned back in his chair and studied the group at the next table. Lois was chattering gaily with Freddie, but every now and then she cast a sharp glance at her brother who was biting his lips and staring moodily at the tablecloth. Jessie Lanyard was trying to make conversation with her husband, but wasn't having much success. She seemed to have recovered entirely from her faint, but her conversation, it seemed to Quade, was high pitched and forced.

Quade sat up. "Look, folks," he said, "I seem to be Murder Suspect Number 1 and the chief of police is going to ask me some mighty embarrassing questions this afternoon. Mind if I talk about it?"

Lois made warning signals with her eyes and Freddie drew himself up stiffly, but Lois' brother came out of his lethargy. "Yes, let's talk about it. We're all thinking about it anyway. Why did my wife faint when the coroner said it was Wesley Peters? Is that what you want to know?"

"No. I want to know why Mrs. Lanyard *pretended* to faint?"

All four of the people at the adjoining table gasped. Jessie's face went white, then red. "What do you mean by that?" she snapped.

"I mean that you were no more faint than I," Quade replied. "I saw your eyes. And your muscles were tensed, not relaxed, when your husband picked you up."

"Mr. Quade," said Freddie Bartlett. "I don't think this is a matter that concerns you."

"But it does," cried Lois' brother. "Jessie put on a scene over there and I want to know the meaning of it. Jessie, why did you faint? Or pretend to faint?"

Jessie's eyes flashed sparks. "Very well, if you must have a public scene, I'll tell you. You know very well that I knew Wes before I married you. Naturally it was a shock to learn that he was murdered—under such peculiar circumstances."

"Why peculiar?" snapped Bob Lanyard. "The dog show was as good a place as any for him to die. He was a—a dog, you know."

"Bob!" Jessie cried indignantly.

"Why did you have to start this?" exclaimed Lois, looking at Quade.

"Because I wanted to make you all mad," retorted Quade. "When people are mad they tell things, and I think there are some things to be told. Don't you think so, Mrs. Lanyard?"

Jessie Lanyard's eyes slitted, "All right, Wesley was in love with me once. And I almost accepted him before I married you, Bob. I didn't want to tell you that, but you insisted on having it. So take it."

Charlie tugged at Quade's sleeve. Quade turned and saw Chief Costello bearing down on the group.

"Hello, folks," said the chief. "Thought I'd find you here."

"You mean your shadow told you we came here," Quade retorted.

"Still at it, young fella, huh? Well, I got some news for you. I found out who owned the gun that Wesley was killed with."

Jessie Lanyard rose so suddenly that she bumped the table and knocked over a water glass. Quade saw panic in her eyes.

"It was his own gun," continued the chief. "He bought it a year ago, got a license to carry it."

The panic remained in Jessie's eyes. Quade hesitated, then suddenly pointed a lean forefinger at her. "But didn't he give you that gun, Mrs. Lanyard?" he asked softly.

Jessie screamed suddenly. She pushed back her chair and it crashed to the floor. Her face was suddenly twisted into a weird gargoyle. "Yes, he gave it to me. Yes, and I killed him. I killed him with his own gun! I'd do it again because I hated him!"

Jessie's dramatic confession exploded like a bombshell in the crowded restaurant. The place seethed with excitement. Lois sat up in her chair, her eyes aghast. Freddie was frozen stiff in his chair.

Bob Lanyard sprang to his feet. His arms encircled Jessie and he caught her tightly to him. "Jessie!" he cried in anguish. "You mustn't! You're over-wrought. You don't know what you're saying."

Jessie began sobbing as if her heart was breaking. Her husband soothed her.

Chief Costello stood back uncertainly. It was obvious the social standing of these people impressed him, made him uncertain. Then he ordered his policemen to clear the restaurant.

Bob Lanyard's soothing quieted Jessie. In two or three minutes she was able to pull herself together, although she still kept a handkerchief covering her mouth and most of her face.

The chief cleared his throat noisily. "I'm mighty sorry about this, Mrs. Lanyard," he said. "But you understand...."

"You fool!" gritted Bob Lanyard. "Don't you know she said that to shield me? Wesley was an old sweetheart. She knew I was intensely jealous of him and when she knew he was murdered, she naturally jumped to the conclusion that I did it."

"Did you?" the chief asked, taken aback.

Quade almost held his breath, waiting for the answer he was sure would come. It did.

"Yes!" exclaimed Bob. "I killed him. I found the gun in Jessie's dresser, took it to the dog show with me and killed him during the excitement of the dog fight. He—he was annoying Jessie again."

"Bob!" That was Lois. "You—you couldn't have! You were right behind me all that time."

"No, you were with Freddie." Bob Lanyard refused to accept the alibi offered him.

Freddie Bartlett blundered in. "Oh, come now, Bob, you know very well we were talking together when the excitement began and I remember your being with us when the dog fight was over."

"Say, what is this?" cried the chief. "Two confessions inside of five minutes. Is there anyone else here who wants to confess?"

"If I wasn't afraid you'd take me seriously I'd toss in my hat," said Quade.

The Lanyards and Bartletts were wealthy local residents who could embarrass Chief Costello in his own bailiwick. He had to treat them with the utmost respect. But Quade, the chief knew, was an outsider and a mere book agent. Fair bait. He turned savagely upon him.

"That's the last damn crack I'm takin' out o' you, fella!" he snarled. "You make just one more yip and I'll not only throw you in the clink but I'll see that you get worked over plenty with the rubber hose. Get me?"

"I get you, Chief." Quade subsided, but his mind worked furiously over the problem. He had a strange hunch that this case had just begun. There had been a hundred or more people in the building at the time Wesley Peters had been killed. And the place had been in an uproar. No one had paid any attention to anyone else because of the commotion. Alibis weren't worth a dime a dozen.

And Wesley was known in Westfield. There could easily have been a dozen people in the building at the time who knew, and perhaps disliked him. Jessie Lanyard was a neurotic. She might say or do anything under stress of emotion. Her husband was a moody, sensitive type.

Chief Costello made a sagacious deduction. "Maybe we'd better not decide anything just yet. All of us know each other and there's plenty of time for getting together. Anyway, it would be much better for all of you to think things over and maybe discuss them with your families and lawyers. If you'll give me your word not to leave town suddenly, I'll make my report and we'll get together later this evening." He departed, taking his policeman with him.

Lois came over to Quade. "I've been greatly disappointed in you, Mr. Quade," she said.

He flushed. "I'm sorry, Miss Lanyard." He rose, turned stiffly and followed Charlie Boston out of the restaurant, although neither of them had been served yet.

Outside, Charlie Boston whistled softly. Quade turned angrily on him. "Cut it, Charlie."

Boston stopped whistling. He walked beside Quade without saying a word. After a moment, however, Quade apologized. "Sorry, Charlie. Nerves. I made some fool plays and I'm sore about them."

Boston grunted assent. "We're out of our class, Oliver. That's all that's wrong. Shall we ditch the books and clear out? It's only thirty miles to New York City. Once there no one from here'd ever find us."

"It'd probably be the smartest thing we could do, but you know how I am. I'm too stubborn to quit something I've started."

IN THE DINING-ROOM of the Westfield Hotel, Quade and Charlie discussed the case.

"That thousand dollars Peters had, that worries me. It's too much money for him," Quade said between bites.

"I wouldn't know myself," replied Boston. "But I've heard there's lots of folks have a thousand dollars."

"Not ham actors. I read Variety, and I know that Peters hasn't been in a show for four years or more. I wish I knew how he got his money. He dressed well."

"Is that the important thing in this case? Seems to me some of those people haven't told all they know."

"Some of them don't know any more than we do, if as much. Hmm, wonder who that is?"

The head waiter was pointing out Quade to a man who had just come into the dining room. He would have been more at home in a Greenwich Village bar than the Westfield Hotel. He was perhaps thirty, tall and hollow-cheeked. There was a three days' growth of beard on his face. His cinnamon-colored coat didn't match his trousers and his shirt had evidently been washed in some communal bathroom and worn unpressed.

He came up to Quade's table. "Mr. Quade? My name's Renfrew, Felix Renfrew. I read in the afternoon papers about— about Wes Peters and came out here."

Quade said, "Have a seat; you interest me."

Renfrew sat down. "Wes Peters," he declared, "was my best friend. The minute I heard he had been killed I grabbed a bus and came out here."

"You may have been Peters' best friend," said Quade, "but I bet you didn't hear about Peters' death in the city."

Renfrew glared for a moment, then shrugged. "All right, I came out with Wes this morning. What difference does it make? Wes was killed, his body found in your booth. There's a lot of talk going around town about your knowing something."

"I do know something. More than you ever will. What'd you come to me for?"

"To find out who killed Wes, that's why!" snapped Renfrew. "Wes was the best pal I ever had and I'm going to stick around until his murderer is found."

Quade gave Renfrew the once over, his eyes insolently staring at the unmatched suit and unpressed shirt. "You were Peters' pal, eh? Roommate perhaps?"

Renfrew flushed. "No, we didn't room together. But—"

"You live in Greenwich Village?"

"Yes, but what's that got to do with it?"

"Perhaps nothing. Wes Peters, if you'll pardon the inference, put on the dog. And when he was found this afternoon he had a thousand dollars on him. Would you be knowing how he got that much money?"

Renfrew shrugged. "Peters always had money. We didn't live together but he paid my rent and visited at my place a lot."

"Why?"

"Why? Well, because there was always something doing there. I'm a playwright, you know."

"I didn't know. What plays have you written?" Renfrew scowled. "I've written eight or ten, but none have been produced. But they're good plays. Only the capitalistic—"

"Oh, so it's like that. Anyway, you always had a crowd of the

Village folks at your diggings. Poets and writers and artists. And Peters liked to pose as a big shot. So he paid your rent and hung around your dump. Right?"

"Something like that."

"And you're worried because your patron has shuffled off? Kinda puts you on the spot. Tell me, where'd Peters get his money?"

"He never told me."

"Where'd he come from originally?"

"I don't know. New York, I guess. I've only known him four or five years. But I always guessed that he got his money from relatives. Who else would send him money regularly?"

"Ah, he got it regularly?"

"Yes, I happen to know because at times he was broke but he didn't worry about it. And he didn't work. Not for the last four years. Before that he was on the stage. He played the juvenile lead in Hidden Faces, I know."

"Jessie Lanyard played in that, too, didn't she?" Renfrew looked puzzled. He said: "I don't know her."

"Well, that wasn't her name then. She's the woman who fainted when Wes Peters was found dead. Or weren't you around then?"

Renfrew flushed. "No, I left right after—well, right after you got through selling books."

"Because you saw Wes Peters coming in and didn't want him to see you around?"

Renfrew chewed at his lower lip, then suddenly rose. "I've got to catch my bus back to the city."

Quade did not try to detain him. When he was gone, Charlie Boston snorted. "Wonder what the hell Peters saw in that."

"The only difference between Peters and Renfrew is that

Peters had money these last few years. Before he got the money, I'll bet, he was just like Renfrew. Dirty finger-nails and all. Well, I guess it was a tough blow to Renfrew at that. He may even have to go to work now."

"It won't hurt him," growled Boston. "Say, what did you say that made him run out so sudden-like?"

Quade grinned reflectively. "I guess I got a little too close. Renfrew had gotten curious about Peters, or maybe, he hoped to find out how and where Peters got his money. So he followed him out here today but didn't want Peters to spot him... You know, this Renfrew interests me."

"Not me," said Boston. "I can find his kind anywhere. What do we do now, go see a movie or something?"

"They've got a crime thriller at the Bijou," Quade said. "But I don't think it'll be as interesting as the one we're in ourselves. Instead, let's go stir up the porridge a bit."

"Back to the dog show?"

"No, I thought we'd brace some of the suspects and others in their own backyard. The Lanyard house."

"Ouch! After the trimming we took from the Lanyards this afternoon?"

LANYARD, SENIOR, HAD money. He must have had scads of it, to keep up the estate that Quade and Boston entered a little while later. It was about a mile out of Westfield and was surrounded by a low, trimmed hedge. The house was Georgian style and contained at least twenty rooms. A smaller house nearby was evidently the servants' quarters. There was also a four-car garage behind the house and a long, low building with wire-enclosed runs in front of it. A dog kennel.

There were a half-dozen cars on the graveled driveway leading up to the house; the smallest a Packard. The cars didn't faze Quade, however. He squeezed his old flivver in between a Packard and a large foreign car and leaped lightly over the hingeless door.

And there was no hesitation in his manner as he rang the front doorbell of the big house. Charlie Boston had the good grace to hang back a bit.

"They got company, Ollie," he protested. "Listen to the music."

Quade had already heard the music, recognized it, too. Mendelssohn's *Wedding March*. That and the several cars outside told him what it was. A wedding rehearsal. Evidently the scene in the restaurant hadn't been allowed to interfere with the Lanyards' plans.

The door opened and a liveried butler looked questioningly at Quade.

"Mr. Lanyard," Quade said.

"Which Mr. Lanyard?"

"Senior. Tell him it's Mr. Oliver Quade."

"Very well, I'll see if he's at home." The butler closed the door.

"It's the suit," Quade said. "I'll have to get a new one. Can't go around society homes with the checkerboard pattern."

The door opened again and a dignified, gray-haired man with a short clipped mustache held out his hand to Quade. "Come in, Mr. Quade. I've heard about you. Glad you dropped out."

Quade winked triumphantly at Boston.

"This way," Guy Lanyard said, leading the way to a room on the right side of the foyer. Quade looked to the left where the organ was playing, but followed Lois' father to the right.

In the library, Guy Lanyard said, "Have a seat, won't you? I presume you want to talk to me about that affair this afternoon. Pretty bad, wasn't it?"

"It was. This is Charles Boston, my friend."

"Ah, yes, how are you, Mr. Boston? You were there too?"

"Me, I found the body," Boston said proudly.

Guy Lanyard winced. "The children have told me about it. And our chief of police left me only a few minutes ago. He's considerably disturbed about the matter. I'm glad to have this chance of talking it over with you, Mr. Quade. From what Lois and Bob told me about you, I gather that you're a man of some—ah, perspicacity."

Quade grinned at the blank look on Boston's face. "Forsaking modesty for the moment, Mr. Lanyard, I'm probably the smartest person in this State. I'm the Human Encyclopedia."

Guy Lanyard didn't seem to know just how to take that, but finally he grinned. "Maybe I'm saying the wrong thing, but if so, forgive me, because I've never met a Human Encyclopedia before. But as I have this opportunity now I'd like to take advantage of it. Can you tell me if Mid-City Service is a good buy right now?"

"I wouldn't know," Quade replied. "I'm not a fortune teller. I impart only *knowledge*, and the devil himself couldn't tell you if Mid-City Service is a good or bad buy right now. I can tell you that it was a good buy a year ago. That's a matter of knowledge. Anything else I could help you on?"

Guy Lanyard's eyes snapped. "Yes. Who killed Wesley Peters?"

Fortunately Quade was spared answering the question. Lois Lanyard burst into the room. "Dad!" she cried and then came to a stop when she saw Quade.

"Hello," she said.

"I didn't know you were having a dress rehearsal," Quade apologized. "I wouldn't have come out."

"Quite all right," replied Lois. "We're finished now. Dad, the reason I burst in—don't you think Honolulu would be more interesting than Europe?"

"Borneo is charming at this season," Quade volunteered.

Lois Lanyard sighed. "We're at it again. Well, let's entertain the others, too. Come along, Mr. Quade."

Guy Lanyard frowned but Quade was willing. "Fine, I'd like another chance to talk with Freddie Bartlett."

Lois passed him in the doorway. She whispered fiercely, "Don't start any more trouble. I've had enough for one day."

The large living-room was full of people; a half-dozen girls, the minister and several well-dressed young men. And Mrs. Lanyard, an older edition of Lois, who still retained most of her youthful beauty. The years had endowed her with added warmth and charm.

Bob Lanyard was walking in and out of the crowd, his ascetic face strained in a frown. His beautiful wife, Jessie, seemed to have quite recovered from the afternoon, for she was chatting gaily, surrounded by several young men.

Freddie Bartlett was in an expansive mood. With most of the girls around him he was expounding on the merits of different honeymoon spots. "Honolulu," he was saying, "has become too common. Singapore is the place today. A month there, then Yokohama in cherry-blossom time."

"How about the county jail?" Quade asked. "I've been told that it's charming at this season."

Freddie Bartlett scowled. "Ah, it's you, Mr. Shade. Always

clowning. How's the—what do you call it in the vernacular—the pitching business?"

"Fair to middling," Quade shrugged. "I've forsaken it for the nonce. I'm in the detecting business now."

"Then you'll be interested to know you'll have some competition tomorrow. Bob has engaged a famous sleuth—Christopher Buck."

Quade's eyelids lowered thoughtfully. Christopher Buck had a reputation that was more than local. He had a good press agent too, for there was seldom a week that some mention of him didn't appear in the newspapers.

Quade drifted over to Bob Lanyard. "I understand you've hired Christopher Buck to do some investigating for you," he remarked casually.

Annoyance came into young Lanyard's eyes. "Yes, with all due respect to Chief Costello, I don't believe he knows what it's all about and I don't believe he'll ever find out who killed this—this Wesley Peters, do you?"

"Not unless the murderer confesses voluntarily."

Bob Lanyard winced.

"I'm sorry," Quade apologized quickly. "I forgot."

"It's all right. But that's just why I phoned to the city and engaged Mr. Buck. Unless the case is solved beyond a shadow of a doubt a few people will still have ideas—and I don't want any reflection to hang over Jessie."

Jessie must have heard her name mentioned for she suddenly excused herself from her circle of admirers and came over.

"Oh, Mr. Quade, I'm so glad you dropped in. You know I've been thinking about you."

"Indeed?"

"Yes, you know I was in the show business before I married Bob. Your little spiel out at the dog show this afternoon; have you ever thought of going on the stage?"

Quade's lips peeled back in a wide smile, too wide. "No, and I'm sorry to say that no Hollywood scout has approached me either."

Jessie Lanyard didn't catch the sarcasm. "Why that act—you know that question and answer stuff—that's great. Properly handled it should be a wow on the stage. I've a friend in Mr. Kent's office and, if you like, I'll give you a note to him."

"Jessie," said Bob Lanyard, "perhaps Mr. Quade doesn't want to go on the stage."

"Why not? With his personality and that gift of gab? Say, I've seen hoofers with less than he's got make good on the big time."

Quade pursed his lips. "You mean I'd have to take up dancing?"

That was a bit too strong. Even Jessie Lanyard caught the sarcasm. "I'm sorry," she said stiffly. "I didn't know I was being funny." She put her pretty nose into the air and went back to her covey of admirers.

"At it again," said Lois Lanyard.

Quade walked to one side with her. "What's this I hear about your brother employing a private detective?"

Lois frowned. "Bob seemed to think Jessie's reputation has been besmirched and he's determined to clear it. Well, she did throw quite a scene today."

"When's Buck coming?"

"Tomorrow morning. I've heard he's a very astute man-hunter. He comes high, at any rate."

"Hmm. You're really going through with your marriage?"

She looked coolly at him. "Of course I'm going to marry Freddie Bartlett. We've been engaged for almost a year and the date has been set for four months."

"I apologize, Miss Lanyard. Shall we wave the white flag?"

"You'll keep it white?"

"Of course. I'm sorry I interrupted this evening. I must be going now."

CHRISTOPHER BUCK WAS not burdened with good manners. He banged on the door of Oliver Quade's room at the ungodly hour of eight a.m. Quade, cursing under his breath, climbed out of the bed and opened the door.

"I left a call for nine o'clock, not eight!" he snarled.

"I'm Christopher Buck," the detective announced grandly.

"So what? I'm Oliver Quade and that gorilla yawning over in the bed is Charlie Boston. A good morning to you." Quade started to shut the door in Buck's face.

But the detective must have worked his way through college selling magazines. He put a foot in the doorway. "Hey!" he yelped. "I'm Christopher Buck, the detective."

Quade opened the door again. "A detective?" he pretended to be amazed. "Why didn't you say so? Come in."

Christopher Buck stepped angrily into the room. "Hey, Charlie," Quade called. "Get up. There's a cop from the local police force here."

"I'm not from the Westfield Police," Buck called. "What're you trying to do, rib me?"

Quade blinked. Then: "I'll be damned. Of course, I've read about you in the newspapers. You're the famous detective, Christopher Buck!"

Buck was so lean that he had to stand twice in order to cast a shadow, but he made up for it in height. He was at least six feet four and his huge, bushy eyebrows and stooped figure gave him a sinister appearance.

"I was engaged by Robert Lanyard to solve the murder that was committed out at the dog show yesterday," he said. "I came to you because I've been told you're the chief suspect."

"Right to the point, that's what I like," said Quade. "Have a seat, Mr. Buck. You don't mind if I dress while you grill—I mean, question me. Take a chair."

"Ow, oh-wuh!" said Charlie Boston, yawning and stretching.

Quade drew his pajama coat off, then unblushing slipped off the trousers. Nude as the day he was born, he searched around for his underwear.

"Sitting on my drawers, Mr. Buck?" he asked. "No, here they are." Calmly he began dressing. Charlie Boston scooted for the bathroom.

Christopher Buck drew a stubby pipe from his coat pocket and filled it. "I've already talked to Mr. Lanyard and Chief of Police Costello. There seems to be some difference of opinion as to just what happened yesterday."

"Some of the dogs got loose and raised a ruckus," Quade said. "Of course everyone in the building gathered around. I left my stand. Then when the dog fight had been stopped and the dogs chained up, I started to go back. Charlie, here, told me then that there was a dead man in our booth."

Buck grunted. "You say some of the dogs got loose? I hear there was only one loose."

"Yeah, that's right. Anyway, he got into the next stall and tangled up with another dog. The second dog was chained, but it didn't affect his fighting ability. It was a swell fight."

"I'm not interested in the dog fight," said Buck, severely. "I'm interested in the man who was killed. He was an old sweetheart of the wife of my client. Tell me more about this Peters fellow. How long had you known him?"

Quade sighed. "He was in the audience when I made my first pitch out there, but that's the only time I ever saw him alive. I know nothing about the murder. And I think I'll have breakfast now."

Christopher Buck scowled. "I don't like it. No one seemed to know this Peters fellow, yet someone hated him enough to kill him. Why?"

"You said you were the detective," Quade reminded him. "Me, I'm only a book salesman."

"Yes, but I've heard about your bragging yesterday. About what a smart fellow you were. Claim to know the answers to everything. Well, who killed Wes Peters?"

"I don't belong to the detectives' union."

Buck started to get up from the chair. It was quite a job, because he was so lean and tall. "You're not leaving Westfield, are you, Quade?"

"No, I'm going out to the dog show today and make a few dollars. Any time you think you've got the goods on me you'll know where to collar me!"

Christopher Buck closed the door ungently behind him.

"I think I'll blow myself and have about four eggs and some ham," Boston said dreamily, coming out of the bathroom.

"O.K., Charlie, better fatten up while you can. It's been a lean stretch. I think we'll get us each a hand-me-down, too."

"Gonna get yourself a nice blue serge?" asked Boston, looking wisely at Quade.

"Why blue?"

"Oh, I dunno. Just thought maybe a loud suit was undignified."

Quade made a pass at Boston, which the big fellow ducked easily. "She's getting married today, you sap."

"Going to the wedding?"

"I wasn't invited."

But Quade did buy a blue serge, after all. It fitted him well and changed his appearance considerably. He finished the job by getting some black oxfords, a blue striped shirt and brown felt hat.

He had a good day at the auditorium, running out of books when there were still some prospective purchasers in the crowd. His pockets stuffed with money, he closed his pitch and strolled out of the building.

He saw a hamburger stand nearby and went over to it. As he stuffed the last of a sandwich into his mouth a voice behind him said:

"Ah, Mr. Quade, I was hoping to find you here this morning." It was Jessie Lanyard, wearing a floppy picture hat and a flowered organdy dress. Her blonde hair was smartly coiffured.

"How d'you do, Mrs. Lanyard?" Quade greeted her. "Won't you have a hamburger?"

"Why, I don't mind if I do. It's a long time since I've eaten one. Not since I got married." She laughed. "You know, one time, when I was out of work I ate nothing but hamburgers for a solid month."

"They didn't spoil your figure," Quade complimented her. He ordered a couple of hamburgers.

"I've decided to overlook your kidding last night," Jessie

Lanyard said brightly. "I really like you, Mr. Quade. You're—you're my sort of people."

"Thanks."

"You know some of the people out here in Westfield are awful snobs," Jessie prattled on. "My in-laws still don't treat me any too well. But I don't care. Even if the in-laws and some of Lois' girl friends give me the turned-up nose, the men like me. You saw them last night."

"I did. You were pretty well surrounded."

Jessie sighed. "Yes, they always rush me. Some of them even—well, that isn't what I wanted to talk to you about. It's about this detective Bob hired."

"Didn't you urge him to do that?"

Jessie smiled prettily. "Well, I did suggest it, I guess. But Bob was so worked up. Seemed to think I had been carrying on with Wes—Mr. Peters. Goodness, I hadn't seen Wesley Peters for a long time. Not alone, that is. Of course he hung around a lot out here in Westfield, but I couldn't very well chase him away, could I?"

"No, of course not. By the way, what'd Peters do for a living?"

"He was on the stage. I played with him in a show about five years ago. I was just beginning then," Jessie hastened to say. "I started very young, you know."

Quade took a deep breath. Then he said, "Mrs. Lanyard, how long is it since you saw Bill Demetros?"

Ketchup dripped from the hamburger to Jessie Lanyard's organdy dress, but she didn't notice it. She was staring too intently at Oliver Quade. "Where did you hear about—him?" she asked, slowly.

"I've always been a great newspaper reader and I never forget anything I read. Your name was mentioned with his several years ago. They even ran your photos together. You were Janet Jackson then."

"I haven't seen him—for five years," she said, looking relieved.

"Since he went to jail? You haven't seen him since he got out?"

"No, and I—I hope I never see him again. I don't even want him to know where I am."

"You changed your name even before you married Bob. Demetros probably wouldn't know where to look for you if he wanted to."

"No, but there wouldn't be any reason for him to look me up. The newspapers were wrong. We were never more than casual acquaintances. I—I must go now."

Quade looked thoughtfully after Jessie Lanyard as she walked to the dog building. Then he left and caught a taxi. Charlie had taken his car to replenish their supply of books.

Quade rode back to Westfield, paid off on the main street of the village, then stood on the sidewalk for a few minutes. A five-and-ten-cent store across the street caught his eye. Smiling grimly, he bought an ordinary toy, shaped roughly like a mature, lethal gun. He had the clerk wrap it in paper and put it in a mailing box. At the stationery counter he bought a box of adhesive address labels.

Then Quade went back to his hotel room. He got a jar of Vaseline from the bathroom, smeared a light coat of it on the water pistol, then wrapped it in paper and put it in the box. He tied the package, addressed a label and stuck it to the package.

He walked with it to the post-office, had the box weighed there, then mailed it first-class.

Returning to the dog show he found Boston fuming because he had been unable to find Quade.

"I brought the books back here an hour ago," he exclaimed. "Where you been?"

"Attending to some business," Quade replied shortly.

Quade made a pitch to a small noon-day crowd and took in thirty-five dollars. He and Boston drove to the hotel and had a late lunch. When they got the key for their room the clerk handed Quade a package. "Mailman just brought this."

"Who'd be sending us a package?" asked Boston as they rode in the elevator to their floor.

"One of my female admirers probably," Quade said.

In the room he cut the string of the package. Quade opened the box, lifted out the paper-wrapped contents and unwrapped it. He exhibited the water pistol.

Boston examined the gun, then snorted. "Someone's ribbin' you!"

Quade scarcely looked at the gun. He was examining the inside of the wrapping paper. The Vaseline on the gun had made recognizable outlines on the paper. He nodded in satisfaction.

"Look, Charlie," he said "run down to the telegraph office and send a wire to the Blake Publishing Company in New York. Have 'em rush us two hundred more copies of our book. We're going to need them before this dog show is over."

"But what about the gun?" protested Boston. "Why would anyone send it to you? I don't like it, I tell you. It's—it's a threat."

"Don't you worry your pretty head about the gun, Charlie. Go ahead, send that telegram."

The moment Boston had left the room Quade took out a knife and scraped the address label from the box in which the gun had been mailed. He addressed another label, glued it to the box, then left the hotel.

He threw the toy pistol into an ashcan a couple of blocks from the hotel. Then he walked three blocks more, entered an alley and sought another ashcan behind the third building from the corner. Into it he tossed the paper box and the wrapping paper in which he had mailed the gun to himself. He'd torn the address label from the box, but left the postmark.

He chuckled. "Maybe a smart detective can make something of a box with a local postmark and paper bearing a little oil and imprint of a gun."

Quade rejoined Boston at the hotel an hour later and the big fellow had his finger-nails chewed half-way to his wrists. "What's all the mysterious stuff, Ollie?" he cried. "You got rid of me on a phony excuse, then you go off somewhere."

"Can't a man attend to his private business affairs?"

"Yeah, sure, but—ah, never mind. What do we do now?"

"You can take the afternoon off, Charlie. I think I'll do some visiting."

"At the Lanyard place?… Well, I hope you don't get burned."

"It's a cold world without some heat," Quade said reflectively. "I've just discovered that I've been cold all my life."

A COUPLE OF cars were parked in the curved drive of the Lanyard estate. Quade parked his own car, then circled the house to the kennels. The dogs started a terrific barking and Quade was about to retreat when Lois Lanyard called from a window in the rear of the house. "Look out! Those sheep dogs bite."

"Ever hear of a man biting a dog?"

Lois disappeared from the window but reappeared at a rear door a moment later. She was dressed in a pink and yellow sport sweater suit and her eyes were dancing with mischief. Quade tightened about the mouth.

"Did you come here to see the dogs?" she asked. "There are more of them at the dog show, you know."

"The dog show? Oh, you mean the dog show where you said you'd be today."

She sobered for a moment. "I couldn't very well get away. Some last minute fittings and—other things."

"Ah! The marriage, of course."

The moment was a tense one, but then a Gordon pointer came dashing out of a dog kennel and bounced up to the wire fence, putting his nose between the mesh. Quade snapped his fingers at the dog.

"Who does he belong to? Bob?"

"Yes, that's Duke, his favorite. I've got the sheep dogs that are at the show. And Jessie has two Eskimo Dogs, huskies. Come, take a look at them."

She led Quade to a pen and whistled. A tawny face appeared in the door of a kennel and after a careful examination was followed by a head. Another dog followed.

"They're beautiful, I think," said Lois, "But pretty shy."

A voice called from the house. "Lois!"

"Yes, Mother?" Lois replied.

"I'm afraid you'll have to come in for that last fitting."

"I'll be right in." Lois turned to Quade. "I have to go now. It's been nice seeing you. Come and see us when we get back."

"From Borneo?" he couldn't help cracking.

She laughed and ran into the house.

Quade drove thoughtfully back to the dog show. Charlie Boston wasn't around the booth and had probably gone to see the rest of the show. Quade ran into Christopher Buck and Chief of Police Costello, engaged in heavy conversation.

The chief did not look cordially at Quade. "Ah, here you are," he said in greeting. "What's the big brain man know today?"

"I know that the prenadilla is a South American fish that travels for hours on dry land," he retorted. "And I know other things. What do you know? About the police business, for instance. Have you pinched the murderer yet?"

"When I do, maybe you won't be so cocky," hinted the chief.

"Still barking up my alley, eh? Well, just for that I'll let you worry over the thing by yourself."

He walked off, but less than two minutes later Christopher Buck popped out in front of him. "Say, Quade, what did you mean about letting us worry by ourselves? You know something?"

Quade looked around mysteriously. "I got an anonymous phone call at the hotel this noon. A man's voice told me to take a look around Bartlett's house—the ashcan for example. What do you suppose he meant by that?"

Buck's lean, lank frame quivered with excitement. "The killer's thrown something away, something important. A clue!"

"What sort of clue would he throw away? The murder gun was found here. It's just an ordinary .32. Peters' own gun. But maybe Peters loaned the gun to someone else and that person loaned it to Fred—to the murderer."

There was no holding Buck after that. He tore off in a lather of excitement. Quade looked at his watch, then sought out Charlie Boston.

"Look, Charlie, in the city the poor people hang around the church door to get a look at the bride. Let's go down to the church in Westfield and get a gander at the folks."

"I could smell that coming," said Boston. "How about the rice, you want to throw some?"

They drove down. The wedding was scheduled for five in the afternoon but curious townsfolk had gathered around the church at a quarter to the hour. Quade parked his car directly across the street, then, throwing one foot across the car door, settled down to wait.

At ten minutes to five a closed sedan pulled up to the chapel door and several people got out. Quade had a glimpse of Lois Lanyard wearing a black silk cape that did not quite cover the white dress underneath. The party moved quickly into the church.

Five minutes later another car drew up and Freddie Bartlett, surrounded by several of his intimates, climbed out and went into the church. Freddie was quite the picture in striped trousers, cutaway tail coat and silk hat.

Quade bit his lip. The ceremony was due to start in another five minutes—unless there was some unusual delay. He wondered if he would have to make the delay himself. But at two minutes to five an automobile siren screeched up the street.

"Now begins the fun," he said, sitting up.

"It's the cops," said Boston. "Wonder who they're going to pinch!"

"Maybe the bridegroom—or me. We'll see. Ah, Christopher Buck is with the chief."

The police car screamed up to the curb before the church. The lanky Christopher Buck sprang from it even before it stopped.

He was clutching something under his arm. Chief Costello and a uniformed cop piled out after the private detective. They charged into the church.

"Holy smokes!" exclaimed Boston. "They're busting right into the wedding and they don't look like they're going to kiss the bride, either. It's a pinch if ever I saw one."

It was. Almost immediately Chief Costello, Christopher Buck, the policemen and Freddie Bartlett came out. Bartlett's clothing was disarranged and he was handcuffed. Even a Freddie Bartlett will become indignant at being arrested while the clergyman is saying the words of the marriage ceremony.

Behind the arresting party, swarmed the members of the family and the wedding guests.

"I don't think there'll be any wedding today," said Oliver Quade.

"You knew something was going to happen here," Charlie accused. "You were too calm about things. I know you, Oliver."

Quade screwed up his face. "All right, I'll confess, Charlie. I had a tip-off from Buck. He had a hot clue that pointed to Freddie. I had a hunch he would butt right into the wedding ceremony to make his pinch. For a while, though, I was afraid he wouldn't make it in time."

"Afraid? You mean you wanted him to bust up the wedding?"

Quade did not answer. Boston threw up his hands in disgust. "O. K., Ollie, if that's the way she stands that's the way she stands. C'mon, let's beat it, they're looking over here!"

Quade saw Lois Lanyard, very lovely in a white satin dress and bridal veil, pointing across the street at him. Christopher Buck, head and shoulders above the crowd, was looking, too.

Quade stepped on the starter and shifted into gear. The car

leaped away from the curb. "They're yelling at us, Ollie," said Boston.

"Let 'em yell. I've had lots of people yell at me in my day."

FIFTEEN MINUTES LATER Quade walked into the dining-room of the Westfield Hotel with Charlie Boston. They were on the soup course when the dining-room was invaded by several determined looking men.

"I'd hoped to get a good meal before going to jail," Quade said to Boston, "but such is life.... Hello, Mr. Buck, what's up?"

"Your number," Buck snapped.

Freddie Bartlett, no longer handcuffed, pointed a lean finger at Quade. "You cheap book agent! Why'd you send this detective to look into my ashcan?"

"Tsk, tsk," Quade clucked to Buck. "A detective should never reveal the sources of information."

"That's the last trick you'll pull in this town, Quade," said Chief Costello sternly. "The idea, trying to throw suspicion on an innocent man just to break up his wedding! Well, it brought out the truth and you're under arrest!"

"What for? For giving information to a private detective instead of a policeman?"

"Cut out the stalling, Quade," snapped Buck. "Miss Lanyard spilled the beans. She saw you unchain that bull-dog at the dog show—the dog fight. You started that dog fight to cover up your dirty work."

"The red flag," said Quade half aloud. "Ask no quarter and give none. All right, I'll come quietly."

Charlie Boston pushed back his chair and took up a fighting stance.

"Maybe you could lick them at that, Charlie," Quade said, "but they'd only get me later. I'll go along with them. Look me up after they've booked me."

"I'll get a lawyer. My cousin, Paul, in New York. He'll put these small town cops through their hoops," howled Charlie Boston. "He's the smartest criminal lawyer on the east side."

But Quade scarcely heard him. He was being dragged off to jail. It was the swankiest jail Quade had ever been in; quite in keeping with the town itself. It wasn't a very large jail, neat cells, a wide corridor and a clean, large bull pen where the guests were permitted to exercise during prescribed periods.

The inhabitants of the jail unfortunately were not up to its standards. They were unfortunates from the city who had wandered out to rich Westfield hoping to better themselves and had fallen afoul of the law. There were eight or ten of them. As the cells adjoined one another and were separated only by bars, communication among the prisoners was easy.

The prisoners knew all about Quade by the time he was locked into a cell and they greeted him with the respect due a capital crime violator.

Quade bore up cheerfully enough that first evening in jail.

He entertained the other prisoners for an hour or two with his fund of knowledge, then pleaded fatigue and they left him alone. Quade examined the bunk and blankets closely and sighed with relief when he found no spots that moved. He threw himself down on it.

An hour later he sat up. "Lord, why didn't I tumble before?" he said, half aloud. He went to his barred door, cried out loudly, "Turnkey!"

The other prisoners took up the cry and a moment later a

uniformed man came clumping into the cell corridor. "What's all the racket about here?"

"It's me," Quade cried. "I want to talk to Chief Costello."

"You wanta confess?"

"Confess, hell," snorted Quade. "I didn't kill that man. But I just thought of something I want to tell the chief."

"Ah, do you now? Well, tell him tomorrow morning. This is the night the chief plays poker and he don't like to be bothered with little things."

"This isn't a little thing. It's important."

"Nuts," said the jailer. "If you keep up the racket I'll turn out the lights on you even though it's only eight o'clock." He went out through the door and slammed it behind him.

Quade yelled for him to come back. The other prisoners, thinking to help him, yelled also. And then the lights in the entire jail went out. The turnkey had kept his threat. Quade cursed and threw himself on his cot. After a while he fell asleep.

A NEW JAILER came around in the morning and asked the prisoners if they preferred the regular jail breakfast of oatmeal and coffee or a more complete breakfast sent from a restaurant, at their own expense. Quade stripped a ten dollar bill from the roll that had not been taken from him and ordered breakfasts for all the prisoners. He was roundly applauded for his generosity.

After breakfast the jailer came into the cell room and distributed a few letters. There were two for Quade. One from Charlie Boston, telling him that he was going to the city to get his lawyer-cousin, Paul, and not to worry about a thing.

The other was an unsigned note, written the evening before. It said merely:

"That was a very detestable thing for you to do. I hope you stay in jail for keeps."

Quade winced as he read the note. He had treated Lois Lanyard pretty shabbily, but still he couldn't regret it. Given time to think things over, Lois couldn't help but realize that she shouldn't marry Freddie Bartlett. In innumerable ways she'd shown that she didn't love him; she was going through with the marriage merely because it had been rather expected of her and because several people, including her family, had been opposed to it. Quade had taken a high-handed way of helping her out of her quandary and sooner or later, he believed, she would appreciate it.

The prisoners' cells were unlocked a little while later and they were herded into the bull pen. The men crowded around Quade then, thanking him for the breakfasts and assuring him that he was the Number One man of the jail as far as they were concerned.

"That's very fine of you, boys," Quade thanked them. "But I'm expecting to get out of here today."

One of the prisoners had not joined in the eulogy to Quade. He was a surly, dark man, who sneered when the others crowded around Quade, but a little later he came up alone.

"Here's something for you," he said.

His hand came out of his pocket and Quade threw himself backwards. The gleaming knife blade ripped his coat sleeve from elbow to shoulder.

The prisoners in the bull pen began yelling, but the knife wielder received the surprise of his life. Quade was totally unarmed, except for his quick wits and lean, strong body. But even with a knife the attacker was no match for him.

He side-stepped the man's second rush and, snaking out a hand, imprisoned the knife wrist. He jerked swiftly on the wrist, then smashed the forearm across a raised knee. The knife clattered to the concrete floor and the prisoner yelped in agony.

Quade stepped back from the prisoner and brought up his right fist in an uppercut. The blow caught the man under the chin, lifted him from the floor and deposited him on his back on the concrete. Quade scooped up the knife. The prisoners crowded around him.

"What the hell's the matter with the Greek? He go nuts?" asked one.

"Greek, huh?" Quade rubbed his chin. "I think I know what's wrong with him. He got a letter this morning, didn't he?"

"Yeah," replied one of the men. "He tore it up in little pieces and flushed it down the toilet."

Quade filled a tin cup with water and sloshed it on the unconscious man's face. The prisoner gasped and began moaning. In a moment he sat up.

"All right, partner," Quade said. "Who told you to carve me up?"

"No one," grouched the prisoner. "I just didn't like your looks."

Quade reached down, caught hold of the man's shirt and yanked him to his feet. "Fella," he said, glaring into the man's face. "I asked you a question and I want a straight answer. Was it Bill Demetros?"

The prisoner looked at the fist that Quade shook in his face and said, "Yeah. He said you was getting in his hair."

Quade threw the man away from him. "I ought to report you

and you'd get a good deal more than you're due to get now, but I can't be bothered with small fry."

The turnkey stormed into the bull pen. "Quade, Mister Quade, you're wanted up front."

Quade brushed off his new blue suit, frowned at the slashed sleeve, and followed the turnkey to the front part of the jail. Christopher Buck and the chief of police were both there and both looking serious.

"I guess we've got to let you go, Quade," Costello said.

"You're convinced that I didn't kill Wesley Peters?"

"Yeah. Bob Lanyard confessed that he did it."

"What? Why, he confessed that a couple of days ago. You don't believe him this time, do you?"

"Got to," grouched the chief. "He left a letter."

Quade became rigid. "What do you mean, he left a letter?"

"He shot himself last night."

Quade gasped. "Bob Lanyard shot himself? He's dead?"

Both the chief and Buck nodded. Quade shook his head in bewilderment. "The letter—could I see it?"

Chief Costello pointed to a piece of paper lying on the desk before him. Quade looked down at it. It was just an ordinary sheet of white bond paper, crumpled, as if it had been clutched in a dead hand. There were two lines of typing on it. They read:

"I killed Wes Peters. He was annoying my wife. Forgive me, Jessie, for making this exit.

Bob."

"When was he found?" Oliver Quade asked.

"About five-thirty this morning," replied the chief. "The caretaker heard the dogs whining and howling and when he went to see what was the matter, there he was. The gun was in his hand."

"He was found in the dog kennels?"

"Yeah, in the vacant stall where Miss Lanyard usually kept those woolly dogs she's got at the show, now."

Quade's forehead wrinkled. Then suddenly smoothed. "Buck, you still interested in this?"

"I've lost my client," growled the cadaverous detective. "But I haven't been paid off yet. What do you want me to do?"

"Go out there and point out things to me."

Buck looked at the chief, who nodded. "My men should be through by now. Let him look around."

They rode out to the Lanyard home in the private detective's expensive roadster. Quade looked at the drawn shades of the house and shook his head. Lois had been fond of her brother. And it would be a terrible shock to the parents, too.

The backyard was still swarming with newspapermen, but a couple of police were keeping them out of the dog kennels. Buck was known to them and they let him pass through with Quade.

The dog house was a long, low building, divided into three individual stalls. There was a door at each end of the building and connecting doors between the stalls. Quade had to stoop to enter and the tall detective had to walk bent almost double. Quade's eyes were gleaming by the time they had entered by the small door into the wire runs.

They passed through the huskies' kennel to where Bob Lanyard had been found in the vacant woolly kennel just beyond. The body had already been removed but the coagulated blood on the floor was mute proof of where the body had lain.

Quade's eyes made a sweeping, searching tour of the sheep dog stall, then he nodded to Christopher Buck. "All right, let's go—" Buck looked at him with narrowed eyes. "That's all?"

"Yes. I just wanted to make sure he didn't commit suicide."

"But he did," protested Buck. "The gun was in his hand."

"Placed there by the murderer. If Bob Lanyard wanted to kill himself, why would he come out here? He could have done it in his room just as well. Someone forced him in here, probably at the point of a gun. Didn't want the people to hear the shot."

"Quade," Buck said thoughtfully, "there may be something in what you say. That confession note was typed, but not signed. Anyone could have written it. I'm going to check up on the typewriters around here."

"That won't prove anything. Almost all the people interested in this matter could have got to one of the Lanyard typewriters. You forgot they almost had a wedding yesterday and there were plenty of guests."

Christopher Buck swore. "I'm still on this case. Christopher Buck never quits until he gets his man, even if his client is murdered!"

Quade almost grinned at the man's dramatic self-appreciation. He left the building and almost bumped into Charlie Boston who was arguing with one of the policemen.

"Ollie!" cried Boston. "I just got back and they told me at the jail that you'd been let out. I brought my cousin, Paul."

"Jail?" cried a cameraman nearby. "You're Oliver Quade, the man who was jailed last night?"

Quade gritted his teeth and smiled. "All right, boys, Oliver Quade was never modest. Bring up your cameras."

They did with a will. They snapped Quade from all angles. It was ten minutes before Boston could drag up his lawyer cousin, a mousy looking man of indeterminate age, who was, in Boston's own words, "the best lawyer on the east side."

"Sorry you won't be needed," Quade said to him. "But as you see, I'm a free man. Give me your card though and I'll give you a ring the next time I'm pinched."

"It'll be a pleasure to defend you, Mr. Quade."

The liveried butler came up then and spoke to Quade in a low voice. "Beg pardon, sir, but could you come into the house for a moment?"

"Yes, I could. Charlie, wait out front by the car."

Quade trudged behind the butler to the house. In the living-room, his face strained and white, was Guy Lanyard. And Lois. Lois, in a black dress and clutching a wadded handkerchief in her hand. Her eyes were dry, but they had been wet before, Quade knew. Quade mumbled his sympathies and Guy Lanyard nodded.

"Mr. Quade," Lois said. "I'm sorry about yesterday. I shouldn't have told the police about seeing you unchain that dog."

"I had it coming to me. It was a dirty trick I pulled on you."

Guy Lanyard cleared his throat. "Lois had the idea that Bob didn't shoot himself."

"He didn't," said Quade.

Guy Lanyard gasped. Lois sprang to her feet. "I told you so, Dad. I knew Bob wouldn't do that. He was moody and all that, but I know he'd never take his own life."

"Someone killed Bob," Quade said.

"Mr. Quade," said Guy Lanyard. "My son had employed—that detective person, who hasn't impressed me much. I wonder if I could persuade you to do some investigating for us. I'd expect to pay, of course."

"That won't be necessary. After the things that have happened nothing could stop me from running down the killer."

Lanyard heaved a great sigh of relief. "That will be some small satisfaction. Even though it won't bring back Bob. Perhaps you suspect someone already?"

"I don't suspect. I know. I've known right from the start, but I couldn't prove it. I can't yet."

"Who is it?" cried Lois. "Tell me and I'll—"

Quade shook his head. "It isn't time yet. I'm going into the city today—on this case—but I expect to be back this evening. Don't worry."

OUTSIDE, CHRISTOPHER BUCK pounced on Quade. "What'd the family want, Quade?"

Quade shook his head, continued walking. Buck swore, caught hold of his arm. "Come clean. I just heard through the grapevine about that fellow who tried to kill you in jail."

Quade stopped. "So?"

"Where does this Demetros fit into the picture?"

"Demetros and Wesley Peters were brothers!"

Christopher Buck gasped. "Say, this Peters fellow *was* dark complected. I get the picture now. Lanyard killed Peters because he was hanging around his wife, and then Demetros killed Lanyard."

"Then all you have to do is find Demetros."

"Yes, but where? Where are you going?"

"To the city. To find Demetros."

Christopher Buck ran back to his own car. He would burn up

the roads to the city, knowing that he could get there an hour before Quade could make it in the dilapidated flivver. Quade wondered what Buck would do if he found Bill Demetros, ex-racketeer and ex-convict.

"First though," he said to Boston and the latter's cousin. "I'm going to the hotel and clean up. The facilities in the Westfield jail aren't as good as those at the hotel."

Seated in the lobby of the hotel, a big Eskimo dog at her feet, was Jessie Lanyard. She sprang up when she saw Quade. "I slipped out of the house when you were out there, Mr. Quade," she said. "I want to talk to you."

The hotel lobby was hardly the place for a private talk. "Come up to my room, Mrs. Lanyard," Quade said. He introduced her to Charlie's cousin, then all three of them crowded into the elevator.

Jessie had the husky on a leash, but the dog was skittish and growled ominously. Charlie Boston promptly backed as far away from the dog as he could. Charlie wasn't afraid of anything in the world except dogs.

In Quade's room, Jessie said, "It's about Peters. You asked me yesterday about him. Well, I came to tell you that he was really George Demetros, the brother of Bill Demetros."

"If you'd told me that yesterday," said Quade, "it would have been news. But I figured it out for myself last night, in jail."

She sat up stiffly.

Quade said, without looking at her, "Tell me, Mrs. Lanyard, wasn't Peters blackmailing you?"

"That was the other thing I came to tell you. Yes, the dirty rat! He blackmailed me. I gave him thousands of dollars and he kept wanting more and more."

"He threatened to tip off his brother about you. Your new name and your whereabouts. Isn't that it?"

Her eyes dropped. "Bill will kill me if he finds me. He's that sort. I was afraid to tell Bob about him. And so I paid all that money to Wes Peters, to keep him from talking. Oh, I know Demetros was in prison all these years, but that didn't mean I was safe. He had friends on the outside, members of his gang who'd do anything he ordered them to, even though he was in prison."

"I can believe that," said Quade. "This morning, here in the local jail, a prisoner got a note from Demetros and inside of a half-hour tried to murder me."

Jessie cried out. "He—he knows then! Oh, I was afraid he did. I hadn't even seen him for five years, but I thought I recognized him yesterday at the dog show!"

It was Quade's turn to be surprised. "Demetros was at the show when Peters was killed?"

"There was a man there I'd have sworn was him. He didn't talk to me and kept his distance but I'm sure it was him!"

Quade looked at her with clouded eyes. Then he sighed. "Thanks for telling me all this, Mrs. Lanyard."

She rose. "I'm going away after the funeral. I couldn't stand it here without Bob—and Demetros loose."

"Perhaps he won't be loose very long. He's known to the police and he'll have a hard time hiding from them. I don't think you have to worry about him, right now. Too much excitement around here and too many police and newspapermen."

"Good-bye, Mr. Quade," Jessie said. She smiled wanly at Boston who heaved a sigh of relief when the Eskimo dog padded out of the room.

"What do you make of that?" Boston asked when the door was closed.

"All roads lead to Athens—meaning Bill Demetros. So I guess we'll have to find him."

"Buck's got a long headstart," said Boston. "But somehow I'm not worried about him. From what I hear this Demetros fellow is a very hard customer, indeed."

BUCK WAS TAKING the easy way of finding Demetros. When Quade, Boston and the lawyer reached the city, the newspapers already carried screaming headlines: "Police Seek Demetros in Murder Quiz."

The story mentioned Buck's name in every other line. He had solved, he claimed, "The Westfield Dog Murders" as the papers called them. And he wanted Demetros. The city police knowing that Demetros made his headquarters here, started a search for him.

Quade bought the paper in the Bronx and read it as Boston tooled the car down to Manhattan. "Methinks Mr. Demetros is going to be rather hard to find from now on," he said.

"That dumb dick!" snorted Boston. "What'll we do now? Head back for Westfield?"

"No, drive down to Twelfth Street. Everyone seems to have forgotten Felix Renfrew. He was, after all, Peters' best friend."

Renfrew lived on the top floor of a five-story brownstone walk-up. He occupied a dingy room containing a studio couch, a couple of chairs, a rickety table and a gas plate. And a typewriter and stacks of paper.

Renfrew was home, but not overjoyed to see Quade and Boston.

"You knew that Peters was Bill Demetros's brother?" Quade asked.

Renfrew shook his head. "I met Bill a couple of times through Wes several years ago, but Wes never told me Bill was his brother. Said he was just a friend. I knew Wes was a Greek though, but he was touchy about it and I never asked him his real name. After all, my own isn't Felix Renfrew."

"What is it?"

Renfrew reddened. "Obediah Kraushaar, but can you imagine a playwright putting that on a play?"

"Renfrew hadn't brought you any big contracts."

"No, but playwriting is a tough racket. I may quit it and go back to Hamburg, Wisconsin. With Wes gone the landlady may chuck me out any day."

"That's one of the things I wanted to ask you about. Do you suppose Wes got his money from his brother Bill?"

Renfrew shrugged. "I don't know, but I imagine so, now that you tell me Bill was his brother. Come to think of it, it was right after Bill went to jail that Peters began getting his money."

Quade looked thoughtfully at Renfrew for a moment. Then he said, almost casually, "Would it surprise you to know that Wesley Peters got his money from Jessie Lanyard by blackmailing her? Threatening to tell Bill Demetros her whereabouts."

Renfrew's mouth fell open and his eyes bulged. If he had known those facts about Wes before, he was a good actor, Quade thought. "Lord!" gasped Renfrew. "I never dreamed that about Wes. But come to think of it, that's why he was always running out to Westfield. He pretended to me he had some pals out there."

"And that is why you went out there? To learn who his friends were?"

Renfrew's mouth clamped tightly shut. And his bulging eyes suddenly narrowed to slits. "What are you trying to do? Spring something on me?"

"I'm trying to get information, that's all."

"Yeah? Well, get to hell out of here!" snarled Renfrew. "I've said the last word to you. Beat it!"

"Don't get tough, fella!" cut in Charlie Boston. "I used to eat a couple of poets and playwrights for breakfast every morning."

Renfrew backed away from Boston. But Quade held out a hand toward his pal. "We'll let him alone, Charlie, for a while. Let's go."

Outside Quade said to Boston. "I got Peters' address. He used to live near here, on Christopher Street. Let's take a look at his place."

They didn't get into Peters' apartment, however, for the very good reason that a hard-boiled policeman, who was parked in it, wouldn't listen to reason or financial coercion. Christopher Buck had sold the New York Police on Bill Demetros.

Quade and Charlie climbed into the flivver, started off. As the traffic light turned red at the corner, a squat, dark-complected man stepped out of a doorway, crossed the sidewalk and stepped on the running-board of the flivver.

"All right, boys," he said. "Drive around the corner and park the buggy."

"Ah," said Quade, "you're Bill Demetros?"

"Yep. I been following you around since you left Renfrew's joint. I knew you'd get around there and to my brother's place sooner or later."

The lights turned green. Demetros rode around the corner with Quade and Boston. The latter, his nostrils flaring, looked inquiringly at Quade. Quade shook his head.

They climbed out of the car. "You came to town looking for me, didn't you?" asked Demetros, as they walked together up the street. The gangster kept his right hand in his coat pocket, a fact that Quade had noted from the moment Demetros appeared.

"Yes," replied Quade. "And I guess we had better luck than the cops."

Demetros raised his eyebrows. "Luck? All right, in here." He pointed to a short flight of stairs, which led to a saloon just below the level of the sidewalk.

There were two customers and a bartender in the saloon. The three looked at Demetros and his "guests" and went on with their conversation.

Demetros and Boston sat down. The gangster scowled at Quade. "Look, fella," he said, "none of this business had really concerned you, so why do you have to butt in on it?"

"What about the lad in the Westfield jail who tried to stick a shiv into me?"

"You got out of that, so why don't you take the hint and stay out of it today? You know, I never liked buttinskys. I know of a few out in the ocean with concrete on their feet."

Quade grimaced. "As a purely hypothetical question, what's your own interest in this thing?"

"I just finished a five-year stretch in Atlanta," Demetros said. "I didn't like it there and I don't want to go back. Or worse."

Quade considered that. It sounded reasonable enough, but still, just how much did Bill Demetros know? Quade cautiously ventured to find out. "You know that Wesley Peters was your brother?"

"Of course," snapped Demetros. "The louse! How the hell do you suppose I got into this?"

"I see," said Quade. "Well, I think I'll be going now."

Demetros slammed to his feet. "You ain't going nowhere."

It was a swell fight while it lasted. Charlie Boston was a howling terror. And Quade was no slouch himself. But the addition of the bartender and the two customers, who turned out to be pals of Bill Demetros, was too much. They and the weapons they brought into the fight, to wit: a couple of black-jacks, a bungstarter and a chair or two.

REGAINING CONSCIOUSNESS WITH a split-ting headache, Quade groaned and sat up. For a moment he thought he was blinded but then he realized that he was in a dark room. He groped in his pockets and found matches. Striking one, he saw that he was in a dingy room, littered with old furniture, junk and kitchenware. From the rough beams overhead he guessed that it was the basement of the saloon in which they'd met their Waterloo.

Charlie Boston lay supine upon the floor near Quade. He was twitching and mumbling, although still unconscious.

Quade saw a cord dangling from an electric light bulb and pulled on it. To his satisfaction it sprang into light. He rose and stood for a moment, shaking his head to clear away the cobwebs. He ached in almost every muscle of his body. And his blue suit was now ripped in a dozen places.

There was a dirty sink at one side of the room, beside an old coal range. Quade went to it and ran water. He laved his hands and face, then caught a peek of himself in a cracked mirror over the sink. He grimaced when he saw the mouse under his right eye.

Charlie Boston was mumbling louder and Quade sloshed water on Boston's face. The big fellow shuddered and sat up.

"What the hell!" he gasped as he looked around.

Quade grinned through split lips. "I thought you were a good fighter, Charlie."

Boston swore. "Fists against fists I'd have licked all four of 'em by myself. But those blackjacks and that chair the bartender conked me with!"

"Pipe down," Quade warned.

The thugs had neglected to search them, probably figuring on doing that later. Quade still had his wrist-watch. It showed one fifteen. "We've been out over an hour," he said.

"And we'll probably be 'in' here until tonight," replied Boston. "Then we'll go on a one-way ride."

Quade looked around the room. There was a trapdoor over-head and he guessed that recalcitrant customers had on occasion been unceremoniously dropped through the floor. There was another door at one side of the room, which no doubt led to an outer corridor and upstairs. There were no windows in the cellar. The only ventilation in it came from a narrow vent which led into another part of the cellar. The air was dank and laden with a thousand old smells.

"Looks like they used to do the free lunch cooking here in the old days," Quade observed. "And there's an awful lot of trash."

"You mean we could start a fire?"

"We'd probably be roasted by the time the fire department got here. Because I don't think our friends upstairs would dash to our rescue in the event we fired the joint. No, it's got to be something better than that."

He began poking around things in a corner. Thoughtfully he prodded a sack of cement, then a smaller sack containing a white substance. "Lime and cement," he commented. "The boys mix a bit of concrete now and then."

"I got a hunch they don't mix the concrete for no building work," scowled Boston. "You heard what Demetros said about pouring it on guys' feet."

"I remember it well. But lime has many uses. You haven't forgotten, Charlie, that I've read my encyclopedia from cover to cover. There are some mighty interesting things in it... Ah!"

He brought up a sheet of tough fiber board. He broke off a corner, tested it with his tongue. "Sulphur it is, Charlie. They soak this fiber with it to make it tough and waterproof. Lot of these advertising signs that have to hang out in all sorts of weather are first soaked in it. There's just one more thing I'd like to find. Look through those bottles around here and see if you can find a bit of ammonia."

A fifteen-minute search failed to produce any ammonia. Quade sighed. "I'll have to try it without the ammonia. Build a fire in the stove, Charlie, and hope the damn chimney still works."

There were plenty of old boxes and other fire material in the room. Charlie Boston soon had a nice fire going in the old coal range.

Quade then broke up the fiber board into small pieces and put them in a big, old cooking pot.

"With better tools I could do a better job, but this will do," he said to Boston. "If I'd only found some ammonia or naphtha we'd have had some real fun."

The pot on the stove began giving off a strong, biting odor after a while. Boston sniffed it. "Damn me if it don't smell like sulphur, Ollie."

"It is. I tasted it. Sulphur melts at 113 degrees Centigrade and boils at 444. But I don't think we can get up a hot enough fire here to boil it. But maybe that won't be necessary."

Inside of twenty minutes the pot on the stove was half-filled with a brownish-green liquid in which floated pieces of fiber. Quade fished out the fiber as well as he could, then drained the hot mixture through a handkerchief into another pan that Boston had washed in the sink.

He let the stuff cool for a while, then stirred lime into it. The mixture began bubbling but Quade worked cautiously and kept it from bursting into flames. Finally when the mixture was completed and cooling, he poured it out on a sheet of newspaper in thin strips.

"Now, Charlie," he said, "don't spit on those strips or there'll be trouble."

Quade carried a sliver of the stuff to the sink and tossed it in. There was water in the sink and the instant the sliver touched it, it exploded into a bright yellow flame.

"I'll be damned," said Boston.

"If we'd had naphtha," said Quade, "I could have made Greek fire, the stuff the old-timers used in their wars. Thinking of Demetros gave me the idea. But this will suit our purpose." He looked at his watch. "It's after three. Time we got out of here. Tear yourself a leg from that old table there. You may have use for it."

Taking the thin brittle strips of lime and sulphur, Quade stuffed them in the cracks of the door leading to the outer corridor. Boston helped him and soon the wide crack was stuffed completely around.

"This isn't going to be a cinch, Charlie," Quade said. "When that stuff starts burning it's going to be just about hot enough to melt the hinges off. We're going to have to smash down the door then and jump through a regular furnace. If there isn't a staircase or a quick outlet on the other side of the door we're going to get roasted alive."

Charlie Boston scowled. "And if we stay here and wait for Demetros to get back it's a tubful of cement on our feet. I'll take a chance on the fire, Ollie."

"All right then, get ready."

Quade took a deep breath, then, with a pan of water in each hand, suddenly doused the sulphur-stuffed cracks of the door.

The result was astonishing. The sulphur and lime exploded into a roaring thread of bright yellow flame. The fire was so hot that it almost seared Quade's face even though he sprang back quickly. The flame, he knew, was only a few hundred degrees cooler than an oxy-acetylene torch.

Quade and Boston waited at the far end of the room, shielding their faces with their arms. Now and then Quade peered over his arm. Finally, after about a minute, he said, "The hinges are gone now, Charlie. A good stiff wallop or two and the door'll go down. Then we've got to make it. And keep your fingers crossed."

Boston caught up the table leg he had torn off and leaped forward. He struck the door a mighty blow and it fell completely off its melted hinges, dropping out into the corridor.

"Let's go!" cried Quade. He covered his face and leaped

straight through the inferno of fire. Scorching heat seared through to his body. For a fraction of a second Quade thought he had lost, but then he stumbled on a stair and began scrambling up it. Behind him he heard Charlie Boston, scuffling and swearing. They fled up the stairs, the fire crackling behind them. Quade beat out sparks on his clothes and he knew that his hair and eyebrows were singed.

A door at the head of the stairs was closed but not locked. They tore it open and burst into the saloon where they had been defeated earlier in the day.

The bartender and one of the two men who had come to Demetros' aid were the only occupants of the saloon. The fight this time was all in Quade's favor, Charlie using the table leg to knock both of the utterly surprised men out of the way. He and Quade left the saloon inside of two minutes.

"The building'll probably burn down," he exclaimed outside. "But damned if I care."

Their battered flivver was still around the corner. Demetros hadn't had it removed. Quade and Boston climbed into it and in a few minutes were bowling north along Seventh Avenue.

IT WAS ALMOST six o'clock when they reached the Westfield Hotel. Dirty, their clothing scorched and torn and their hair singed, they caused the hotel room clerk to exclaim in horror when they entered. But they breezed past him to the elevator.

Quade was putting on a clean shirt when someone in the corridor began a sledge hammer tattoo on their door.

"Christopher Buck, the world's greatest detective," Quade remarked. "I recognize his gentle knocking."

He let Buck into the room. "Where've you been?" Buck cried.

"Talking to Bill Demetros."

"You got him?" Buck cried eagerly. "Where is he, in jail?"

"Not that I know of," replied Quade. "Matter of fact we lost an argument with him."

Buck saw the remnants of Quade's blue suit on the floor. "You were in a fight!"

"No, I got the black eye from a canary. It kicked me."

Boston came out of the bathroom, several strips of adhesive tape on his face. "You shoulda been along, Mr. Buck," he grinned largely. "You would have enjoyed it."

Buck shuddered. "I abhor physical violence. A man with brains doesn't have to resort to it."

"Brains?" exclaimed Boston. "Man, where we were your brains would have got you a concrete block."

Christopher Buck wrapped himself into knots and dropped into a chair. "What're you going to do next, Quade?" he asked.

"Gather in the murderer," Quade replied bluntly. "Before there is another killing."

The telephone tingled. Quade picked it up.

"This is Felix Renfrew," said an excited voice. "I'm over here at the bus station. I just got in. I've got something very important to tell you."

"Come right over," Quade told him. He hung up the receiver and turned to Buck. "Sorry, but I'm having a visitor. You'll excuse me, won't you?"

Buck scowled. "Holding out again, huh?"

"Look," said Quade, exasperated. "You've fooled around on this case long enough. Your client is dead, so why the hell don't you take a powder?"

Buck blustered but Quade shoved him through the door. Quade turned to Boston, his eyes gleaming. "This thing is breaking fast, Charlie. Felix Renfrew is coming up here. I think he's going to give me the proof I've been trying to get."

"That Demetros knocked off young Lanyard? Hell, I knew that long ago."

Five minutes passed, but Felix Renfrew did not show up. Quade fidgeted. "Wonder if Buck ran into him and bought him off to spill it to him. That man would do almost anything to get credit for breaking a case." He held up a hand suddenly. "Listen, isn't that a police siren? Lord, I wonder…."

Quade bounded off the bed and out of the room. He took the stairs to the first floor, three at a time, and burst through the lobby. People were rushing by on the street, heading for a spot in the next block where a large crowd had gathered. Quade caught hold of a man's arm. "What's happened?"

"Man's been shot!"

It was Renfrew, of course. Quade found Chief of Police Costello and his entire force herding the curious back from the huddled body.

Costello was very unhappy. "More killings!" he snapped. "It's getting to be an epidemic around here."

"How'd it happen?"

"No one seems to know exactly. He was crossing the street and someone took a shot at him from an automobile. Only one or two people around and they thought at first the noise was just a backfire. Only natural. Up to now, people haven't been in the habit of firing off guns on our Main Street. What happened to you?"

Quade touched the mouse under his eye. "I got tough to the

wrong man. Well, you still satisfied that Bob Lanyard committed suicide?"

The chief cursed roundly. "I been out to the Lanyard house.
The old man and his daughter claim it was murder. This
Renfrew killing makes me wonder now."

Quade saw the lank figure of Christopher Buck forcing
through the crowd and slipped away. He walked to the hotel
and climbed into his disreputable flivver.

Ten minutes later he rang the bell at the Lanyard home.

"Miss Lois Lanyard," he said to the butler.

"I'm sorry, she's not at home."

Quade frowned. "Mr. Lanyard then."

The butler led Quade into the living-room where Guy
Lanyard was sitting by the rear window, moodily looking out
toward the dog kennels.

"Where'd Lo—Miss Lanyard go?"

"To the dog show. I thought it best for them to get out for
a while."

"Them?"

"She and Jessie both went. Poor girls."

Quade left abruptly and drove to the dog show—fast. It
was around dinnertime and attendance was slight. Quade
went swiftly from aisle to aisle but saw neither Lois nor Jessie
Lanyard. He did, however, run into Freddie Bartlett. The
wealthy playboy gritted his teeth at sight of Quade. "Here
you are, I've been looking for you all day." Freddie spoke as he
would to a servant.

"The hell you have," snapped Quade. "Where's Miss Lanyard
and her sister-in-law?"

"What business is it of yours?" sneered Bartlett. "You've been around them just about enough. I was looking for you today to see that you didn't annoy any of us any longer."

"Oh, hell!" snorted Quade. "Are you going to try to lick me?"

"Someone seems to have started the job," Bartlett said ominously, "but I'm going to finish it. You didn't know I was light-heavyweight champion of my university, did you?"

Quade sighed, stepped forward and smashed Bartlett a terrific blow on the point of the jaw. Bartlett staggered back against a dog partition. His eyes rolled wildly as he struggled to keep his feet.

"So you want to fight?" Quade asked. He lashed out with a left hook, and Freddie Bartlett hit the wooden partition and slid down it to a sitting position. He wasn't out, but he sat there goggle-eyed. "And now," Quade said, "where's Lois?"

Bartlett looked up stupidly. "I—I don't know," he mumbled. "They were here, then they said they were going for a drive up River Road. Jessie said something about going where it was quiet. Woods down there—"

Quade left Bartlett sitting there. He dashed to the exit of the building, then on sudden impulse ran back. He found the Old English sheep dog aisle and stepped into one of the stalls, the one occupied by Oscar, Lois' first-prize winner.

The dog was a bit skittish, but Quade spoke soothingly to it and unchained it. Leading it by the chain, he started again for the exit.

The show secretary was coming in just then. "Here, here, you!" he cried. "You can't do that."

Quade did not even answer. He brushed the man aside and rushed out to his car. He put the dog in the front seat and climbed in beside it. In a moment he was scooting out of the fair grounds.

Quade didn't know the section of the country around West-field, but during the last few days he'd seen the river several times and instinctively headed toward it. The road beside it was a winding one. There were a few houses and farms on both sides of the road, near town, but when he got out a mile or two, the farms gave way to thick woods. Quade cursed furiously. There was no fencing along the side of the road and every now and then there was a winding wooded lane or road, cutting off from the main drive. Jessie and Lois could have turned down any of these roads and he would miss them.

Quade stopped the flivver beside a small road and listened. There were fresh tire tracks leading into the road, but it did not necessarily mean anything. This was a populated country and someone used these roads every day. He stepped on the starter, but suddenly switched it off again. He strained his ears, but heard nothing. The dog beside him growled deep in his throat. Quade looked at it and his eyes flashed.

"Bark!" he cried, in a sudden command. The dog was startled and barked warningly. "Louder!" Quade cried, making a pass at the dog. The dog barked and bared his teeth threateningly.

And then Quade heard it—a wolf-like howl rising to a mournful note and dying out. It came from the woods ahead and not so far away. Quickly Quade stepped on the starter of the flivver and slipped the gears into second. He stepped on the throttle and the car leaped into the narrow winding road. As he drove he bore down on the horn. The noise excited the dog beside him even more and it barked. And from ahead, came the answering howl of a dog. The flivver burst into a clearing and Quade brought it to a stop in a cloud of dust. Ahead was a bright yellow roadster, Lois' own car. Oscar, the sheep dog, began barking excitedly and tried to get out of the car. Quade sighed in relief, kicked the door open beside He saw the girls then. They were in the back of the clearing, near an old stone house. Jessie had the big Eskimo dog with her. It was bristling at the approach of the sheep dog and Jessie had to speak to it to keep it from attacking the woolly as the latter bounded across the clearing to his mistress. "Hello, there!" Lois called as Quade approached. "How'd you happen to find us?"

Quade jerked his head toward the husky. "The dog. He howled."

Lois looked at him in surprise. "You mean you recognized his howl? But you've only seen him once or twice."

"I know, but this happens to be the only dog in this neighborhood that doesn't bark. You're a dog raiser; you ought to know that an Eskimo dog, being descended from the wolf, does not bark—he howls."

"The Human Encyclopedia himself," said Jessie.

Quade looked at her. Jessie was unsmiling. "Yes," he said. "I got that information out of the encyclopedia. It was a good thing to know."

"We were just about to start home," said Lois. "Jessie wanted to explore this old house first. It's deserted."

"Some other time," said Quade. "Let's go back to Westfield now."

"Why, has something happened?" Lois' eyes clouded.

"I'll tell you later," Quade held out his hand to Jessie. "Let me have your bag."

Her eyes widened, but he took the handbag firmly from her grasp. It was heavy and he could feel the outline of something hard in it.

Lois' forehead was creased as they walked to the cars. Something seemed to be annoying her. Quade's rudeness, no doubt. At the car he maneuvered to hand Jessie into the seat first, then took hold of Lois' elbow.

"I'll drive," he said firmly.

He handed her into the car, then stowed the two dogs into the rumble seat, chaining each to a side, so they would not be forced together too much.

Quade walked around and slipped in under the wheel. He could feel Jessie beside him, her body tensed. She knew that he knew.

No one said a word until they reached the Lanyard house.

"Your father's in the living-room," he suggested, guessing that the old man would still be by the window overlooking the dog kennels. He was. By the look on Guy Lanyard's face Quade knew that he had guessed the truth during his absence.

"Renfrew, Wesley Peters' pal, is dead," Quade said.

Lois gasped. "Dead!"

"The police captured this Demetros," said Guy Lanyard. "Costello phoned just a few minutes ago. He resisted and is in a bad way. Probably won't live. He'd come to Westfield to—"

Lois suddenly looked sharply at her sister-in-law. "Jessie," she said slowly, "who was that dark man you talked to at the dog show this morning? I asked you about him before and you didn't answer."

"I'm going to my room," Jessie said.

Guy Lanyard looked at Quade. The latter held his gaze for a moment, then looked at Jessie's handbag in his right hand. He extended it to her. "Here's your bag."

Jessie's teeth were sunk into her lower lip. She took the bag, turned and walked out of the room. Quade heard her heels as they clicked on the stairs going up.

"Thank God you got to Lois in time," Guy Lanyard said.

Lois turned to Quade. "What does he mean? What's the matter with her? Why wouldn't she answer me about that man? Was he…?"

There was a sharp explosion upstairs. Quade relaxed. Guy Lanyard slumped into his chair.

"It's best this way," Quade said.

"That was a shot!" cried Lois. Her eyes were wide. "Jessie! Jessie!"

AN HOUR LATER Quade dropped wearily onto the bed in his room at the Westfield Hotel. Charlie sat on the other bed, biting his fingernails. "The dame!" he swore. "You knew it was her all the time!"

"Not all the time, Charlie. She fooled me there at the start. That confession of hers. It was on the level and that's what threw me off the track.

"If she'd stopped with Peters' death she'd probably have got away with it."

"What mistakes did she make?" asked Boston. "I didn't get any. Hell, I never even suspected her."

"But I knew she killed her husband the minute I read the suicide note he was supposed to have left. Remember what it said? 'Forgive me for making this exit.' Making an exit is an actor's expression. Bob might conceivably have picked up such a phrase from his wife, but his speech ordinarily was scholastic and precise. In his most tragic moment he would not have used slang.

"But aside from the note, Jessie gave herself away by killing Bob in the dog kennels. Remember the layout?"

Boston considered that for a moment, then shook his head. "What's wrong with that layout? She didn't want to kill him in the house maybe on account of the noise."

"It would have been far safer for her to have done so. Don't you see, Charlie? The dogs are loose in their kennels. She could have forced Bob past the pointers, but after shooting him she could never have gone back that way. The pointer, Duke, would have torn her to pieces. Dogs smell blood quickly and sense death. And Bob probably cried out when she shot him. No, after shooting him she left by way of the husky kennels, her own dogs.

"Get it now. *No one* could have killed Bob and left by the pointer kennels. And *only Jessie* could leave by the Eskimo kennels. Those dogs are half wild and in the middle of the night would have attacked anyone but their mistress. So it had to be Jessie."

"I'll be damned!" exclaimed Boston. "But did she have to kill Bob?"

"Perhaps, perhaps not. But one murder leads to another and after she killed Peters she had to kill her husband. You see, Jessie made her big mistake years ago when she tried to throw over Bill Demetros. Demetros wasn't the sort of man who liked his women to leave him, at least not until he was through with them. And he wasn't through with Jessie. She changed her name, but Bill would have caught up with her probably, except the Government caught up with him about then and sent him on that five-year visit to Atlanta.

"Then Jessie got into that show with Wes Peters. That was

a bad break for her, because he turned out to be Bill Demetros' brother. When Jessie found out she threw him over. Or maybe she met Bob Lanyard about that time. Lanyard meant real dough to her. And safety.

"She married Bob. And then it turned out that Peters, even though he was supposedly not like his gangster brother, was even worse. He blackmailed Jessie about her former association with a gangster and threatened always to tell Bill where she was unless she paid plenty."

"You mean she paid heavy sugar just to keep that rat Peters from writing his brother that Jessie had married a rich guy?" demanded Charlie.

"That's about the size of it. Jessie knew Bill pretty well. She knew that he would get word to some of his pals on the outside and it would be too bad for her. So she paid off... and then Bill got out. Inasmuch as Wes had played around with his brother's girl he figured he'd better skip. He needed money for that. So he went to his mint, Jessie, and demanded one last big roll.

"She couldn't get enough money. So she gave Peters that thousand that was on him when he was found dead and stalled him. She got an opportunity and gave him a lead slug instead of more money. She might even have taken to carrying the gun figuring to kill herself with it. But when she got such a swell chance in the dog show she up and let him have it.

"It was her first murder and she was pretty shaky about it, so when we went after her hot and heavy there at the start, she broke down, admitted it. Then when her husband tried to take the blame and she saw that no one really wanted to believe she had done it, she began covering up.

"But Bill Demetros must've got to her, because all of a sudden

I found Demetros on her side. Which wasn't at all according to Hoyle. Took me a little time to figure out. Demetros had been away for five years and I imagine his lawyers and fixers had come pretty high, so the old safety deposit box was probably pretty empty. He knew Jessie was scared stiff of him. So he showed her how she could come into a big chunk of dough and by splitting with him, live to spend it.

"It was smart figuring on Demmy's part. By knocking off her husband Jessie could come into a half million or so. Then Lois happened to see Jessie with Demetros and questioned her. That made Lois next on her list. I didn't know the reason when I went after Lois and Jessie today, but I knew Jessie was desperate and I wasn't taking chances on Lois being the next victim."

"That all sounds pretty straight," said Boston. "But where'd this guy Renfrew fit into the picture?"

"Renfrew finally figured out Wes Peters' soft thing, or maybe he didn't see it until after we told him about it. Anyway, he suddenly got the bright idea of taking up where Wes left off, not knowing that Demetros had shuffled a new deal. Renfrew phoned Jessie to put the squeeze on her. Which signed his death warrant. Demetros got to him and told him a few things and then Renfrew got panicky and wanted to come to me, to blow up the thing and save his life. So Demmy killed him."

"Uh-huh," said Boston. "What about Lois' romance you busted up?"

Quade's ears turned red. "Why, she gave me an invitation to come out some time—What the hell you grinning about, you big ape?"

"Nothing," said Boston, his face as sober as a Kansas prohibitionist's.

If You Want to Write, Well Write

HOLLYWOOD—SO, YOU WANT to be a writer? If not, you are, by survey findings, a rare exception indeed. Nine out of 10 people more or less secretly entertain the ambition of some day hitting the literary  big-time through short stories, novels, movies or television.

So declares Frank Gruber, generally accepted as the most prolific and versatile author in the entertainment field today. To satisfy his own curiosity, Gruber, who has written 325 TV shows, 33 novels and 60 motion pictures, conducted a poll on the subject of the writing yen. He discovered that just about everyone is at least subconsciously a repressed author.

"The point is," he chuckled, "while everyone wants to be a writer, you find precious few who will sit down and write!"

Writing, in Gruber's opinion, while an art, should be approached in a businesslike fashion. The successful people in his profession don't toss off saleable items lightly, he insists. Any story or script should be approached in the same carefully planned manner a builder would erect a house or a tailor would make a suit.

"The so-called 'serious' writers in my profession would undoubtedly frown on such a description," admitted Gruber, who has been getting words into print—and picture—for more than 25 years. "In fact, because of my attitude I've been accused of being what is known as a 'hack.' Well, let them call me a hack—or anything else. If selling everything you write makes you a hack, I guess I'm one. But a hack's pay can be pretty good, too!"

There was no boastful note to Gruber's voice in pointing out that his work "sells." Creator of the popular "Wells Fargo" series starring Dale Robertson, and "The Texan" featuring Rory Calhoun, he is one of the most productive writers anywhere. His latest bestseller, "Town Tamer," is being converted into still another TV series. His books are published in 33 countries and have sold over 50,000,000 copies. With the old West his chief subject, he turns out at least one a year.

"That's just because Westerns are the vogue right now," he explained. "There was a period when I concentrated on mysteries—because they were popular. If they happen to be the rage next year, I'll switch back to them."

A farm boy native of Meadowland, Minn. (Pop. 50), Gruber let nothing stop him once he decided to write. In 1931, at the worst of the depression, he arrived in New York with enough money to keep going for a week—just long enough to dash off his first story. He took it to an agent who returned it with the blunt statement, "this is absolutely unsaleable."

Undaunted, he submitted it himself to the now defunct Liberty magazine. When it was accepted, he vowed he'd never work through an agent again. And he hasn't, preferring to do his own negotiating,

"Faith in one's self," he emphasizes, "is all important to the writer. During my first year I sold about 50 percent of my output—for the last 15 years my record has been 100 percent. But one thing I've learned: never get discouraged by a rejection slip! I once tried 35 different editors before finally making a sale. Later I learned to study each magazine's requirements.

The same is true of television, only more so. One should write with a particular show or star in mind."

Gruber takes a dim view of writing the "great American novel." It's a trite expression that nobody really understands, he points out. Many so-called literary greats are quickly forgotten and not even read 20 years after their "wonder" works are published, he believes.

"I wouldn't want to set myself up as an authority," Gruber concluded, "but the one piece of advice I'd give anyone who wants to write is 'do it—don't talk about it.' First of all, decide exactly what you want to write for. Plan it just as you'd draw up the blueprint for a house. From then on everything depends upon one thing—your talent."